THE VICTIM OF THE SYSTEM
A Novel

by

Steve Hadden

TELEMACHUS PRESS

Cover designed by Cover Quill

Cover art:
"Allegheny County Courthouse skyway over Ross St in Pittsburgh" by Dllu under Copyright © ID 80919946 © Mike D. Tankosich/Dreamstime.com

Interior Periodic Table:
Copyright © iStock/825083434/MicrovOne

Edited by Julie Miller

Published by Telemachus Press, LLC
7652 Sawmill Road
Suite 304
Dublin, Ohio 43016
http://www.telemachuspress.com

Visit the author website:
http://www.stevehadden.com

ISBN: 978-1-948046-03-9 (eBook),
ISBN: 978-1-948046-04-6 (paperback)
ISBN: 978-1-948046-06-0 (hardback)

Categories: Fiction / Thriller / Suspense

Version 2018.06.27

Acknowledgements

As always, this book would not be possible without the help and support of my wife, CJ, who gives me her love, encouragement and insights. Thanks to my early readers, Martha Martin, Matt Adams, and Jacqueline Tirado who inspire me to do my best. Thanks to Steve and Terri Himes, Mary Ann Nocco, and the entire team at Telemachus Press. I'm grateful for the assistance of the team at The Editorial Department including Julie Miller, Doug Wagner, and Ross Browner. Special thanks to Johnny at Telemachus and to Rena at Cover Quill for the great cover.

Dedication

To Martha, Dave and Mario,
this one is for you.

Also by Steve Hadden

The Swimming Monkeys Trilogy

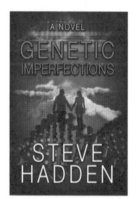

Genetic Imperfections

The Sunset Conspiracy

THE VICTIM OF THE SYSTEM

CHAPTER 1

JACK COLE KNEW they were coming for him next. He waited in the dense shrubs with a vengeful patience. He reminded himself he was here for a reason—one that justified the action. He fought back the dark sensation that this was wrong. *Thou shalt not kill* had been drilled into him at Saint John's. But this was the only way to end it—to be safe.

His hand shook as he gripped the heavy rifle and took aim at the front door of the mansion across the private cul-de-sac. He settled the jitter with the thought that this man had killed his dad.

He leaned back against the tree and braced for the kick. Then, through the bushes, he saw a sliver of light widen as the front door opened. He dropped his head and took aim through the scope. He'd been watching the lawyer's house for days.

The thick door swung open and his target stepped out, closing the door behind him. Jack hesitated when he came face-to-face with him through the scope. Still, he steadied the heavy rifle and squeezed the trigger.

The blast slammed his back against the thick tree. The kick felt stronger than it had when he'd fired it on his first hunting trip with his father, just two months ago. As he scrambled to regain his balance, he saw his prey—the man responsible for destroying what was left of his family—fall against the front door of the red brick home, his white shirt splattered with blood and his face paralyzed in shock. Blood smeared as the man grabbed at the door, apparently reaching for someone inside. Finally, the attorney collapsed with his contorted body wrapped around his large legal briefcase.

Jack stood and froze, shocked by the carnage he'd unleashed. When the door swung open and a panicked woman rushed out, he came to his senses.

In seconds, Jack secured and covered the rifle and began his escape. Halfway down the cul-de-sac, he was sure someone had called 911. As he calmly pulled the red wagon his father had given him on his ninth birthday, he heard the police cars responding. They raced through the expensive suburban homes toward 1119 Blackbird Court.

The two cars turned onto the cul-de-sac and slowed when the patrolmen passed a mom and her children standing in their driveway, gaping at the terrifying scene. At the deep end of the cul-de-sac, the police cars screeched to a stop. Their doors sprang open and two officers swept the area with their guns drawn. The other two rushed to the porch. The woman cradled the man's body, screaming wildly. Blood coated the porch and covered the woman's face and arms.

Jack fought the urge to run and wandered out of the cul-de-sac. Two other police cars and an ambulance raced past. Over his shoulder, he saw the paramedics rush to the porch. Then Jack turned the corner and lost sight of what he'd done—and he began to cry.

Six Months Later

CHAPTER 2

IKE ROSSI HATED this place. Not because something had happened here. Instead, it was something that hadn't. It represented failure. A rotting failure that he placed firmly on his own shoulders. While it had been twenty-two years, the wound was as raw as it was on that dreadful day he'd tried to forget for most of his adult life. Now, after years of dead ends, he was here once again to close that wound.

He waited on the hard bench in the massive lobby of the Allegheny County Courthouse flanked by murals of Peace, Justice, and Industry. Despite their ominous presence, he ignored them. He'd never found any of those here.

As nine a.m. approached, the lobby swelled with people making their way to their destinies. Their voices and the clicks of their best shoes echoed through the massive honeycomb of thick stone archways as they wound up the network of stairs leading to the courtrooms on the floors above. Nameless faces all carried their tags: anger, sadness, fear, and arrogance. Those who were above it all, those who feared the system, and those who just saw money. While he'd always heard it was the best system on earth, he was painfully convinced that justice deserved better.

Three benches down, Ike's eyes locked on a small boy who was crying and leaning into a woman's side as she tried desperately to comfort him. When he recognized Jack Cole from the flood of news reports over the last six months, he didn't feel the prickly disdain that had roiled in his gut as he watched the initial reports on TV. At first, he'd condemned the ten-year-old boy as another killer—one who took the life of someone's parent. But as the case unfolded he'd discovered the boy had lost his father. The constant wound Ike kept hidden in his soul opened a little wider. He knew what it was like to lose a parent.

According to the reports, Jack Cole's father had committed suicide as a result of a nasty divorce from Brenda Falzone Cole, the estranged daughter of one of the richest families in the country. Jack, a genius ten-year-old, had shot and killed his mother's family law attorney—not exactly what Ike expected from a kid. When he was finally identified in video from a neighbor's security camera and questioned, he shocked investigators by admitting the act.

Claiming he didn't have a choice under Pennsylvania law, the prosecutor was trying the boy as an adult. Jack faced a murder charge. Due to his young age, both sides wanted to fast-track the trial. It was scheduled to start next Monday, just a week away.

The boy looked up and caught Ike's gaze. Despite his best efforts, Ike couldn't look away. Tears streamed down Jack's face, but at the same time, his eyes begged for help. A mix of fear and generosity accumulated deep in Ike's chest. He knew the boy sought the same help he'd sought for himself years ago, but the prospect of exhuming that pain warned him to stay away.

Still, yielding to a magnetic force that had no regard for his own protection, Ike stood, smiled, and walked to the boy, ignoring the condemning stares from the people eyeing Jack. Reaching into his jacket pocket, he pulled out a small Rubik's Cube he carried to amuse distressed kids on long flights to distant oil provinces.

He stopped in front of the pair and asked the woman, "May I?" while he showed her the toy. The dried streaks down her cheeks told him she shared the boy's pain. He recognized her from the news reports but didn't want to remind her that millions of people were now witness to her custody battle with Jack's mother's family—and the progression of her devastating pretrial defeats at the hands of the district attorney.

"Oh, that's so kind of you," she said, nodding gently.

Ike gave Jack the toy and sat beside him. Jack's smallish build and timid posture made it hard to believe he was ten—and he'd killed someone.

Jack sniffled and wiped his nose with the back of his arm.

"Here, honey," the woman said as she handed him a Kleenex. Jack wiped his nose and immediately began twisting the cube, ignoring Ike.

"I'm Lauren Bottaro," the woman said. "This is Jack. I'm his aunt."

Ike reached out. "Ike Rossi."

Her eyes flamed with familiarity. She seemed stunned. "You're Ike Rossi?"

Jack handed the cube back to Ike. "Done!"

Ike wasn't sure what startled him more, the look on Lauren's face or the fact that Jack had solved the cube in less than a minute. "That's great, Jack." Ike offered Jack a high-five, but Jack awkwardly hesitated. Finally, he slapped it and Ike returned the toy. The tears were gone, replaced by a proud smile. Ike looked back at Lauren, who'd apparently caught herself staring at him.

She seemed to regain some composure, and a serious expression swept across her face.

"Mr. Rossi, can I ask what you do, now?"

Ike hesitated, hearing more than just that question in her voice.

He looked up and saw Mac Machowski, grinning.

"I'll tell you what he does."

Ike could have kissed Mac for the timely rescue.

Mac counted on his thick gnarled fingers. "He fixes things that can't be fixed. He keeps fat cats from getting kidnapped—or killed if they do—and he's the best damn investigator I've ever seen."

Ike noticed Jack had stopped playing with the Rubik's Cube and was listening intently to Mac, along with Lauren.

Ike smiled. "Mac, I'd like you to meet Lauren and Jack."

Mac tipped the bill of his Pirates cap to Lauren. "Ma'am." Then, extending his meaty paw, he knelt painfully and came face-to-face with Jack. "Nice to meet you, young man."

Jack nervously looked away but reached for Mac's hand and shook it.

"Jack. What do you say?" Lauren said.

Jack faced Mac. "Nice to meet you, sir."

Mac's joints creaked as he reached to the floor and pushed himself up. "You ready there, partner?" he said to Ike. "We gotta catch him before he leaves the courthouse at nine."

As Ike stood, Lauren rose with him. "So you're a detective?"

Ike threw a nod toward Mac. "He is—a retired homicide detective. I'm a private security and investigative services consultant in the oil and gas business."

Lauren tipped her head back, as if enlightened. "That makes sense now."

"What makes sense?" Ike said.

"I saw your name written on my brother's day planner."

The claim jolted Ike. "My name?"

Lauren nodded again. "Did you speak to him?"

"No, I've never talked to your brother." Ike was sure investigators would have checked the planner, but he'd never been questioned.

Jack reached up and tugged on Ike's forearm. "Can you help me?"

Those eyes were begging again.

Lauren gently pulled Jack's hand from Ike's arm. "I'm sorry," she said. "He's been through a lot."

Jack kept his eyes, now wet again, locked on Ike. "My dad wouldn't do that to me. He wouldn't kill himself."

Ike was frozen by Jack's stare. It was as innocent as any ten-year-old's. A primal desire to protect Jack stirred in Ike's heart. He didn't want to believe the kid—but he did.

Lauren hugged Jack. "It's okay, honey." She looked back at Ike and Mac. "We have no right to ask you th—"

A thick, towering woman with dark brown hair and a stone-cold stare wedged into the space between Mac and Lauren. She studied Mac, then Ike. "What's going on here, Lauren?"

Ike immediately recognized her from the news reports. Jenna Price represented Jack. For the last two months she'd been billed as a hopeless underdog, and the string of losses so far—other than prevailing at the bail hearing—supported that label. A basketball player-turned-lawyer, she was battling a DA who so far showed little mercy. She worked with her father in their tiny firm, and every talking head said she didn't stand a chance.

Lauren said, "Jenna, this is Ike Rossi and Mac ... I'm sorry?"

"Machowski," Mac said as he shook Jenna's hand.

Jenna gripped Ike's hand and held it as she spoke. "My dad said you were the greatest quarterback ever to come out of western Pennsylvania."

Ike always had one answer to that comment to quell any further discussion of his accolades. "That was a long time ago."

"What are you doing now?" she asked.

Jack leaned around Lauren and nearly shouted, "He's a detective. He can help us!"

Lauren hugged him tight again. "Shhh."

"A detective?" Jenna said.

"A private security and investigative services consultant."

Jenna nodded and held her gaze but said nothing.

"We gotta go now," Mac said, looking at his watch.

Ike stepped back from Jenna. "Stay strong, Counselor." He nodded to Lauren. "Ms. Bottaro." Then Ike offered a handshake to Jack.

Jack sheepishly held out the Rubik's Cube for Ike. Immediately, Ike felt Jack's awkwardness.

"You keep that, Jack." Ike raised his hand for another high-five. Jack took the cue this time and slapped it. "Ladies," he said, turning with Mac and walking down the hall.

As they reached the stairs at the end of the corridor, Ike glanced over his shoulder. He could see Jack edging around the two women to keep his eyes on Ike, with the Rubik's Cube clutched in his hand. Ike turned back to the stairs.

"You okay?" Mac said. Ike nodded and started up the stairs to meet a man he despised. A man who might finally deliver the key to *his* parents' murder.

CHAPTER 3

IKE KNEW HE'D rather set himself on fire than have a conversation with Vic Cassidy. But he needed what little information Cassidy might have. Cassidy called himself a detective, but he'd been nothing but a roadblock since he took over Ike's parents' case eight years ago—a cold case, he'd said. Buried under the avalanche of unsolved murders committed over the last five years along the Liberty Avenue corridor, their case was lumped in with those of drug dealers and gang members who didn't exist when Ike's parents were killed outside the bar in Bloomfield. Now, according to Mac's sources inside the department, there was finally a new lead.

Ike followed Mac into one of the district attorney's meeting rooms on the third floor of the courthouse and wrestled his rage into its box. He assumed Cassidy was working on a trial and trying to show off his stroke. He spotted Cassidy in the back of the cramped room hovering over an open file.

Mac bull-rushed him and extended his hand, keeping him seated. "Vic. Thanks for meeting with us."

"Your waste of time, not mine."

The only person who despised Cassidy more than Ike was Mac. Both men's postures foreshadowed a dogfight, but they played the game and held their tempers. Mac had always suspected Cassidy had planted cash from the evidence room in Mac's locker eight years ago. The IA investigation that followed had provided enough heat that even Mac's reputation couldn't overcome the chief's political fears. Mac had been allowed to resign with the full pension benefits he needed to care for his wife, Doris, who'd been diagnosed with brain cancer five months earlier. He'd left without a fight. Oddly enough, the chief was convicted of embezzlement shortly after.

Cassidy was dressed in a brown herringbone blazer that was well above the budget for a detective. He glanced at Ike, then back at his file. "I should have guessed he'd be with you."

Mac stepped closer. "They're his parents, you—"

"It's okay, Mac. He knows who I am." Ike wanted to get to the point of the meeting.

Mac stepped back. "Joey said there was a call to the station over the weekend about the Rossi case. Said you checked it out."

Cassidy didn't look up and flipped to another page in the file. "It's nothing."

"Let us be the judge of that," Ike said.

Cassidy slammed his hand on the page. "Who the hell do you think you are?"

Ike lunged forward, but Mac pulled him back. Ike rested his six-foot-three frame on his hands on the table, stopping face-to-face with Cassidy. "I'm one of only two people in this room who give a shit about solving this case." Ike allowed Mac to pull him back.

"Okay, okay, let's settle down."

"Who called, Vic?" Mac said.

Cassidy held his stare on Ike. Ike didn't flinch. Cassidy's eyes always held lies. Ike knew if he didn't back down there was a fifty-fifty chance they'd get the truth.

Finally, Cassidy returned his attention to the file. "It was some ancient crackpot at a nursing home for the demented."

"And?" Mac said.

Cassidy looked up at Mac. "And nothing. Her son called. Said she was dying and wanted to clear her conscience about something regarding the case. I went there and she couldn't remember her name, what day it was, and every minute I had to remind the old bat that *she* asked for *me*."

Mac looked over his shoulder at Ike. Ike read his expression. Mac thought it was another dead end.

"What was her name?" Ike asked.

"I don't know."

"You interviewed her and you don't know?"

Cassidy stood. "Hey, dipshit, I don't have to tell you anything."

Mac leaned in between Ike and Cassidy. "What was her name and where was she, Vic?"

Cassidy seemed to spot something in Mac's eyes. Ike knew Mac had leverage on Cassidy, but Mac never said what.

"Emma Sosso. Homewood Nursing Home." Cassidy sat down and nearly ripped the next page he yanked from the file.

"Thanks, Vic. What you working on?"

Cassidy glared up at Mac but then leaned back and smiled. "That kid's case."

"The Cole case?"

"Yup. Easiest one yet. The kid's guilty as hell. Got all the evidence locked down. Just a matter of time."

"You're handling Jack's case?" Ike said.

Cassidy crossed his arms. "Well, well. On a first-name basis, are you?"

Ike could see Cassidy took sick pleasure in the fact that Ike knew the boy.

"How'd that case come to you?" Mac said.

"Handled his father's suicide. They thought I should handle this one, too—you know, keep it in the family." Cassidy chuckled.

Ike thought of Jack asking for his help. He'd like nothing better than to make a fool of Cassidy, but his gut said to stay away from the kid. He'd felt the bottom drop out of his heart when he'd met him. It was the same feeling he'd had when the resident assistant at Penn State gave him the phone and a younger Mac Machowski introduced himself as a homicide detective and told him his parents were dead. He'd promised himself to avoid that sickening feeling for the rest of his life.

"You're an asshole," Ike said.

"At least I'm not some washed-up jock trying to play detective."

Ike again took a step toward Cassidy, who stood.

Mac blocked his path and pushed against Ike. "Let's go, Ike. We're done here."

Ike backed out of the room, his stare locked on Cassidy. He wasn't done—not by a long shot.

CHAPTER 4

JENNA PRICE KNEW she was representing a killer. But she had bigger problems. It was two p.m. sharp and she heard the shuffling outside the conference room door. The other side's cockiness was surging, and the old two-bedroom house that had been transformed into her father's Cranberry Township law practice was smaller than the opposing counsel's lobby. With their arrogance reinforced by the inferior setting, they'd go for the throat.

She glanced at her dad, who'd suggested he be present only to keep the meeting to three-on-three. He was relaxing in his chair, calmly fluttering through the pages of notes he'd made for another meeting. He knew this was part of the strategy: make them wait just a little to signal control and a lack of eagerness. Hell, he'd taught it to her. It was part of the home-court advantage—an advantage she'd been quite fond of during her playing days at Pitt. Time and time again she'd seen it create a subtle unease in her opponents and a cradle of confidence for her and her teammates.

She certainly needed an edge. Four years out of law school she was risking her father's law practice to prove her case against the ambitious Allegheny County district attorney and a jury carefully selected from the public that had already condemned her client. She'd taken the case all because of something Jack had said to her. She believed him immediately. She didn't know why.

That didn't matter. She trusted her instincts above all else. They'd taken her to the women's Final Four, to the top of her class in law school, and back to a successful role in her father's practice. While it wasn't the role she'd dreamed of, it had kept her close to her brother.

When she doubted that decision, she'd simply visit her favorite lunch spot. It was nothing special to see—a simple sandwich shop in Cranberry. But to her it was a magical place. She'd known the owner all her life. He'd opened the shop two days after her father set up his practice two blocks away, just off Freedom Avenue. She remembered spinning on the red stools and leaning on the Formica counter to get to the strawberry milkshake her father would buy for her on the days she came to see him for lunch.

But now it wasn't the special childhood moments with her dad that gave Julian's Sandwich Shop its magic. It was the electric enthusiasm of her younger brother, Michael, when he floated down the counter greeting and serving every customer as if they were royalty. Sometimes, the joy wasn't returned, usually by some small-minded jerk who thought the outward trait of Down syndrome represented a less-than-complete person. Customers like that were ignorant bullies who deserved the immediate and voracious excoriation by the regulars. Just like the regulars, Jenna had always had Michael's back, and would for as long as she lived.

But today she had a chance to demonstrate that she was better than the elite firms she'd shunned. The most powerful family in Pittsburgh represented by a firm fifty times larger than theirs was suing Jack's aunt, Lauren, for custody.

Kristin, her father's assistant who'd watched over Jenna when she'd hung out in her dad's office as a kid, gave two gentle knocks on the door. Jenna paused, closed her eyes, and imagined a glowing steel core inside. It had worked before every game and before any challenge she'd faced so far in the profession. She raised her head and shared a confident nod with her father and stepped over to Lauren, who sat rigid at the table nervously picking the lint from her navy wool sweater.

"Remember, I've got this. Stay calm and look relaxed. I'll do all the talking. Don't let them bait you into saying anything."

Lauren gave her a trembling smile. "I'm ready."

"We're ready, Kristin," Jenna said.

They entered the conference room and took their seats without introductions. After a month of battling in the custody complaint, no introductions were necessary. Jenna eyed Brooks Latham across the table. His short snow-white hair was cut close and perfectly in place. Even his eyebrows were brushed. His white starched collar perfectly contrasted his dark-blue suit, red tie and tanned face. He returned her stare with a certainty that exuded the wealth and power of the founder of the largest law firm in Pittsburgh. To his right was Ed Mayer, the newly promoted family law lead at Latham's firm and the man she'd battled for the last month. Her pulse picked up as she imagined punching the smug grin from his face. Joseph Falzone, patriarch of the Falzone empire and her client's grandfather, sat to Latham's left, hands folded tight, appearing ready to crush these minions he faced. He looked like Latham's twin. Jenna reached for Lauren's hand and gave it a gentle squeeze.

Two months ago, Lauren had walked through the doors of Jenna's father's practice in Cranberry Township and asked for Jenna. She explained that a close friend had recommended her. She didn't have much money, but she believed her nephew. Her brother, she said, had not killed himself, and the people who did would come for young Jack Cole next. The claim was sensational, considering the indisputable evidence that Jack had killed Franklin Tanner.

Tanner was a legendary family law attorney who'd represented Jack's estranged mother, Brenda Falzone Cole, against her husband,

Tom. Tom had proved Brenda unfit, mainly due to her excessive coke use and severe personality disorder, but in the process Tanner had nearly destroyed him. Now Jenna had the good fortune of facing Brenda's father and one of Tanner's founding partners in Latham, Tanner and McKee.

Jenna had used every ounce of her being and every resource she and her father could muster to persuade the judge to grant bail, even though Pennsylvania law dictated that Jack be tried for murder as an adult. It was not a popular decision. Jack would remain in his aunt's custody as requested in Tom's will. Jenna was preparing for the trial, which was only a week away and, at the same time, dealing with Falzone's custody complaint.

She pulled her shoulders back and used every inch of her six-foot-two frame to rise above the men. "Gentlemen, this is your dime."

Latham locked on to her and didn't say a word. Finally, he turned to Mayer and nodded once.

Mayer jumped right in. "Ms. Price. As you know, the judge wanted us to try to settle this one more time. Mr. Falzone is the boy's grandfather and with the terrible consequences his grandson is facing, he'd like to assume legal custody."

"Not happening, Mr. Mayer," Jenna said, leaving no room for doubt.

"Ms. Price, I'm sure Mrs. Bottaro is a fine mother to her own son, but she's a widow with limited resources. Her lack of supervision resulted in allowing her nephew to commit murder. I don't think the judge will look favorably on that. Mr. Falzone is Jack's grandfather and a pillar of the community. He can bring significant resources to his aid and defense."

The insult didn't go unnoticed. "I'm his defense counsel and Mrs. Bottaro is his legal guardian. Despite your efforts to prove her unfit, she's stood strong. The results of the psych evaluation are in and we'll take our chances with the judge."

Mayer leaned forward to continue, but Joseph Falzone stopped him with his raised hand. "Ms. Price, are you sure you want to do that?"

Jenna understood the threat. Falzone built far-reaching enterprises from oil to construction and had amassed a fifty-billion-dollar fortune. Politicians and judges sought his counsel and his funding. Judge Kelly was no different. But there was no way she'd turn a ten-year-old boy over to this bully. Lauren was a great mother. She worked from home for a tech company and raised her son, Jimmy, and now Jack. She'd lost her husband in Afghanistan. Still, she was a rock. Those boys were lucky to have her.

She looked at Lauren and smiled. Then she glowered at Falzone. "Yes, we'll take our chances."

Falzone's face tightened as he froze for a moment. Then he bowed his head, acknowledging Jenna's position. He leaned over and whispered something to Latham. Latham whispered to Mayer, and the two attorneys rose.

Mayer packed his single sheet of paper into his folio. "Ms. Price, Mrs. Bottaro." Then he and Latham left the room.

"What's this?" Jenna said. "This meeting is over." She stood and guided Lauren to her feet.

"Just a minute," Falzone said as he raised his palm. "Hear me out."

Jenna stopped, holding her file in her arm.

"Mrs. Bottaro, all I want is to spend whatever time I can with my grandson. I can help both of you." He pulled a business card from his suit pocket and produced a pen. "It would be worth a lot to me to be able to do that." He hesitated and glanced up at Lauren. "I noticed you speaking with Mr. Rossi. Hire him and this doesn't happen." He returned his attention to the card and wrote something on the back, rose, and laid the card face up on the table. He paused and scanned Lauren's face, then tapped the card with his index finger and left.

Lauren gave Jenna a quizzical glance, then reached down and picked up the card. She flipped it over, read it, sighed, and covered her mouth. She rotated the card in her trembling fingers and held it up to Jenna.

Five million dollars

A bully with a shitload of money.

CHAPTER 5

JENNA LEANED BACK in the conference room chair and it gave a familiar squeak. She studied her father as he flipped the business card between his fingers. She knew that expression. When she was a kid, it always came in advance of a flurry of late nights without her father at the dinner table. It was a fragment of light in a case with nothing but empty darkness.

Finally, Jenna's father pinned the card to the table with his index finger and faced her. She raised her eyebrows and waited.

"Why such a ridiculous offer?" he said.

"I know. And why is he afraid of this Ike Rossi?" she added.

Her father shifted and sat up straight in the chair. He eyed Jenna and nodded toward Lauren, who was locked on her phone, texting with the sitter, checking on Jack. Jenna got the message. It's always the client's decision, no matter how obvious the answer is. But this wasn't obvious. Five million dollars was life-changing. Lauren could look at it two ways as far as Jenna was concerned. Five million for Jack's life. That answer was obvious. She'd spent hours with Lauren going over the criminal case. She'd gotten to know her well. A widow who lost her husband in Afghanistan and was raising her son on her own. Then her brother died, and now she had Jack. She never complained and seemed to love them both. Still, it was five million dollars. She'd seen that kind of money change people—even the saintliest.

"Lauren?"

Lauren finished typing and returned her phone to her purse.

"As the client, it's your decision. We'd recommend turning down Mr. Falzone's offer, but I know it's a lot of money. What Mr. Falzone was saying, or not saying, is true. He probably knows the judge personally and has some financial tie to him. There is a chance we could lose the custody case, but in the bigger picture, you have to consider the impact on the outcome of Jack's trial. I believe what Jack has said and I think there is a case to defend, but we need more hard evidence and time is running out."

Lauren looked down the table to Jenna's father, then down at her folded hands.

"I'll never turn Jack over to those people. They don't care about Jack. They never did. He's a special boy and he needs people that understand him."

Jenna shared a smile with her father. "That's what we wanted to hear."

Lauren wasn't smiling. "We could lose? I could lose Jack?"

Jenna saw the tears filling Lauren's eyes. She reached for her arm. "It's only one outcome. It may be that the judge awards some visitation but you'll keep custody of Jack. Or he could deny the request. You've done all you can and you've passed the evaluations with flying colors. You're a great mother."

Lauren forced a smile and pulled out a Kleenex and wiped her eyes. She sighed and patted Jenna's hand. She stuffed the tissue into her purse. "So, we need more evidence?"

"Yes. We need something to back Jack's claims."

"How do we do that in six days?"

Jenna stood and walked to the end of the conference table and picked up Falzone's card. "Five million dollars."

Her father, Ed, proudly nodded.

Jenna continued. "Falzone was willing to pay five million for us to stop right now in the custody battle. On the surface, it looks like an effort to buy Jack. But he also said something else: the offer was null and void if we involved this Ike Rossi." She held the card out. "Why?"

"He's afraid of Rossi. He's afraid of what he might find," Lauren said.

"Exactly."

"That means there's more. There's more in the criminal case against Jack that someone is hiding. That something may confirm some of what Jack has told me."

Jenna remembered her conversation with her coach before their legendary run in the NCAA tourney. Trying to accomplish what seemed impossible was a sure formula for failure. But breaking it down into minute steps was the key. Back then, it wasn't win the tourney, win each game, or even win each half. It was win on every play—every time down the court. No focus on the outcome of the game or the tourney. It worked until the final game, late in the second half, when Jenna traded Cinderella's slipper for a torn ACL. She'd let them down then, but this time she'd drive to victory.

"Jenna? So how do we do that in six days?" Lauren said.

"We need a full court press. After six months of digging, our investigators have turned up nothing. So we use what the other side fears most."

"Ike Rossi?"

Jenna held out the card. "Ike Rossi."

Lauren stood with her purse. "Let me talk to him. Let me talk to Ike Rossi. He and Jack had a connection—I know it. I'll convince him to help."

Jenna considered the offer. She hated money and how it bought verdicts. She wanted to win—for Jack, of course, but deep down she had something to prove. She was just as good as any of them. So far, they hadn't shown her any respect. She was holding her own, but she'd lose if they didn't turn up evidence to support Jack's claims. His young life would be over and her father's practice would be a shambles along with their reputations. She would be the has-been they claimed she was. The question was whether she was willing to put that in the hands of Lauren and a stranger named Ike Rossi.

In that moment, she decided she'd go with her instincts. She glanced at her father, who gave her the expression he always did: he was in full support of whatever she decided. She turned back to Lauren.

"Okay. Go get us Ike Rossi."

CHAPTER 6

FOR JOSEPH FALZONE, the ride down I-279 into the city took forever. There were tremors afoot and the epicenter seemed to be around Ike Rossi. He wasn't afraid of Rossi, he was afraid of not knowing the odds. He'd run numbers for his father in his youth and gambled and lost several times in the oil fields of Texas. But then he deciphered the odds and played them to his advantage, and he hit it big.

The briefing from his sources said Rossi was good. A former Penn State chemical engineering student athlete who, upon his parents' murders, had come home. With the help of the detective who'd investigated the murders, he won an internship with the Pittsburgh Police Department. At the same time, he enrolled at Point Park University and earned a master's degree in criminal justice. Upon graduating, he landed a job in corporate security at a local oil company. When a Houston-based company purchased his firm, Rossi started consulting on private security and investigative services. The report said he rarely failed.

The word was he'd been recently contacted regarding the suicides of the CEO and CFO of one of Houston's largest oil companies less than eighteen months apart. Joseph hoped the large retainer and the specter of facing off with the Falzones would be enough for Rossi to stay away from Lauren Bottaro and her attorney. But the file also revealed he was a man who'd surrendered his Penn State football scholarship at nineteen to come home and raise his nine-year-old sister. Worse yet, he'd always been obsessed with finding his parents' killer. That pointed to a man of principle and justice. He couldn't handicap the chance that Rossi would agree to help Jack.

Joseph couldn't risk it. The multibillion-dollar enterprise he'd built wildcatting in West Texas was in jeopardy. But that wasn't what occupied his mind late at night. It was the risk to his family. Information was hard to protect, but information was the one thing that could topple his empire and crush his family. He couldn't take that chance. He'd have to attack.

His driver dropped him at the private elevator in the executive garage of the fifty-five-story building he'd constructed upon his triumphant return to Pittsburgh in the mid-eighties. In true Pittsburgh tradition, it was a fifty-five-story finger in his abusive father's face. A year later he bought his father's failing glass company, and two years later flipped it for three times the price. His father died that same year. Joseph liked to think he'd had a hand in hurrying his father along.

On the ride up to his office, he stretched his starched collar and readied to face the family. Erin, his second wife of thirty years, would be waiting to hear the outcome of the settlement conference. She cared deeply for Jack, even to the point of thinking it might be best for Jack to stay with Lauren Bottaro. Nick, his oldest son and twin to his daughter, Brenda, would be eager to hear that Jack was in their control. Unlike his stepmother, Nick was quite aware of what was at risk. For him it was more than the company or the family, it was personal. His own freedom, perhaps his own life, was in the hands of a ten-year-old boy.

And Shannon, Joseph's daughter with Erin, would be there to help spin the result to the public. She'd been a gift to Joseph. With her brother, Patrick, gone, she was the most competent of all the children. She ran the Falzone Foundation and handled all the PR for the company and the family. Erin and Shannon knew nothing of the risks to the family and the company, and he needed to keep it that way.

The elevator stopped and he tensed for battle. The door opened and he pivoted to the right and headed down the long mahogany hallway to his office. He strode with determination and heard his footsteps echo loudly, announcing his arrival. He saw Erin step out of the doorway to his reception area. Despite her smile, her eyes revealed concern. He gently hugged her and led her into his office.

"Give us a few minutes, Stephanie," he said to his secretary. He closed his door and dropped his black folio on the corner of his desk and faced Erin. She dropped her purse next to the folio.

"How did it go, darling?"

Joseph paused. "There was no settlement, but I made them an offer."

"An offer?"

He held her by the shoulders. "Honey, I just want this to be over. I want our grandson to have the benefit of his grandparents. So I made an offer they couldn't decline out of hand."

"How much?"

"Enough. You don't need to know the details."

"What did they say?"

He could see her optimism eroding. "Nothing yet, but don't worry."

"I *am* worried Joseph. I'm worried about Jack."

"He'll be with us soon."

"I just want what's best for him. His trial starts Monday. That's a week. The papers say he'll be convicted. I don't want our grandson in prison."

He pulled her to his chest and did his best to hide the battle ripping up his insides. He didn't want Jack to go to prison, but he didn't want his only full-blooded son to either. He couldn't admit that his grandson had simply become a pawn he had to control. To save them all.

"I'm doing all we can, dear."

She pulled back. "You know his aunt doesn't seem to be a bad person. He seems happy with her. Can we just help them both?"

"That's why I made the offer."

A commotion in the outer office caught his attention.

"Mr. Falzone," he heard Stephanie say. "Your father said he didn't want to be—"

The door flew open and Nick barged in. "Did you get him?" he said, ignoring his stepmother as he always did.

Joseph flashed his anger with one look.

Nick glanced at Erin. "Oh, sorry. Hi, Erin—did we get him?"

"Not yet."

"Not yet? It's only a week away!"

Nick had always had a temper. Joseph blamed that on his mother, who was an unstable narcissist of the grandest proportions. It was the affliction he'd divorced. She'd taken a payoff to leave Nick with him at the age of nine. Nick had been mad ever since. But he was smart and he had great business sense. He'd doubled the value of their oil holdings in three years. So Joseph always gave him the benefit of the doubt, a position he'd questioned ever since Patrick's death. But Joseph needed to shut Nick down before Erin got suspicious.

Joseph moved close to Nick. Nick was a foot shorter and Joseph could still intimidate his son. "They're considering the offer. That's it. I don't want to hear any more, Nick."

Erin's expression showed her disdain for her stepson's disrespect. "Darling, I still think we should do what's best for Jack."

"This is the best for that little criminal," Nick said and glared at Erin.

Joseph launched another warning. "Nick."

Erin dried her eyes and stuffed the tissue into her purse. She dropped the purse into the bend of her elbow. "I thought at some point you'd get some manners when you grew up. You're forty-two and we're still waiting."

"You're not my mother."

Joseph saw Erin's eyes soften as she spotted someone over Nick's shoulders. Shannon knocked on the door frame.

"Can I come in, Father?"

Joseph waved her in.

Shannon walked to her mother and gave her a long hug. "Love you, Mom," she whispered.

Shannon was the rescuer. She had unmatched instinct and timing. She kissed her mom on the cheek and then touched Joseph's shoulder and air-kissed his cheek. "Hi, Father." Then deadpanned to her stepbrother. "Nick."

Nick just flicked a feeble wave in her direction.

The greetings said it all. For Joseph, blending his families had been like building a bomb. Especially when one member bled contempt. One misstep might destroy it. But for Joseph, this was all still worth saving.

Shannon looked at him and raised her eyebrows.

"Nothing, yet," he said.

"All right," Shannon said. "We're still getting a flood of inquiries for comments on the custody dispute and its effect on the trial. It's not just local. It's the *Journal,* the *Times,* and *USA Today,* along with every major network."

"I know. Keep holding them off with the statement. No comment on pending legal matters."

"Okay. I'm also having lunch with the editor from the *Pittsburgh Post-Gazette*. Just keeping channels open for when we need them."

She was the smartest in the family. It was a shame she was only twenty-six. Joseph had so much more for her to do.

"Oh, and don't forget the banquet's tonight. It's the kickoff for the Special Olympics and you're the featured guest."

"Wouldn't miss it for the world."

Shannon took Erin's arm. "Come on, Mom. I have some great letters to the foundation I'd like to show you."

Erin leaned over and Joseph hugged her. They passed by Nick as if he weren't there.

Nick stepped to the door and closed it.

"You need to show more respect for Erin," Joseph said.

Nick smiled and walked back to his father. "We've got much more important matters to deal with. We need to control the kid."

"I offered them five million. That could be enough. I also have Judge Kelly on the hook."

"If that kid's father told him about the data or anything about Patrick, we're both done."

"I know. You think I'm not focused on that?" Joseph soothed his temper as he went behind his desk. "We have another problem."

Nick looked as if he'd been punched in the stomach. "What now?"

"I saw Bottaro and Jack talking with a guy named Ike Rossi in the courthouse."

"Oh, shit. Rossi? One of the guys at the club hired him and said he was the best he'd seen."

"I had Brooks check him out. He is good. Too good. I made the offer contingent on not hiring him."

Nick leaned on his knuckles on the desk. "You tipped your hand?"

"Had to. We can't afford to have him digging. You know it's impossible to fully secure data these days. And who knows what Cole had copied?" Joseph's temper flared as he thought about the cesspool Nick's transgressions had put them in. He shot out of his chair. "And what you did was unforgivable."

Nick recoiled. "I know, I know. I'm sorry, Dad. I didn't mean to."

Joseph had to believe him even though his intuition said otherwise. Exposing Nick would end Joseph's marriage and Erin and Shannon would be gone. They were the best things in his life.

"Do you think Rossi will help them?" Nick said.

"Don't know. But we need to be ready. I don't like the odds. We need insurance."

Nick's expression changed instantly from one of remorse to one of satisfying anticipation. He'd had the same look when he confessed to laying his twin sister's dead cat on her bed. It worried Joseph. "I've got some insurance, Dad."

"Don't do anything without checking with me. I don't want to know the details, but don't do anything. You got me?"

Nick's confidence had returned. He bowed his head in agreement.

"Now get out of here. I need to get something done today."

"You got it, Dad."

Nick left and Joseph dropped back into his chair. He scanned the skyline and traced the rivers mingling at The Point. All of this could be gone. He hated being here. He was relying on a son he'd gambled on—and thought he'd made the right decision. Right up until it wasn't. He was facing a choice between a grandson and a son—a choice he didn't want to make.

CHAPTER 7

IKE WATCHED THE Pirates' first baseman swing and miss as
they went down in order in the bottom of the first. He sipped the ice-
cold Guinness his sister had ready. This was his sanctuary. He'd
owned the place since Maria had graduated with her degree in music.
It was the perfect fit. Despite Maria's immense talent as a singer,
composer, and pianist, she wanted to stay close to home. She played
three nights a week and tended bar and managed the place the rest of
the time. She loved working in the same place where people from all
over Pittsburgh used to come to enjoy her mother's cooking.

Their name was on the London pub-style storefront, halfway
down Liberty Avenue, in Pittsburgh's Little Italy, Bloomfield. His
mother had worked here for as long as he could remember. She'd
said it was her favorite place on earth. Some thought it morbid that
he would buy the bar on the alley where his parents had been brutally
murdered. But not him. He found great joy here and felt a close connection to his parents' memory.

Mac sat to his right on the stool he'd occupied every night since
his wife, Doris, had passed six years ago. He took a long draw on his
beer. "They don't look good tonight."

"Eight more innings, my friend," Ike said, patting Mac on the back.

"The top of the order never does good against lefties," Maria said as she appeared behind the bar drying a clean mug.

"The Rossis—my eternal optimists," Mac said, raising his mug.

Mac was the reason they all were here. He and Doris had guided Ike and Maria since they'd met on that painful night. Ike had been lost, but Mac had been more than just the detective assigned to his parents' murder. He got Ike a part-time internship with the Pittsburgh Police and persuaded him to enroll at Point Park University. While Ike worked and went to school, Doris watched over Maria and took her from school to the Boys & Girls Club in Lawrenceville. Slowly, with all the loving care from Mac and Doris, the wounds healed and a new family formed. It didn't replace what Ike and Maria had lost, but it gave them the sense of caring and be-longing Ike needed to survive being a brother, parent and breadwinner.

Ike took another sip and thought about heading home early to start preparing for the case in Houston. The chairman of the board of an oil company there had called him and asked for his help. He'd work on a retainer of $200,000. The cops had signed off on the sui-cides of the CEO and the CFO eighteen months apart, but the fami-lies and chairman needed more. The police didn't have all the facts.

"Hey, look at that," Mac said. "Turn it up, Maria." Mac looked at Ike. "That's the kid. That's the kid we talked to in the courthouse today."

Maria turned up the volume. The breaking-news graphic said the defense team's last-minute motion for a change of venue had been denied. Jack looked sad and displaced. It was two-month-old footage from after his arraignment.

"The case of the decade will start on Monday," the reporter said. "Young Jack Cole, the ten-year-old who shot and killed attorney

Franklin Tanner, will be tried as an adult for murder. If convicted, he'd face a sentence of at least twenty-five years to life. Tanner, a father of two, had represented Brenda Cole in the divorce proceeding brought by Jack Cole's father, Tom, who was later found dead in the family's garage from carbon monoxide poisoning. Pittsburgh Police said evidence at the scene showed it to be a clear case of suicide. Jenna Price, Cole's attorney, had this to say to KQDA's Lon Henderson."

They cut to a clip of the woman Ike had met at the courthouse. She loomed over the reporter and stared into the camera. "This is a travesty. My client is not guilty of murder. The DA should be ashamed of bringing such charges against a child for his own political gain. And this venue is tainted by the flood of media coverage that has been completely unfair to my client."

They cut back to the anchor. "Pennsylvania is one of two states that automatically try juveniles charged with first- or second-degree murder as adults. The state currently has more than five hundred prisoners that were convicted as juveniles. That's far more than any state in the nation. Now, back to the game."

Maria still held the remote as she turned to Ike. "You talked to him today?"

Ike eyed Maria and put his beer on the bar. "Yes, I did."

"He looks so scared. What did he say?"

"Not much." Ike returned to his beer and hoped that was enough. He didn't want to get into it with his sister. He didn't want her to relive their agony, even sympathetically.

Mac dropped his mug hard on the bar and shot a look of disappointment at Ike. "He asked Ike if he'd help him."

Maria locked her widened her eyes on Ike's. "He asked you to help him? What did you say?"

"His aunt was there and cut him off. She was embarrassed he'd asked."

"Will you help him?" she said.

Ike saw the pain in Maria's eyes. He knew where this was going. "Maria," he said shaking his head. "I understand how this makes you feel. It gets to me, too."

"No, Ike. That little boy lost his father. His attorney thinks he's innocent. Someone needs to help him."

"He has an attorney. I'm sure they know what they're doing." He gave Mac a *thanks a lot* look.

"I read that they don't stand a chance." She put both hands on the bar. "You know what it's like to lose a parent." She'd hit the nail on the head. Ike *did* know what it felt like. The pain was always there somewhere. Safely hidden away until something triggered it. And this was triggering a tidal wave. He didn't want to get close to this. He didn't want to get involved. He didn't want to risk failing again. But something had been nagging him since he'd met Jack. He did want to help him, he just couldn't.

"Maria, the aunt said no. I have to go to Houston Wednesday."

Maria pushed back from the bar and took in everything going on in the restaurant. Then she smiled at Ike. "Tiga?"

Ike smiled back. "Tiga." It was their code word. The word they came up with in therapy when Maria was ten. It meant "There I go again." They both used it when their emotions about their parents' death were hijacked and projected onto another situation. The word always de-escalated the situation and brought them closer to the mindfulness the therapist had taught them.

"You ready for dinner?" Maria asked Mac.

"Yes, ma'am."

Maria nodded to the waitress at the end of the bar, who headed into the kitchen.

Mac grinned and finished his beer. "You know, he is a good kid."

Maria threw the bar towel at Mac, and Ike just dropped his head and chuckled. But something was grinding in Ike's gut. It was a feeling Mac had taught him to listen to. But this time he pushed it down and turned his attention back to the game. The Pirates were down two in the second. *Damn.*

CHAPTER 8

IKE WATCHED THREE more Cubs cross the plate, heard the collective sighs of the remaining patrons, and gave up on the game. The Pirates were down 8–2 in the eighth and the cash registers began to clang out the final damages. But Jack's plight still tugged at Ike's attention.

He checked his watch and saw it was nine thirty p.m. He and Maria had an agreement: one of them always kept an eye on Mac. Without Doris, they were all he had left. He turned to Mac. "So much for optimism. You need a ride home?"

Mac shrugged and showed him his half-empty mug. "When this is done." Mac took a gulp. "You going to check out that lead from Cassidy?"

Ike's urge to punch something, like Cassidy's face, returned. "Tomorrow morning. I'm heading to Homewood to check her out."

"Cassidy's an asshole, but don't get your hopes too high. I heard she has Alzheimer's."

"I hear you. But this is the first and only lead in years. I gotta go."

Ike watched Maria wiping down the far side of the bar. She deserved it. Closure. She'd deserved it since she was nine. So did he. He'd follow any lead anywhere. All it took was one.

Just beyond Maria, the front door opened and Ike's urge to punch someone disappeared. It was Lauren Bottaro. She stopped the last customer headed for the door and they exchanged words. Then the customer pointed in Ike's direction. The helplessness and guilt of a nineteen-year-old stirred somewhere in the basement of his soul.

She walked around the bar and Mac eyed her as she passed and acknowledged him with a nod. He tipped the bill of his Pirates cap and drank the last of his beer. She looked troubled. Who wouldn't? She brushed back her dark hair with her fingers and looped it over her left ear. She presented her hand.

"Mr. Rossi."

Ike shook her hand. "Mrs. Bottaro."

"It's Lauren, and Ms. I need to talk with you about my nephew." She looked more determined than at the courthouse. The embarrassment was gone.

"He seems like a good kid," Ike said guardedly.

"He *is* a good kid. That's why I'm here. Mr. Rossi, what they're doing to him is wrong. They're trying to end his life."

Ike shifted in the stool. "It's a terrible situation. The DA does seem determined even though he claims his hands are tied by the law."

"It's not just the DA," she said, raising one eyebrow. "There's something else."

Ike saw Mac, ever the detective, lean closer over her shoulder.

"Someone is coming for Jack, and probably me and anyone else that's in the way."

Ike took a tangent, testing where she was headed. "I'm sure it feels that way, with the public and the media coverage."

Lauren's eyes ignited and she stepped closer. "No, Mr. Rossi, someone is coming to kill Jack."

Ike stiffened but resisted taking the bait. "Did you tell the authorities?"

"They don't believe us."

"Is there any evidence?"

Lauren's expression faded from frustration to enlightenment. She set her purse on the bar. Maria worked herself closer and Ike introduced her.

Lauren continued. "Jack's not the typical ten-year-old. You've seen him. He's not as playful or outgoing and doesn't have close friends. He's crazy smart and deals with the world on a different plane than the rest of us. But there is one thing he's never done—with me or my brother—and that's lie. He tells the truth, regardless of the consequences."

"I think I saw most of that at the courthouse," Ike said. "But who's trying to kill him?"

"I don't know. But I know what he told me."

Now Mac and Maria were in such proximity that they were part of the conversation. Lauren paused. Ike nodded toward them. "They're good. They help me all the time."

Lauren eyed Maria and then Mac, then returned her attention to Ike.

"First of all, he told me his father would never kill himself, and I agree with that. Tom was the happiest I'd seen him after that last court appearance against Brenda." She glanced at Maria. "His crazy ex."

"Why was that?" Ike said.

"He'd won. He stopped her from getting her hands on Jack again. Before they divorced, she'd gone off the deep end. Screaming fits in front of Jack, leaving the house at two thirty a.m. to 'work out,' which turned out to be an affair with a coke head. She started using and Tom had enough. He filed for sole custody and the judge temporarily agreed. That's when it began."

"What began?"

"The trashing of Tom. Joseph Falzone had disowned his daughter because of her antics. She was a blemish on the family's image. He'd had enough, too. But then he suddenly got involved and hired an attorney for Brenda."

"Tanner?" Mac said.

"Yes. Franklin Tanner. He called Tom's partner and told him Tom was in trouble and he should make him clean this up before it destroyed the company's image. Tom was livid and embarrassed. He loved his company almost as much as Jack. Tanner's team created every lie you could think of: affairs, child neglect, even drug use by Tom. It did take its toll on him, but only because he knew he couldn't stand to lose Jack. They're the same. Two peas in a pod. They were very close and spent every minute they could together. Tom taught him things. Helped get him out of his shell."

Ike eyed Maria, then Mac. They seemed to be on the same page. "That sounds terrible. But it sounds like an acrimonious divorce, not grounds for murder." Out of respect, Ike stopped short of saying that maybe Tom was hurt more than she knew. Maybe he'd been hiding it.

Lauren's dark eyes flashed again. "I know. But here's the catch. Jack said his father told him he knew something very important. Something that some people may not like. Jack said those people were coming for them—and they killed his father."

Lauren stopped, and the silence filled the bar. Maria and Mac waited for Ike's response.

Ike asked the first question he always asked in a case. "What evidence exists to support that?" As soon as the words left his mouth, the voice that came from his darkest place railed against getting involved. Asking that question was just like dipping your toe in the pool—you intended to jump in.

Lauren's determination faded. "None. Jenna's detectives haven't turned up a thing."

Mac's face soured.

"But that's why we need you."

"I'm sorry, Ms. Bottaro."

"Lauren."

"Lauren. I have two other cases I'm working on and I'm already committed. I'm leaving town Wednesday."

"Jack doesn't stand a chance against them. The DA, Falzone, and his lawyers." Lauren looked away and tears welled in her eyes. "They'll take his life away. After he's already lost his father, they'll destroy him."

Maria handed Lauren a tissue from behind the bar. Lauren acknowledged the kindness and dried her eyes.

"You're my last chance—his last chance."

Ike spotted Maria grab another tissue and wipe her own eyes. Mac dropped his head. As much as he hated to, Ike readied to refuse again. "I just can't—"

"I have this," Lauren said, pulling a business card from her purse. She offered it to Ike as if it were the Holy Grail.

Ike took it and read it. *Joseph Falzone, Chairman, CEO and Founder.* Falzone's business card. So what? He raised his head to reply, but before he could, Lauren said, "Turn it over."

Ike flipped it over. *$5,000,000.* It was handwritten. Ike's mind ignited with the possibilities. Did she write it? Did Falzone? A memo? An offer?

"That's what Joseph Falzone offered for my nephew's life."

An offer. An offer like Lauren Bottaro had surely never dreamed of and would never see again.

Her face hardened and she leaned close enough for him to smell her sweet perfume. "And he said it was no good if I hired you," she whispered.

The words rattled through every nerve ending in his body before consolidating into a determination he'd felt only once before. The voice inside raged louder and harder against helping. It was if he were about to jump into a pitch-black abyss.

"He said that to you?" Maria asked.

Mac asked with his eyes, *What now, buddy?*

Ike examined the card again and tapped it against the back of his other hand. He looked up at Lauren. "I need to think about it, maybe check a few things out. That's not saying I'm in. Can I let you know tomorrow?"

Lauren grabbed her purse. "That's more than what I came in with." She fished a pen from her purse and grabbed a napkin from the stack at the edge of the bar. "Here's my number. We only have five days, so please call as soon as you can." She smiled at Maria and Mac. "Nice meeting you both." Then she left the bar.

Maria spoke first. "Did you hear that? Five million. And Falzone said it's off if she hires you. Sounds like a desperate man."

"Sounds like a man afraid something would be found out," Mac said.

"Hang on, you guys. We don't even know this is legit. She could have written it herself. And before you two go signing me up, I have a job in Houston and I gave *them* my word I'd help."

Mac just leaned back and folded his thick arms.

Ike's iPhone vibrated and he pulled it out. It was an e-mail message.

"Holy shit," Ike said.

There was no text, just a math expression: *3–53+8x2+19*

"What's up?" Mac said.

"I just got an e-mail from Tom Cole."

CHAPTER 9

IKE HELD HIS phone in his hand and stared at the e-mail. He stood at the edge of the abyss and this was his invitation. Despite his best efforts to resist, it was pulling him in.

He was certain the kid felt as he had when his parents were killed. He needed to know. He needed the truth. He needed closure. But closure for Jack would come at a cost to Ike. Those nasty, sticky thoughts he kept locked in the darkest corner of his mind would be released again if he helped the kid. He'd spent his adult life wrestling them, trying to get his own closure. But it never came—just the guilt of his failure to uncover the truth for himself and for his sister. He didn't want to face such failure again, especially where the price was the life of a ten-year-old boy.

He'd moved upstairs to his office above the bar. The building had been there for more than seventy years. Two stories with an attic. The second story had a storage room, a small office that looked more like a closet where the previous owners had managed the bar, and two small apartments. Ike had converted one of the two apartments on the floor to an office. He'd modeled the entry door after the district attorney's office in the county courthouse, including the

stenciled glass. It helped unlock his curious side, which was para-
mount in his line of business.

Mac tapped on the glass and entered. "Maria is closing up with
the others. Said she'll be up when they're done." He threw a nod at
the phone. "Anything?"

"I called Lauren when I got up here. She was adamant she didn't
send it to get me involved. Said she deleted all of Tom's personal e-
mail accounts three months ago. His partner told her he'd keep his
business e-mail open for a while to field any business follow-ups he
might have missed, but she thinks he would have shut it down by
now. She said no one would have access."

Mac moved next to Ike and examined the e-mail. "Can your guy
get the IP address? Nail down the location?"

"He's working on it. I forwarded it to him. I should hear back
soon."

"The obvious answer is minus 15," Mac said.

"Yeah. If you do the math that's it. It means nothing to me."

"Me neither."

Ike pointed at his phone. "I thought it could be a way to disguise
the numbers. Seven numbers. Could be a phone number—no area
code. I used 918 and 724 and came up with nothing. And 353 is the
area code for Ireland, but there's not enough numbers for an inter-
national number."

"Too many numbers for a street address," Mac said.

"I thought it could be an alphabetic code, but 53 doesn't work."
Ike kept scanning the expression, but nothing jumped out.

Mac grabbed a pen from Ike's desk and scribbled the numbers
on a pad. "Could be a four-number combination to a safe?"

Ike weighed Mac's theory. "That's a possibility."

Ike grabbed the pen and just wrote the numbers with no spaces.
"Could be a serial number. And it can't be GPS coordinates." Ike

leaned back to get a broader perspective. It hit him immediately. He turned to Mac.

"The biggest issue here is I just got an e-mail from a dead guy. Now it's either someone, like Falzone, screwing with me to waste my time or it's someone else."

"Who?"

Ike's phone vibrated with a call. "I have no idea," he said as he answered the call. His tech guy was on the other end. "What'd you find?"

"No traceable IP. Whoever sent it didn't want to be found. They used TOR."

"You got me there?"

"The Onion Router. You can subscribe through several services. It encrypts the VPN tunnels and bounces around the world. The NSA guys might have something, but I can't trace it."

"Okay. Thanks."

Ike relayed the information to Mac as Maria walked in.

"You still working on that?" she said with a smile.

Ike knew his sister well. "I'm not signing on."

The smile never left her face. "Oh. Okay."

"I have to be in Houston. I'm committed. I've never stood up a client and I won't start now."

Still the smile. "I understand."

Ike ignored her. His thoughts shifted to his own closure. "What did you think of Cassidy's lead yesterday?" he asked Mac.

"Interesting. A call from out of nowhere directly referencing your parents' case. Cassidy is sloppy. He doesn't want the case to thaw. He thinks it's a loser for him."

"There's something there. I can feel it. I'll head to Homewood and check it out tomorrow. I'll give her some time to wake up and get going—probably there around eleven in the morning."

Mac nodded. He always let Ike run with his instincts. "Just don't be disappointed. Alzheimer's does terrible things to a person's mind. Had one of the guys on the force who had it. Erased most everything."

While Mac's warning irritated Ike, he knew it was Mac's way of looking out for him. He loved him for it.

Maria was still smiling, but Ike didn't ignore it this time. "And I'm going to stop by Tom Cole's office and talk to his partner." He gave Maria his fatherly look. "But I'm not taking this case. Just in case you're curious."

Maria didn't reply. She looked at Mac. "You ready to head home?"

Mac hugged Ike and followed Maria out of the office. Ike opened his e-mail again and looked at the numbers. Then he saw the case file from Houston on his desk. Something his father used to tell him came to mind. *Your word is your character. Stand by it no matter what.*

He closed the e-mail, opened the file, and began reading.

CHAPTER 10

IKE LEFT HIS Mount Washington condo early Tuesday and beat the traffic out of the city. He'd opened all the windows on his deep blue Shelby Mustang and reveled in the unseasonably warm air swirling through the car. A decent night's sleep had cleared his mind and his focus had returned.

He knew by taking this drive he was admitting that his curiosity regarding the e-mail, and his ego regarding Falzone's warning, were getting the best of him. He'd get to Cole's Seismic Services in Southpointe by seven and catch Cole's partner before his day got going. He'd prove to himself that his participation in the kid's case was fruitless and call the kid's aunt and respectfully decline. But that wasn't his prime mission today. He'd dispense with the kid's case and head back into the city to the Homewood Nursing Home and talk to Miss Emma Sosso. It was the first live lead in his parents' case in seven years—and Mac always said it only took one to break a case.

Ike turned into the parking lot from Town Center Boulevard. The five-story glass, steel, and brick building sparkled in the sunshine. A few golfers just down the hill were taking advantage of the warm September day. He walked into the entry and directly to the woman seated at the large check-in desk.

"Ike Rossi here to see Robert Scott."

The young woman picked up the phone. "Ike Rossi is here for Mr. Scott." The receptionist hesitated. After checking Scott's calendar and not seeing an appointment, Scott's assistant was checking with her boss.

The receptionist covered the phone. "Mr. Rossi, Mr. Scott is busy. You can leave your card and I'll see that he gets it."

"I'm not selling anything," Ike said. "Tell him I'm here about information regarding his partner's death." Ike's bomb had been detonated and the woman's face went crimson. She relayed the message minus Ike's tone. She hung up the phone and said, "He'll be right down."

A security guard in a dark-blue blazer appeared from a room behind the desk. Ike instinctively sized him up. He was unarmed and Ike quickly determined he could easily be incapacitated. He breathed deeply and quieted his mind. It was the nature of his business, but he was sure it wouldn't be necessary. The security guard was there for show.

The elevators behind the card-activated security turnstiles opened and a dark-haired mustached man of about forty, dressed in khakis and a polo shirt, emerged. The guard stepped to the turnstiles and whispered as the man carded through. He walked up to Ike, trailed by the guard, and offered his hand with an expression that said he was ready for the worst.

"Bobby Scott, sir."

Ike shook his hand. "Ike Rossi."

"I know who you are. I just Googled you."

"I was speaking to Lauren Bottaro last night and I have some questions regarding her brother."

"Did she hire you?"

"We're discussing it."

Scott looked puzzled. Then acquiesced. "Sure. Anything I can do for her."

Ike didn't want to do this in public. "Can we go somewhere private?"

"Yes."

Scott turned, gave the guard a wave, and led Ike through the turnstiles and up the elevator. They passed his assistant and entered his office. It was sparsely furnished and adorned with plaques announcing various oil or gas discoveries Ike recognized from his days working in the exploration and production business. A few pictures on the back credenza showed Scott was a family man with three young children. This would be easy.

"Sorry for coming unannounced, but something came up."

Scott squirmed in his seat. "No problem. How can I help you?"

Scott was structured and a bit stiff. He clearly had a technical background and was uncomfortable outside the numbers.

"First, I need to know if you deactivated Tom Cole's e-mail account."

Scott looked puzzled. "Yes. We did that two weeks ago. Why do you ask?"

"So, it would be impossible to send an e-mail from that account?"

"Yes. Did someone hack his account or something?"

"I'm sorry, but I can't say."

Now Scott looked as if he were sitting on thorns.

"Can you tell me about Tom—how you met and got this all going?"

"Tom and I met at the University of Texas. We were both undergrads. Our sophomore year we became roommates and remained that way through our PhDs."

"In geophysics?"

"Yes. Our focus was sub-salt seismic interpretation. That was just emerging back then in the Gulf."

Ike wanted to connect with Scott in some way, so he said he understood that sub-salt seismic interpretation was a challenge, since the deeper oil and gas targets in the Gulf of Mexico were covered by a layer of salt that varied in its geometry and composition. That effectively distorted the seismic waves that bounced off the layers of rock below, making it difficult to image a target reservoir with a drilling rig that cost a million dollars a day to operate.

Scott seemed impressed with Ike's knowledge and stopped squirming. "That's right. Long story short, Tom came up with a technique a few years ago that provided a much better image than anyone else. Using it, our clients had an unprecedented string of discoveries. Tom continued to refine it and the business rocketed to what it is today."

"Impressive," Ike said. "I hate to have to ask you, but what can you tell me about Tom's attitude leading up to his death?"

Scott's face darkened. "I didn't see it coming." Scott leaned back and looked out the floor-to-ceiling window. "Tom seemed okay. Sure, the crap with his ex was shitty, but he expected that. He never should have married her."

"How so?"

"Tom didn't date much when we were in school. He had a few flings, but I got the sense he was holding back for some reason. Then three years after we started this company, Brenda came along. I could tell from the start she wasn't good for him. But they met at a party and a one-night stand set him up. Then, once she moved in, I think he felt obligated. He ignored her previous two marriages, which had ended quickly and badly, and he married her. I think he thought he could help her—that it would be different with him."

"Do you think he was depressed about his divorce?"

"Not really. He seemed happy when they awarded him temporary custody of Jack. But that's when the shitstorm started. They made up stuff, accused him of crazy things. They even called me and said he was in trouble and I needed to get him to settle before it took our company down." Scott leaned forward. "I think that was the worst. The lies, the shame—that really hurt him."

"Do you think that's why he killed himself?"

Scott shook his head. "I don't know. I can't see him killing himself. He had Jack. He'd never do anything to hurt him."

"What about work? Was there anything unusual going on here?"

Scott's attention drifted out the window again. "You know, now that you mention it, about two months before he died he started on a project for a client, using a new technique he'd developed. He was tight-lipped for the entire project."

"That's not unusual in your business, confidentiality?"

"No. But this was a little different. He *personally* worked on the final data set. Kept it on his personal workstation. Said the client wanted to keep it tight. Once he'd processed the data he removed all the files and said he returned them to the client at their request. He was a little different after that."

Ike saw Scott's eyes widen. "Different? How?"

"He never seemed at ease. I felt like he was always thinking about something else. I wrote it off as part of the custody thing with Jack. But he seemed worried. The strange thing was the client. I don't know why he'd even do the work himself."

"Can you tell me who the client was?"

"Sorry. I'm bound by the confidentiality clause in the contract: location, the data, the client."

"Did you tell the detective about this?"

"Detective Cassidy never asked."

Ike sensed a thread of energy pulsing in the back of his mind. It was like the hair standing up on his Lab's back when she sensed a threat. What if Tom didn't kill himself? What if Cassidy didn't do a thorough job? These were the same cops—the same justice system— that couldn't give him closure after twenty-two years.

"Can you tell me anything about them?"

There was a raging ethical debate going on in Scott's eyes. Then he pulled out his lap drawer, typed something into the keyboard, and smiled at Ike. "I need to use the restroom. Would you like some coffee?"

"No, thanks."

Scott stood and glanced at the monitor, then Ike. "Feel free to enjoy the view."

Scott left the office and Ike walked around the desk. The web page was of the typical corporate format he'd seen hundreds of times. But the name turned the pulsing energy in his mind into a lightning bolt.

Falzone Energy.

CHAPTER 11

IKE ARRIVED AT Confluence Assisted Living in Homewood just before ten. Bright sunshine warmed his back when he exited the Shelby. His mind crackled with anticipation and possibilities. As he approached the entrance that disguised the place as a chalet, he shook off the thought that there might be more to Jack Cole's case than he thought. Still, he had no intention of taking the case in the face of this opportunity and his commitment to be in Houston tomorrow. He'd convinced himself he'd share what he'd learned with Lauren when he called and be done with it. Right now, he'd focus on coaxing as much as he could from Miss Emma Sosso.

He walked to the sign-in desk and wrote his name, then Emma Sosso's, and scribbled an illegible room number in the log book.

The older woman at the desk pulled her attention away from the computer screen. She was probably sixty but fit and well-dressed. Her smile was infectious.

"Welcome to Confluence." She looked down at the log book. "Oh, you're here to see Emma."

Ike spotted her name badge. "Good morning, Grace. I'm Ike Rossi. Emma and my mom were close. I was in town and I thought

I'd visit Miss Sosso. She was always good to me." A lie, of course, but a necessary one. He wasn't sure how secure the facility was.

"How nice. She's in our memory care facility. It's on the fifth floor. Up the elevator and you'll see a door with a keypad. Just punch in 710204 and the door will unlock. She'll be in the activities room down the hall to the right. If you don't see her, just ask one of the aides."

"Thanks, Grace."

He made his way through the lobby, then past the sitting area, a small movie theater, and a hair salon and reached the single elevator. A few residents were headed to the sitting area for some activity. A blue-shirted woman welcomed each one as she helped them into the sofas and chairs. Some walked well, some shuffled, and some struggled with their walkers, staring at their feet as if commanding them to obey. Ike spotted a man and a woman, each helping the other. For a moment, he envisioned his own parents. That's how'd they'd be now. Old but active and kind. He drove the thought back down before the sadness could reach his throat. The elevator chimed and he made his way to the fifth floor.

The door was heavy steel with a push bar. Above it, a sign read "Welcome to Our Neighborhood." He punched the code into the keypad and pushed the bar. The door opened and he entered the hallway. In front of him, a door had a miniature shingled pitched roof over it. To either side of the door was about four feet of siding. Ike looked to the right and left. Every door was adorned the same way. There were sitting areas at each end, one imitating a park and the other a lake shoreline, complete with sound effects.

He made his way down the hallway and passed a woman who gave him an empty smile. She tried one apartment door and then crossed the hall to another and continued the zigzag wandering down the hall. He wanted to help, but he sensed the pattern made her comfortable. Still, it saddened him. He approached two open double doors to his left and heard a TV. A blue-shirted girl wearing a name tag leaned against one of the doors. Stopping between the doors, he looked in. The walls were lined with residents with varying degrees of physical handicaps and awareness. It was worse than he'd expected.

"Hi, sir. Can I help you?" the young girl said.

"I'm here to see Emma."

She looked into the room and then walked toward a white-haired woman, seated but draped over her walker. "Emma, dear, you have a visitor."

The woman strained to raise her eyes, but her head didn't follow. She spotted Ike and gave a childlike smile. The aide helped her stand and Emma shuffled with her walker to meet Ike. The confusion was obvious but the smile stayed.

Ike decided to take command. "Emma, I'm Ike. You and my mom were friends."

"Oh, how nice," she said, turning her neck but still not raising her head. It looked painful.

"Can we visit over here?" Ike pointed to the park setting at the end of the hallway.

She started to make her way in that direction. Ike patiently walked at a snail's pace beside her. He'd always had immense respect for his elders. His father and mother had seen to that. They reached a padded park bench facing a fake lakeside beach.

"Is here okay?"

Emma kept smiling, rotated with her walker, and positioned herself above the bench. Ike helped her sit, then dropped beside her.

"How are you this morning?" Ike said.

"Oh, I'm fine. You're such a nice young man. What's your name?"

"Ike."

Emma just smiled. In her eyes, Ike could tell she was barely keeping up with the conversation.

"Emma, my mother's name was Luciana. Luciana Rossi."

"That's a pretty name. She widened her eyes. And what's your name?"

"Ike, Miss Sosso." Ike had read that with Alzheimer's, long-term memory sometimes lingered, depending on the stage of the disease. He was banking on that. "Miss Sosso, something happened to my mother a while back. I thought you might remember something about it."

"What's your mother's name?"

Ike was patient, but each time she asked he drifted away from hope and closer to hopelessness. "Luciana Rossi. She worked at Carmine's on Liberty Avenue."

Ike saw something click in Emma's struggling mind. Her face shifted to fear and concern. "I told her not to do it."

Ike's brain ignited a rush that shuddered through his body, but he remained calm. "Do what, Emma?"

The smile returned and she remained silent.

"Emma, what shouldn't my mother have done?"

"What's your mother's name?"

"Luciana. Emma, what shouldn't she have done?"

Still the empty smile. "What's your name?"

Ike held his frustration. The woman was clearly struggling. "It's Ike. What shouldn't my mother have done?"

The smile vanished and she was searching, straining for an answer. Nothing came. She began to seem a little agitated and Ike saw confusion in her eyes. She'd had enough. As much as he wanted answers, he refused to put Emma under any stress. She didn't deserve it.

"It's okay, Emma. We can just sit here. Where are you from?"

She knew that answer. "Bloomfield. I lived there with my mom and dad."

"That's nice."

"My mom let me help her in the kitchen. I liked to cook," she said proudly.

"My mom liked to cook, too."

"That's nice."

Emma looked off into a place Ike hoped he'd never see. She didn't say another word. As each second passed, Ike's despair ate away at him. He hated this feeling. It happened every time he ran into a dead end on his parents' case. It was a stew of worthlessness and guilt. He told himself that it was nothing compared with what Emma was going through. But she wouldn't remember. He'd never forget.

After they'd sat for an hour, the aide came over. "Emma, it's time for lunch. Will your visitor be joining us?"

Ike declined and watched Emma shuffle away into the dining area along with any hope of solving the case. But she had told him something. If it was reliable, which was unlikely, his mother might have been involved in something that got his parents killed. Right now, Ike just didn't want to believe that. His frustration built as he left the building and thought about what might have happened if the police had found Emma years ago.

The frustration grew into a smoldering rage and he knew what he had to do. It was what he always did when he felt this way. He got into his car and pulled a new burner phone from the glove box. He punched in the numbers and the man answered.

"Set it up. Tonight," Ike said. He hung up and slammed the phone into the console.

CHAPTER 12

IKE STUDIED THE contents of the flat-panel monitor on the wooden desk in the center of his office above Rossi's. Late-afternoon light leaked through the stenciled glass on his office door and the music below his feet grew more audible, signaling the beginning of Wednesday's happy hour. A tone preceded the reminder that blocked the document he'd been reading. It told Ike it was four p.m. and time to call Lauren. Instantly, he felt he'd stepped on a high wire with no net. It was a simple call—one he'd made many times before—but somehow this was different.

He'd been scouring police reports, confidential documents, and financial statements provided by GCP Energy in connection with his commitment in Houston. He'd immersed himself in that work all afternoon and distracted himself from thinking about the dead end in his parents' case, and the black hole the kid's case represented. Hours earlier, he'd decided to tell Lauren he couldn't help Jack and then he'd head to Houston. The reasons were solid: he had a contract and had accepted a retainer and given his word to the client. GCP's chairman had indicated there was an uneasiness among the executive team, the board, and their families—they wondered who would be next. It was affecting not only their families but everyone in the company, and the bottom line was suffering. They needed to be certain that the deaths of their CFO and CEO were not, in fact, murders. The chairman had information that made him wonder, and he needed Ike to run it to the ground.

That was it. He'd tell Lauren he'd given his word. And his father had said to never break that promise. His commitment. The reasoning had sat well when he decided to turn her down, but now he'd have to tell her. The image of Jack sitting on the courthouse bench alone, eyes begging, didn't help.

Ike picked up his phone as he stood and looked out onto Liberty Avenue. Traffic was thickening thanks to the shift change at West Penn Hospital down the street. He entered the number Lauren had given him and leaned against the window frame.

"Hello?" Her voice sounded full of expectation and hope. He hated to do this.

"Lauren, this is—I—"

"Mr. Rossi. So nice to hear from you. I thought we'd hear from you today."

Ike heard Jack and another boy yelling and laughing.

Lauren covered the phone, but Ike still heard. "Boys, boys. I'm on the phone with Mr. Rossi. Please go in the other room."

She wasn't making this easy.

"Okay," she said returning to the call. "Jack and my son, Jimmy, finished their homework and I let them get out the Star Wars gear."

"Sounds like fun."

"It is. It's just a joy to watch them play. Jimmy is the only one Jack plays with these days."

Ike sank even lower against the window but stayed silent.

"So, I'm assuming you're calling me with great news?"

There was no easy way to do this. Ike decided he'd ease into it.

"First of all, I wanted to let you know I went to Tom's office this morning."

"Great, already on the job."

"No, no. I'm sorry but I just went by to see if there was any information regarding that e-mail I received."

Lauren said nothing, but Ike heard the boys' voices fading and a door close.

"They'd disconnected his e-mail, so it didn't come from their office. It couldn't have. But I found out he'd been working on a project for Falzone's oil and gas subsidiary."

"They were a big customer before he married Brenda. He didn't like it, but he just kept it separate." Lauren's voice had turned cold. "Are you going to help or not, Mr. Rossi?"

Ike shook his head. "I can't, Lauren. I'm committed to go to Houston." There was silence on the other end. He heard a sniffle. Then he continued to give the reasoning he'd given himself. He waited for her reply.

"Mr. Rossi"—her voice cracked initially but turned determined— "let me get this straight. You're going to abandon us—abandon Jack to face his fate on his own against those people so you can go to Houston and help some big corporation who has an army of lawyers to do whatever they need."

"I'm so sorry, but I gave my word. I have a commitment."

"That's a piece of paper, Mr. Rossi. Let me tell you about commitment." She was yelling now. "My late husband died in the hills of Afghanistan because he was committed. It was his second tour. He could have stayed home with Jimmy and me, but he was committed to the freedom he was fighting for. He was committed to the families of the thousands of people who died in those towers. That's a commitment." She began to cry. "You can save this boy's life. I know that—and I think you do, too. You can always go to Houston and patch up your precious reputation, but you can't undo what's about to happen to Jack."

Ike wanted to get off the phone with her. "Lauren, I'm sending a report about what I did today to your attorney. Have her check out the leads described in there."

"So that's it?"

"I'm sorry, Lauren."

"Yes, you are," she said and ended the call.

Ike jammed the phone into his pocket. "Shit!" He grabbed the sports duffel on the side chair before launching himself out the door and slamming it behind him.

CHAPTER 13

IKE DROVE NORTH, out of the city, window down, toward what he called "The Farm." The fresh, cool evening air raced through the car and chilled his skin. He was in that place again— the place where he felt like he was standing atop a fifty-story building and looking over the edge. He was boxed in by another dead end in his parents' case. He was trapped between his word, something he'd never broken, and a helpless kid battling the same system that had failed to deliver justice for Ike. The anger and frustration had him charged like a capacitor ready to discharge its deadly voltage. The Farm offered an avenue to discharge. It was quicker than therapy and Ike got paid for it. He'd embraced the expectation of relief.

As the last remnants of daylight vanished into darkness, Ike pulled to the entrance six miles outside Harmony. It was rolling Pennsylvania farm land and the only meaningful light in the thick darkness came from the halogen beams of his Shelby Mustang. He rolled to a stop across from the speaker just before the gate. He pushed the button.

"Yes."

"It's me."

The gates opened and he eased the clutch out and prowled past the whitewashed fence and thick tree line, down the smooth black asphalt. Ike began to focus on the techniques his father had painstakingly taught him over the years. He envisioned every move and every counter. He knew inattention now would equal pain for a week. He flexed and released each muscle, ensuring their collective responsiveness.

The Farm was a ninety-acre property owned by Phil Moretti, a wealthy trust-fund baby whose family had earned their fortune through the glass business as a front for organized crime and gone legit a generation ago. He'd parlayed that fortune into an even bigger one by buying up natural gas royalties around western Pennsylvania before the boom. He was a braggart who paid for all the connections he could. Ike would much rather punch him out than take his money. But Ike wasn't here for the money, not by a long shot.

The tree-lined road opened to a smaller gravel parking lot next to a large white corrugated-steel building with four large garage doors. He was sure it had been built as a stable for the guy's car collection. But the collection had been liquidated, down to one Lamborghini and a Corvette that sat just outside the open center door. At least twenty cars were spread around the gravel and the grass beyond. Ike guessed the owners had all paid six figures or more for each one. These were people with money. Sports figures, bankers, company founders, and even a few Mafia bosses from the old days—all here to see him. He pulled next to the Vette and got out. He grabbed the duffel from the trunk and headed through the door.

The bright lights assaulted Ike's eyes, and as expected, Moretti was right inside waiting.

"There he is. Ike"—he waved—"come over here and meet these guys."

Ike walked to Moretti and the four other men while he eyed the small crowd surrounding the boxing ring. Moretti grabbed Ike's hand and shook it. "You ready?"

Ike bit his tongue. "Always."

Moretti went through introductions. Two of the men were retired founders, one was another trust-funder, and the last was an enforcer from the Penguins.

"Ike here won the state championship single-handedly."

"I remember the play," the trust-funder said. "Christ, they still show that clip all the time. You were the best quarterback to come out of here, including the two Joes"—he looked at the hockey player— "Namath and Montana." The hockey player seemed to be sizing up Ike.

Ike said what he always said. "That was a long time ago." He shook their hands, excused himself, and walked into the makeshift dressing room to the left. He changed quickly and was joined by Alfredo, a barrel-chested fifty-eight-year-old Mexican immigrant who'd helped his father prepare for the countless kickboxing matches back in the eighties. Ike always felt closer to his father when he was here. A tristate champion until a well-placed kick cratered his knee and ended his passion, he'd taken Ike to nearly every match. Once old enough, Ike became his sparring partner. At the time, he couldn't believe his father would hit him that hard, but now he silently thanked him.

Alfredo pulled the tape from the bag and wrapped his hands. "You sure you want to do this again?"

Ike gave him a gentle smile. "Yes, Alfredo. I have to."

Alfredo knew why. They'd had a running conversation for the past ten years.

Alfredo finished and held Ike's fist. "Be careful today. This one is a giant."

Ike just nodded. Size didn't matter.

Alfredo slipped on the thin gloves, made the sign of the cross, and left.

It was time. Ike ignited the rage. He breathed deeply and punched his gloves together. He thought about his parents, and then he thought about Vic Cassidy and his dead end. He thought about Jack sitting alone in the courthouse. He imagined lead in each fist and an iron shield on his body. He let the beast out of the darkness and stomped out to the ring.

The ring was empty: no corner men, no announcer and no referee. He spotted his opponent immediately. He towered over the ring, at least six feet eight and pushing 280. He looked perfectly proportioned and toned, with long flowing blond hair. He was built like the defensive ends he'd dodged the first few years at Penn State. Quick and powerful. Where did he get these guys?

Still, he was ready. Once they entered the ring, Ike's impression of the man shrank. Size didn't matter. They never used names, but Ike named each opponent in his mind. *Thor.*

"Okay, gents," Moretti yelled from the side of the ring, "betting is closed. Here we go."

He picked up a bell and the hammer and struck it. Thor charged through the center of the ring, growling. Ike took three steps. He planted his left foot as Thor threw a right at Ike's cheek. Ike stopped it with his left. And drilled Thor's temple with his right. The impact stopped the big man's momentum, and Thor's anger switched to surprise. But he could take a punch. His head felt like concrete. Thor squared up and danced to Ike's left, reassessing his approach.

Doubt. Once doubt entered their minds, Ike knew he had them. He hit Ike hard with a combination, hard enough to make him want to end this. Ike stepped in, picking off Thor's jabs and neutralizing his reach. He thanked his father again. Ike imagined his parents' killer and what he'd do to him. Then Jack's image burst into his mind. A fatherless boy against the system. Against Falzone. Alone. And Ike had to stand by his word.

A left hook caught Ike by surprise, but he'd been hit harder. The anger of it all gathered in his fists as if a giant weapon were being charged to fire. He saw the opening, blocked another left, and launched an uppercut. It connected and rocked Thor to his heels. The small crowd rumbled, and Ike followed with a left, then a right to the chin. The left stunned Thor and the right dropped him. The crowd of rich lawbreakers groaned, then cheered. Thor was out.

Ike dropped his arms and stepped back as a doctor entered the ring and watched Thor regain consciousness. Ike let out a long breath—the anger was gone. He walked over to Thor and helped him to his feet and headed to the corner where his apparent girlfriend waited with tears in her eyes. Thor still looked as if he were in another zip code.

"You fight well and hit like a freight train. Thanks for the bout," Ike said.

Thor stopped and looked at Ike with incredulity. "You ain't no quarterback. You're great, man. Just great."

Ike handed Thor off to the doctor and his girlfriend. "Water, ice and rest," he said to the girlfriend. "He'll be fine."

Ike turned and watched the crowd gather around Moretti, collecting payouts. The odds were usually thin when Ike fought, since he'd never been knocked down. He stepped between the ropes and Moretti broke away from the crowd.

"You call me any time," he said, grinning as he plucked a neatly banded stack of hundreds from his sport coat and handed them to Ike. "Never seen anything like it." He turned and walked back to the crowd.

Ike returned to the dressing room long enough to slip on some sweats and collect his bag. He drove into the city in silence as he always did after a fight. It was a time to be with his dad, or at least his memories of him. He talked about the visit with Emma and wondered what his mom would have been doing that might have ended their lives. He talked about commitment and how his father had told him that his word was everything. Never break it. And finally, as he headed across the Fort Duquesne Bridge, he told his father about Jack.

Instead of crossing the Monongahela and heading to his place on Mount Washington, he looped into the city, to Lawrenceville. He pulled into the lot of the Boys & Girls Club. They'd taken such good care of Maria. He knew there were other kids, good, innocent kids who needed help.

He left the car and walked to the glass doors with his bag. He pulled out the wad of hundreds, stuck them into an envelope, and slid it through the slot beside the door.

Just above the slot, taped to the inside, was a letter and a picture of a young boy, probably six or seven, displaying a wide toothless smile. The writing was blocky and the young author had made a noble attempt to stay inside the lines. The letter thanked the donors, volunteers, and the Boys & Girls Club. But it was the last line that hit him harder than any punch that Thor had thrown.

I was alone, my mommy and daddy were lost, and I did not know what to do. But my Aunt Jenny took me to you and you helped me. Thank you for making me happy.

A seven-year-old. Ike dropped his head, then turned and looked up into the night sky. "Sorry, Dad. I'm breaking my word just this one time."

He got into his car and headed into Bloomfield.

CHAPTER 14

IKE TOUCHED THE welt on his cheek and wished he were still in the ring. Pacing past his office window again, he looked at his phone for the third time. The tension wound up like a spring charging for its recoil. Soon, he'd be trading away the one thing his father said to never let go.

It was 10:20 p.m. and he had an hour advantage to Houston, but soon it would be too late to call. He wanted to clear the first call so he could call Lauren. His rule was that a call before the eleven o'clock news was fair game. It was a family tradition, once he reached thirteen, to be sent to bed by his parents immediately afterward. He guessed Lauren would be up until eleven but her kids would be in bed. The news in Houston came on at ten. It was time.

The phone was heavy in his hand, and he didn't want to dial. But that was the plan: the chairman in Houston first, then Lauren. He touched the contact on the screen, placed the phone to his ear, and remembered the fight.

After three rings, the chairman, William Archer, answered. "Archer."

Ike could hear plates and glasses clanging in the background. "Mr. Archer, this is Ike Rossi."

"Funny. I used to worry about private caller IDs, but now they're the important calls. You in Houston?"

Ike shoved his doubt aside. "No, sir. There's been a development. I'm going to be delayed."

Archer's Texas drawl thickened. "Delayed? What? Son, I hope someone died."

"No, sir. But I can't come tomorrow." Ike heard footsteps as the background noise faded and then abruptly ended with the slam of a door.

"Look here, Mr. Rossi. You and I have a contract. I paid you a $200,000 retainer. I have two dead executives and the others worried to death about going to work. You get down here, now."

"I'll wire the money back, sir, and if you can't wait a couple of weeks, I can recommend someone who'd do a great job."

"If I wanted someone else, I would have done that. You were recommended to me by five different people. They said you were a man of your word. The only one to call. Are you going back on that?"

Ike hit the windowsill with the heel of his hand. "Unfortunately, I have to. I'm sorry."

"You're going to be more than sorry. Do you know who you're screwing with? I'll have my general counsel and our best outside firm all over you. I'll smother you with a breach-of-contract suit and be sure your name isn't worth shit in the business."

Ike straightened up. "You need to get a grip, sir. And know who *you're* talking to. My word is still as good as any contract. I have a kid's life in the balance, and you or your team of lawyers can't stop me from doing the right thing. Those fancy-suited lawyers can make all the noise you'd like. The fact remains I'm delayed.

"I'd be happy to help you once I help him, but not before," he continued. "You can bluster all you want, but it won't accomplish anything. Call me, send me an e-mail, or have one of your legal lackeys send me a new contract if you agree to the change. If not, my offer stands to give you a great recommendation. Good night, sir!" Ike almost dislocated his finger ending the call. He tossed the phone onto his desk.

Ike heard Maria's footsteps. He remembered the look she'd given him when he walked through the bar. The same one he always got when she suspected he'd fought. Her silhouette appeared at the open door and she tapped lightly on the glass.

"It's okay."

She made a beeline for him, examining his face. "You did it again, didn't you?"

"I'm going to help the kid."

She stepped back. "What?"

"I'm going to help Jack."

She lunged and hugged him.

He saw Mac in the doorway. "Might as well join the party," Ike said.

"Am I interrupting?"

"No I—"

Maria released him. "No. He's helping Jack."

Mac raised his bushy eyebrows.

"She's right," Ike said.

"What changed your mind?"

Before he could answer, Maria said, "He was fighting again."

Mac scowled. "Let's pretend I didn't hear that."

"Let's," Ike said. He picked up a folder from his desk and handed it to Mac.

"What about Houston? Won't they be mad?" Mac said.

"Already called him. Mad, but I'm out for now."

Mac glanced through the file, then closed it. "Something's not right here."

Ike picked up his phone from the desk. "Yeah. And I'm about to find out." He dialed Lauren's number. Maria held her breath but still grinned.

Lauren answered on the first ring. "Hello."

"Ms. Bottaro?"

Ike heard a huff on the other end.

"Mr. Rossi. It's late," she said as if she were talking to an ex.

"I'm going to help. I'm going to help Jack."

Another huff. "What do you mean? Help?" Lauren was still ice-cold.

"I'm 100 percent committed now."

A long silence, punctuated by a sob. "What changed?"

"Let's just say I had a talk with a very wise man. Jack doesn't deserve to face this without my help."

"I can't pay you, Mr. Rossi."

"It's Ike, and I wouldn't take it if you could."

Lauren's voice returned to the optimistic tone Ike remembered. "Why would you do this?"

Ike thought about his answer. For the first time in a very long time, he opened that place he guarded from everyone and let something escape. "If not for me, then for Jack. And maybe, if for Jack, then maybe for me."

Ike noticed that the smile had left Maria's face.

"I don't understand," Lauren said.

"It's about closure. Closure for Jack. His father died and he doesn't accept how or why. I've been there, Lauren. I've been there for twenty-two years. I won't let that be the case for Jack. I promise you." A strange new feeling overtook Ike for a few seconds. The abyss was still there, but it felt as if someone were standing with him. Someone or something. It was certainty and determination and pride and love all indistinguishably mixed.

Lauren's voice strengthened. "There's a meeting at eight a.m. at Jenna's office tomorrow."

"I'll be there."

Another pause.

"Ike?"

"Yes."

"I can't thank you enough."

Ike kept his guard down. "No need to thank me. See you tomorrow."

He ended the call and Maria and Mac stood silently, as if they'd just seen the Resurrection.

Ike's words echoed in his head.

If not for me, then for Jack. If for Jack, then maybe for me.

CHAPTER 15

IT WAS FIVE minutes to eight and Ike's navigation system told him he'd arrived—he wished it hadn't. He pulled onto the concrete drive that was ten times bigger than necessary for the three-windowed brick home converted to the law offices of Price and Price. While it might be a nice practice here in Cranberry Township, it was ten times smaller than all the law firms he'd worked with. He envisioned an ant being crushed under the foot of the justice system, and the abyss in his gut widened a little more.

As he stepped from his car, he examined the four other cars in the lot. An SUV and three sedans meant Lauren and Jack were already here, along with the Prices and their assistant. The fall morning chill evaporated the dullness of the long ride as he trotted up the walkway. He knocked on one of the wooden double doors as he entered. He spotted a woman, gray and probably in her sixties, twisting something in her hands. Jack sat next to her.

"Mr. Rossi!" Jack said as he snatched the Rubik's Cube from her hands and stood, displaying it to Ike like a trophy.

"Hi, Jack. How's it going?"

"I was showing Mrs. Duncan how to do this."

"As I remember, you're pretty good at it."

Jack stuck out his chest and grinned at Mrs. Duncan. She stood and reached across the desk. "I'm Kristin Duncan, the Prices' legal assistant."

"Ike Rossi," he said, shaking her hand.

She stepped past Jack and said, "Jack, honey, please wait here." She eyed Ike. "Mr. Rossi, they're all in here if you'd follow me."

The hall was six feet long with only one door, which she opened. Ike saw Jenna and Lauren on one side of the conference table as he entered. Thick files were stacked to Jenna's left. He didn't notice the man immediately across from her until he was in the room and Kristin had closed the door.

"I'm Edgar Price," the man said. "You must be Mr. Rossi."

"Call me Ike, sir." Ike shook his hand. His thin frame and curly gray hair didn't match his strong grip.

"Then call me Ed."

Jenna reached across the table. "Mr. Rossi."

The same grip. "Ms. Price."

"Oh, if you're calling him Ed, you're calling me Jenna."

He'd remembered her run to the Final Four—everyone in western Pennsylvania did. That season she broke the all-time season-scoring record for women *and* men. The men's mark had stood since 1970 when Pistol Pete Maravich closed out his career at LSU. She'd scored more points per game than legends like Larry Bird, Oscar Robertson and Stephen Curry. She'd carried the Panthers through the tournament as if possessed. She still looked as if she could take the court and compete. Ike could always spot the fire of competition.

Lauren stood and offered her hand

"Lauren." Ike shook her soft hand.

She covered Ike's hand with hers and held on, smiling. For the first time, he noticed her dark eyes locked on his. "Mr. Rossi, it's great to have you with us," she said.

Ike settled in next to Ed, then felt the group staring at him, waiting.

"We ready to go?" Ike said.

Ed slid a new yellow tablet in front of him, and Ike connected the dots. "Oh. Sorry," he said, sliding the pad back to Ed. "I don't take notes—better for listening."

Ed and Jenna shared a glance. Then Jenna slid the stack of files across the table.

"These are key files you'll want to review. You'll see we've gone through the prelims, and unless something breaks our way, we're going to trial in five days."

Ike slid the thick files from the stack and spread them in front of him. "What's your strategy?"

"DA McCann has made his case for murder one. He's trying to prove Jack willfully, deliberately and with premeditation planned and executed the killing of Franklin Tanner. We're going to agree to those facts."

"What?"

You'll see it's very difficult to dispute the evidence in the responding officer's report, the investigator's initial assessment, the emergency medical personnel's report, and the forensics. Jack did it—without question."

"Self-defense or mental incapacity?"

"You are a quick study," Jenna said.

Lauren rose, and Ike sensed the details of Jack's crime were upsetting her. "I'm going to check on Jack," she said.

Ike and Ed stood as she left the room, then returned to their seats.

"Sorry about that." Ike looked at the door.

"She's had a hard run," Jenna said. "She's had to deal with the custody hearing as well as the criminal trial prep. She's been dragged through the mud by the other side. She's mortgaged her house in

Shadyside to get Jack's bail and pay us, which we refused, but she insisted. And she's raising her own boy, Jimmy, at the same time."

"When's the custody hearing?"

"Judge wants to finish on Friday. Our forced mediation was yesterday." Jenna threw a nod at the door. "Her psych test came back great. The examiner said it was one of the best she's seen."

"So Falzone will lose?"

Ed leaned in. "No. The judge is connected to the Falzones. We're preparing to fight a visitation order."

Ike couldn't imagine being forced to spend time with the Falzones while the trial was going on. "Jack must be scared."

"I'd say determined."

Ike sent an expression of incredulity in Jenna's direction.

Jenna responded with an icy glare. "He's determined someone was behind all of this. He said they were coming for him."

"Tanner?"

"Yes, Tanner. And others who he can't name. Said he overheard his father talking about it two days before he died."

"So, self-defense?" Ike asked again.

Jenna settled back in her chair and looked at Ed.

"We have no evidence to support any of Jack's claims," Ed said.

"Nothing?"

"Nothing until we got your memo and the five million-dollar offer from Falzone."

"They're hiding something," Ike said. "And there's a connection between Tanner and the Falzones."

"Right—through the law firm."

"So it's self-defense." Ike said.

Ed locked eyes with Jenna, then tilted his head toward Ike.

"We've prepared a backup defense. It levers Jack's social awkwardness and his problems with other kids."

A wave of disappointment and sadness for Jack rose inside Ike. "He's just a kid. There's nothing wrong with him. He's just extremely smart. You do this to him now, say he was somehow defective, that will wreck him. He'll carry that for a lifetime."

"We know—we know." Jenna leaned into the table on her elbows. "That's why we need you. You have to find evidence Tom's death wasn't suicide. If you show that Tanner was somehow involved in Tom's death and threatened Tom's family—we don't have to go that way."

Ike let the words wash over him. Produce evidence in five days that hadn't been uncovered by six months' worth of work by two detectives working for the Prices, or Jack's life is over. He let the pressure build, his mind running wild with it. That pressure, that fear of failure, he'd harness and turn loose on the case.

"Okay. Any luck with the e-mail?"

Jenna pulled it from the remaining thin file next to her. "I showed it to Dad and Lauren. Nothing."

"Did you ask Jack?"

"Not yet."

"Mind if I talk to him? I won't show him the e-mail or tell him it's from his father. That would be too much for him. Too confusing."

"Agreed," Jenna said, sliding the copy to Ike. "Already discussed it with Lauren. She's okay with it, as long as she's there."

"Alone," Ike said. "I talk to Jack alone."

"Why?"

"I think we have a connection. I want to build on that. Lauren is someone he seems to want to protect. She'll be in the way."

Jenna scoffed. "I'll let you tell her that."

"Be happy to." Ike slid the e-mail aside and grabbed the thick folder on the top of his stack. He pulled the suicide file. "Anything in here?" he said as he opened it and flipped through the pages.

"Scene was processed as a suicide from the start. Detective Cassidy leaned heavily on the crime-scene investigator's report and the note Tom left on his printer."

Ike flinched at the mention of Cassidy's name, then hoped it went undetected. He slowed his page turns as he got to the photos of the garage where they found Tom: a three-quarter-inch garden hose messily duct-taped to the exhaust of a BMW 530, the other end pinched in the driver's-side window. The keys loose in the cup holder in the console. Tom Cole's ashen face, looking forward but cocked awkwardly against the headrest. *Jack should never see these.* Ike studied the photos again.

"What is it?"

"Not sure yet. But I know Cassidy and he likes shortcuts. Can I take this?" Ike closed the file.

"Sure. Those copies are for your use," Ed said.

"Did you depose his ex?"

"Yes. It's there," Jenna said.

"The Falzones?"

"No way. Judge wouldn't allow it."

"Why not?"

"I'm sure you know about the death of their son, Patrick, about eight months ago."

"Car accident. What's that got to do with excusing them from being deposed?"

"Judge said they were grieving his death and now the loss of their ex-son-in-law. Their attorney argued alongside the DA that it wasn't relevant to the Tanner murder. The judge quashed the subpoenas."

Slowly the plan was forming in Ike's head. Tom Cole's death, the Falzone connections, and go from there. They'd spent more time reviewing the files and the insanity theory. Ike was disgusted with that option. He imagined what it did to Lauren.

But they were right. Evidence for self-defense was nonexistent. To get anything, he'd have to get through the defenses of one of the wealthiest families in America—and find fault with the work of the detective that had held him at bay in his own parents' case for the last eight years. All in five days. He pulled out the e-mail again and looked at the expression on the page.

"I'd like to talk to Jack now."

CHAPTER 16

IKE WAITED IN the conference room for Lauren. In many ways, this would be the most difficult interview he'd ever conducted. Under conditions that rattled the coolest and silenced the most talkative, he'd questioned hundreds of people ranging from egotistical executives to hardened criminals to the most honest and humble workers on the planet, but he knew he had to walk a fine line with Jack. Push him too hard and he'd clam up and never trust Ike again. Too soft and Jack would be convicted despite unknowingly holding the key to his freedom buried in his brilliant mind. Even so, he had to build trust quickly and then press Jack for answers. But first, he had to convince Lauren he had to do it alone.

Lauren slipped past the open door. Her soft welcoming smile triggered an unfamiliar stirring inside. She looked more rested, and her skin glowed from the benefit of some sunshine. Ike suspected she was a runner. Her lean figure and toned muscles were sculpted from more than chasing two young boys around the park. As a rule, Ike didn't pay attention to those things most of the time. Over the years, he'd proved a poor judge of women.

She closed the door and sat in the chair next to Ike. "Jenna said you needed to talk to me?"

Ike could feel her warmth and regretted what he was about to do. He knew she was an extraordinary mother, now to two boys, and she'd kept them close and away from the media, the public, and upsetting questions.

"I'd like to speak to Jack," he said.

"Okay. I thought you might need to do that. We'll be happy to talk with you. Let me go get him." She stood.

"Lauren?"

She stopped and turned back.

"Please have a seat."

Her warmth disappeared. "What is it?"

"I need to speak to Jack alone."

Based on the fire in her eyes, Ike girded for an assault. His question had obviously ignited her motherly protective instinct. He felt like a hiker between a mother bear and her cub.

"What do you mean, alone?"

Ike carefully pressed on. "I think it's important for Jack and me to talk. I think there may be a connection between us. And he clearly is worried about protecting you. That might prove an impediment."

"You think he won't tell the truth in front of me?" she asked as if cross-examining Ike.

"No. I don't think he'd ever lie to you or in front of you, but he may not tell me the whole truth. And we need that." Ike reached out and covered her hand on the table. "I wouldn't ask this of you if it wasn't important. We only have four and a half days until trial."

Lauren looked at his hand covering hers and then at Ike with a mix of warmth and uncertainty. "Okay. But please don't show him that e-mail. It will just upset him."

"I won't show him the e-mail, but I'd like to show him the mathematical expression. I won't tell him how I got it."

Lauren didn't answer. She held Ike's gaze for a moment and then nodded. "I'll get him."

She left the room and thirty seconds later returned with Jack.

Jack glanced up at Lauren, then at Ike. He stuck out his hand. "Thank you for helping me, Mr. Rossi."

After shaking his hand, Ike offered him the seat next to him. Pulling the Rubik's Cube from his pocket, Jack sat down.

"I'll be just outside," Lauren said, kissing the top of his head and eyeing Ike.

Lauren left and closed the door and Jack resisted making eye contact. Jack scanned the room, stopping on every item as if cataloging its contents. Ike sensed the awkwardness.

"So, you like that Rubik's Cube?"

Jack picked up the cube and looked at Ike. Jack's eyes were a brilliant blue and overflowing with an alert energy Ike had never seen. "I do. Did you know there are 43.5 quadrillion combinations and only one correct one?"

"No, I didn't, but I did know that the inventor's name was Erno."

Jack chuckled. "That's a funny name."

"Well, in Hungary, where he lived, I'll bet it was just fine."

Jack nodded in agreement and twisted the cube a few times. Ike knew he needed to press on but wasn't sure Jack was ready. Then, suddenly, Jack locked eyes with Ike. "Are you sad your mom and dad were killed?"

Caught by surprise, Ike simply answered. "Yes. I miss them every day."

"And it was a long time ago?"

"Twenty-two years. How did you know about my mom and dad?"

Jack went back to fiddling with the cube. "I looked it up online. You were a great football player, too."

"I was pretty good."

Jack locked his eyes on Ike again. "I really miss my dad."

Ike could feel the sadness he saw in Jack's eyes. Too much pain for someone so young. Ike leaned in face-to-face with Jack. "I know, Jack. It must be really hard."

Jack seemed to catch himself and flushed the sadness from his face. "Can you help me?"

"That's why I'm here."

Jack cautiously glanced at the closed door. He returned his focus to Ike and raised his eyebrows. "Can you stop them?"

"Stop who?"

"The people who killed my dad. They're coming for me and my Aunt Lauren."

"How do you know that?"

He glanced at the door again. "I heard my dad talking about it."

Ike's instincts were alerted. "Can you tell me what you heard?"

Jack nodded. "Just don't tell Aunt Lauren."

"Why not?"

"I don't want to scare her. If she gets too scared she might leave."

Ike put his hand on Jack's shoulder. "I know for sure she'd never do that. But if you tell me, it might help me help you."

Jack stared at the cube. "First he told me that he loved me. He looked worried. He said he was working on a very important project and couldn't spend as much time with me as he liked. I understood. He told me that my mom was doing everything she could to get me away from him."

"What did you think about your mom?"

"She was mean to me and my dad. But my dad said that she had some problems and it had nothing to do with me. He said she still loved me but that she was sick and couldn't help it."

"That sounds very hard."

Jack looked at the floor and nodded.

"Jack, can you tell me what else you heard your dad say?"

"Yeah. I was outside with my telescope and had to come back in to get another lens. He didn't know I had come back inside. He was in the garage talking on the phone and I heard him say that if something happened to him, to take Jack and his money and get away from here. Then he said that Tanner was wanting to destroy him. He said they were trying to stop him and would do anything,"

"Did you ask him about it?"

Jack shook his head. "I ran outside—then—" Jack started to cry. "My dad was killed the next day. And I didn't stop it. So I stopped Mr. Tanner. He was coming for me. I knew he was after me."

Gently, Ike cradled Jack in his arms. As Jack wailed, Ike felt his tears. He felt his pain and his sense of guilt. They were all too familiar. The door cracked open and Lauren peeked in. Ike gave her his silent assurance that it was okay. Then Jack pulled back a little and looked at Ike with his wet eyes. "Can you help me?"

Ike hugged Jack again and looked at Lauren. "Yes, I will, Jack. Yes, I will."

With a couple of staccato breaths, Jack stopped crying, leaned back, and wiped his nose with his forearm.

Ike grabbed the tablet in front of him and wrote down the mathematical expression: $3-53+8x2+19$.

He slid it in front of Jack. "Do you know what this means?"

Jack examined the tablet.

"That's easy. Minus 15."

Ike waited, but Jack began handling the Rubik's Cube again. It meant nothing to him.

"Okay, Jack. You okay?"

Jack just nodded.

"Let's go see your aunt."

As Ike and Jack walked out of the room, Jack reached up and took Ike's hand.

CHAPTER 17

IKE KNEW THIS was a bold move, but time was running out and risks needed to be taken. Jack's trouble was deep and thick, and going slow or standing still would be like standing atop quicksand—he'd sink in the morass of the legal system and be smothered and choked by the overwhelming facts against him. As he turned from Grant Street and entered the parking garage under Falzone Center, he pegged his odds of seeing any Falzone at less than 5 percent. He'd see Bigfoot first. They'd hide behind their offices, their card-driven turnstiles, and a wall of corporate security to stonewall him. That's what he'd do in their shoes. But this was sending the message, and five million dollars said it would strike home. It would exert pressure—and pressure leads to mistakes.

He exited his car and checked his e-mail as he always did. His eyes froze three messages down. *Tom Cole.* Another e-mail. When he opened the message, there was just one line: *4+3−53+8+74.*

Two of the numbers had been in the last expression and it had seven numbers in all, just like the last one, but this one had no multiplication. Anchored in place next to his car, he ran through the possibilities and discarded his leading candidate. Because there were now two expressions, there was little chance they were four-digit combinations to a safe somewhere. Phone numbers went out the window for the same reason. That put him back to nowhere.

And who the hell was sending these? His tech guy said the IP address couldn't be traced, and there was a possibility that Cole had set up a program to automatically send these messages. But from where? And why? What did they mean? Ike held on to the theory that someone could simply be sending him junk to misdirect his attention and waste time. Those people might be in this building fifty-two stories above him. He stuffed the phone back into his pocket and headed to the lobby.

The door to the parking garage elevator opened and Ike experienced déjà vu. He'd been in corporate lobbies like this before. The short hallway opened into a massive marble lobby. To the right, rows of security turnstiles flanked by blue-blazered security personnel guarded the elevator banks. Straight ahead, two young women perched behind a granite enclosure emblazoned with platinum block letters spelling *RECEPTION*. Beyond them, three guards manned a security desk that was twice as large as reception. One was obviously glued to a bank of monitors hidden by the granite wall surrounding the desks. The other two were scanning the lobby. As Ike approached, one of the security guards eyed him closely, then picked up a phone. With cameras spread across the entire area, Ike was sure he was captured on their system. He slowed his gait slightly, as if stalking prey—more pressure.

Reaching the receptionist, he pulled a business card from his pocket and handed it to the girl on the right.

"Ike Rossi here to see Nick Falzone."

"Do you have an appointment, Mr. Rossi?"

"Mr. Falzone should be expecting me."

She dialed her phone and adjusted her headset. Ike readied for the rebuke. He peeked over her shoulder and saw all three guards focused on him. He'd been thrown out of much nicer places by much larger men. Resting an elbow on the desk, he turned and watched the traffic on Grant—and waited.

CHAPTER 18

NICK FALZONE HATED answering these questions. It wasn't just the probing nature of the inquiries but also the questioners and the implication that he may not have all his bases covered that pissed him off. Joseph and Brooks Latham, his father's bulldog, had been with Nick since eleven, going over the facts in the custody battle with Bottaro and the facts of the criminal cases as they knew them. Only Joseph knew the stakes Nick faced. Even Latham, who'd been at Joseph's side since the beginning, couldn't be trusted with such explosive and deadly information. But Joseph's hackles had been raised when Latham had described Ike Rossi's movements over the past twenty-four hours.

Nick loved his father, but he suspected that everything he'd given Nick was driven by guilt. When his parents divorced just after his ninth birthday, his mother took his twin sister and his father took Nick. The fact that his mother chose Brenda over him haunted him for years. He'd had trouble in schools all the way through Yale. Not grade troubles—he was smarter than all his classmates—but his classmates always pissed him off, and he settled scores with his mouth and his fists. When he was about to be tossed from Yale despite his father's legacy, his father stepped in, and after a year of intense therapy, Nick tamed his anger. He'd told them it was gone. But that was a lie. Once his father had given him the chance to help run the oil and gas company, he created billions of dollars in value and ascended to the top job. Now he hated anyone questioning his authority and decisions or telling him what to do, including his father.

They had reviewed the critical elements of the custody battle and Latham was near certain they'd get visitation at a minimum. That wasn't enough for Nick. He'd just as soon put a bullet in the kid now and eliminate any chance of spending the rest of his life on death row. But Joseph had him on a much tighter leash now and he needed to be careful. Latham shifted the discussion to the criminal case.

"I've been assured by McCann that the boy would be convicted in less than a week," he said. "It was the closest thing to a slam dunk that I'd ever heard from the district attorney. Despite the changes in the Pennsylvania sentencing requirements, I think a life sentence is still on the table. The premeditation and coldness of the killing of a father of two, along with the public sentiment against the kid, is just too much pressure on Judge Nowicki. The boy will be incarcerated for at least twenty years and probably life."

Nick watched his father's expression sour.

"Can we intervene at sentencing?" Joseph asked.

"Yes. As a concerned grandparent asking for the court's mercy. I think that would play well with the public and the jury. But your best outcome is to have him in a juvenile detention center until he's eighteen, and then he's in an adult correctional facility. No chance of parole for at least ten years, probably more. Life without parole is still a possibility."

Joseph settled back, deep into the leather chair. Nick hated his father's consternation. Grandson or not, the boy could destroy the company and end Nick's freedom.

"I'm assured we can control him in both places," Nick added.

Joseph sent a daggered look in Nick's direction. "I don't want him hurt—not in any way."

The scolding stung, as it always did from his father. He wanted to strike back, to tell him the kid would destroy his legacy and his wealth if he knew what Nick suspected he'd done. But he held his tongue. He'd take care of things himself if and when the situation arose.

"What about the custody hearing? I'm assuming if we get visitation, that carries through to visits at the facility."

"Yes. Until he's eighteen," Latham said. "The poker club is meeting Friday. First one without Franklin." He dipped his head. "I'll confirm the outcome there. Should be no prob—"

A knock interrupted Latham and Shannon opened the door and leaned in.

"Ike Rossi is in the lobby asking for Nick."

Almost immediately, Nick's face heated up. Rossi was the second-worst thing that could happen. He quenched his temper with the thought that he could handle Rossi. While his father feared him, Nick had a solution. "I should see him," he said, settling himself.

Everyone in the room looked at him as if he'd gone mad.

"I'd strongly advise against that," Latham said, looking to Joseph for support. "I told you earlier our investigator said Rossi has already been to Cole's Seismic, and he met with the Bottaro woman and Jack at the Prices' office this morning. He's on the other side. He's taken the case."

Joseph held back and Nick took advantage of his hesitation.

"Rossi can be managed. I won't tell him anything. But I'd like know what questions he has. That way we'll know what angle he's taking and what he thinks he knows."

Latham wagged his head and turned to Joseph again. "Look. There's only five days to the criminal trial. Stonewall him and he gets nothing. The facts are all with us right now."

"But what if he talks to the kid?" Nick said. "What if *he* somehow figures out what the kid may know? What if he makes the link to Tanner and then back to us?"

"All in five days?" Latham shot back.

Nick looked to his father for an answer.

Joseph leaned on his elbow and stroked his chin. He turned to Shannon. "What do you think, sweetheart?"

Nick wanted to come out of the chair. He hated that his father would even ask his half-sister about this. He loved his father, but *he* was the heir to his father's legacy—not some twenty-six-year-old ditz.

Shannon stepped in and closed the door. Ignoring Nick, she said, "Well, Father, I think that exposing Nick may not be a good idea. But he has a point. I understand Mr. Rossi is very good at what he does." Pausing for effect, she looked at Latham. "Maybe Brooks and I can go down and tell him he won't meet with Nick or anyone else but we'd be happy to pass on any inquiries."

Latham shook his head again. "Stonewall him, Joseph."

Nick drilled the table with his fist and stood up. "Dad, that's bullshit. I can handle him."

Joseph raised his palm to Nick. "Sit down."

Nick didn't sit.

"Sit. Now."

The command convinced Nick he'd have to handle Rossi on his own. Later. He sat down

"Go down there and do what you suggested," Joseph said to Shannon. "Let's see what's on his mind. But don't engage in discussion. Only what you described."

Latham looked like a scolded dog, but he stood up and left with Shannon and closed the door.

"She can't handle this. It's my ass on the line here," Nick said.

"It's all our asses. And she'll do fine." Joseph rose and left the conference room.

Nick knew he'd waited too long. But he wouldn't wait any longer.

CHAPTER 19

THIS WAS NOT what Ike had expected. After being guided through the maze of security by some secretary and a guard who looked like a square-shouldered enforcer, he was deposited in a sterile miniature conference room somewhere on the first floor of the annex attached to Falzone Center. He was told Shannon Falzone would see him if he didn't mind waiting. Normally he'd be offended by being handed off to the public relations spin mongers, who usually were so hell-bent on the spin that they'd lose sight of the truth, but he'd seen her on the news. Confident, direct, and seemingly competent. Best of all, she was a Falzone. She'd take his words and deliver them to the heart of the beast.

And he'd choose his words carefully, as if handling rocket fuel. He wanted to create an environment to get them worried, out of their fortress of comfort and pressured into action. But he didn't want to tip his hand. Too much detail about his suspicions and they could go scorched earth. They'd destroy anything that was even close to damning evidence, if it even existed, along with any chance to save Jack. Still, he'd light the rocket and try to thread about a dozen needles in less than five days.

Through the translucent panels lining the wall against the hallway, two silhouettes moved toward the door. The taller, larger one hesitated before reaching the door, faced the shorter, slender one behind it, and said something indistinguishable but in an instructional tone. The slender shadow dipped her head and opened the door.

Ike recognized Shannon Falzone. Her poise and confidence were obvious as she marched to the opposite side of the table, trailed by a dapper man in his seventies with well-groomed white hair and a tan he clearly hadn't gotten in Pittsburgh. She was more impressive in person. While her hair, makeup, and clothing were meticulous and she could pass for a fashion model, her eyes glowed with intelligence.

She folded into the chair, clasped her hands in front of her, and smiled. "Mr. Rossi. I'm Shannon Falzone, head of public and government affairs for Falzone Enterprises. This is Brooks Latham, managing partner of Latham, Tanner and McKee."

Ike was impressed with her opening play: no handshake, steel-like eye contact, and all business.

"We understand you asked to see my brother, and as you must have imagined, he is unavailable. We also understand you may be working with the firm representing Jack Cole, and as you can understand there will be no contact with any of my family until all pending matters are resolved."

Ike leaned back in his chair and slowly scanned the pair, conveying his unyielding confidence with a grin he once reserved for slobbering middle linebackers.

"I must say I'm very impressed. Despite your statement, I still have a Falzone face-to-face. I suspect that means you were sent here to hear what I had to say." Ike leaned forward. "I wanted to talk to your brother about the work that Tom Cole was doing for him. But I'm willing to give you both a bonus. Here goes. I'm looking into Tom Cole's death. That means any link between the deceased Mr. Tanner and your family, which by Mr. Latham's presence is obvious.

I've also found that Cole was doing work through his firm for Falzone Energy. Now, I find it odd that your father and Mr. Latham and his colleagues are dragging Miss Bottaro through the mud to gain custody of Jack, despite the wishes expressed in his will."

Shannon's stare intensified but she remained silent. He was hitting home.

"I'm curious why that's so important to you five days in advance of his murder trial." He continued. "I'm also curious about any tactics used by Mr. Tanner, God bless his soul, against Mr. Cole under the direction of your wacky sister, Brenda Falzone, who all of a sudden seems un-disowned. Would the head of public and government affairs have a comment on that?"

Ike folded his arms and settled back in the chair. Shannon stared at Ike, then silently turned to Latham, who whispered in her ear. She quickly sent a text.

With her eyes on fire, she targeted Ike. "Mr. Rossi, you may think you are entitled to some special treatment in this town either because of your notable but failed football career or because of some sense of sympathy for the murder of your parents. I assure you, neither of those things give you any right whatsoever to come in here and insult my family with your smug questions."

She stood with Latham. Ike noticed the shadows of Lurch and his sidekick approaching the conference room door. He hid his fists under the table and reminded himself he wasn't in the ring

"We're done here," she said. The conference room door opened. "These gentlemen will show you out."

Ike bobbed his head as he stood up and threw a disregarding glance at the guards in the doorway. Then he turned back to Shannon. "I'm a long way from done." Ike left and winked at the guards as he passed.

As the guards followed him down the open stairway from the annex into the lobby, Ike took in every detail. After counting six cameras, he noted the receptionist giving a key card to a woman with a briefcase who wore a visitor's badge on her blouse. She cleared the turnstiles with the key card and headed to the elevator bank. The security team, other than the two goons behind him, was down to one guard on the monitor bank. Still trailed by the two goons, he made his way to the parking garage elevators and down to Level 2. Despite his certainty that he could take out both guards, he politely turned as he stepped from the elevator, said "Have a nice day," and headed to his car.

CHAPTER 20

JOSEPH FALZONE NEEDED to know the risks. With Ike Rossi now involved, both his business empire and the blended family he'd painstakingly built with Erin over the last thirty years could unravel if Rossi pulled the right threads. Sitting at the desk he'd used for the last forty years, he drummed his fingers on the blotter and waited for Shannon to return.

Joseph was no stranger to risk. It was in his DNA. His hardnosed father, Marco, had come from Italy with nothing and found work in a Pittsburgh glass company. He'd worked his way up while running numbers for the gangster owner on the side. When the owner suddenly died, Marco took over the business and the illegal lottery. At thirteen, Joseph enthusiastically joined his father's business and learned all about understanding the odds and managing risks.

Knowing he'd never survive working for his father, he'd taken his pay to the horse track and paid for his MBA from Yale. He followed two trust-fund classmates to Midland, Texas, and lost what little he had left wildcatting in the Permian Basin. But he quickly learned the risks of the oil business and how to lever his payoff by using other people's money to do it. A string of gargantuan discoveries followed and propelled Falzone Energy into the big leagues. After building one of the best technical teams in the world, he'd studied the odds, participated in the drilling of three separate billion-barrel discoveries in the deepest water in the Gulf of Mexico, and expanded business there.

Now the risks were unknown and growing. Oil prices had collapsed and the leverage was crushing his balance sheet. His oldest son had taken an ungodly risk to save it and, in the process, did what Joseph knew would be unforgivable. The last time he'd felt this way, his first marriage ended in a devastating divorce, and his twin children, Nick and Brenda, had been divided up like property. The scars on Nick and Brenda for that move were deep and lasting. He hadn't paid attention to his own feelings or his first wife's motives before they married. Looking back, if he'd studied the odds, he never would've taken that chance. The marriage, and having children with that shithead, were the biggest mistakes of his life. He'd promised himself he wouldn't make another one.

Shannon appeared in his doorway with Latham, and Joseph waved them in. He picked up the phone and instructed his secretary to tell Nick to join them. Shannon and Latham were the most trusted members of his inner circle. He valued Latham's judgment and loved Shannon's moxie.

Thirty seconds after he was summoned, Nick burst through the door and slammed it shut.

"What are we looking at?" he said, standing behind Shannon and Latham. Neither turned to face him. Joseph gave Nick his best evil eye to settle him, then nodded for Shannon to proceed.

"The meeting was short, Father, but this is what we learned. First, Rossi said he was looking into Tom Cole's death. He was particularly interested in work done by Cole's firm for Nick and Falzone Energy."

Joseph noticed Nick's face sour and redden and was happy Nick was behind Shannon and Latham, out of their fields of vision. "What else, Shannon?"

"He mentioned something about Franklin Tanner's tactics and your involvement in Tanner's selection, and he questioned why you were pressing for custody only five days from the trial."

Joseph cornered his anger and harnessed the uneasiness building in his gut. Most of Rossi's claims were nonsense—just probing questions intended to cause panic. However, Rossi had identified that thread, the one that could destroy all Joseph wanted and loved. He looked at his lifelong friend, Latham. "How do you assess what's going on here?"

"It looks like a fishing expedition. I don't think we should have met with him. Stonewall him, Joseph." Latham's face said much more. Latham recognized that Shannon knew nothing about the mess at Falzone Energy, and Joseph had warned Latham to keep it that way. While Joseph trusted his friend, he wasn't sure Nick could hold his mud much longer.

"Thanks, Shannon. Brooks. I'll think about this and let you know if I need anything else. Nick and I have a few things to discuss about the business."

Shannon glanced back at Nick and then at Joseph. "Thanks, Father. I'll be across the hall if you need me." She closed her folio and left with Latham.

Nick gently closed the door, faced Joseph, and leaned back against it with his arms folded. Joseph hated the stare that followed. Nick's arrogance was exceeded only by his business acumen, and therein lay Joseph's dilemma.

But this look wasn't about business—it was about Nick's hide. In different ways, Joseph still loved all his children, Nick included. He wasn't willing to trade Nick for his business—that just wasn't an option. If Nick went down, it would crush Joseph, since he felt his mistakes long ago shaped Nick's shortcomings, and the problem would be exposed. The business would go down with him anyway. Joseph's only choice was to get Nick back under control.

"Have a seat. And keep your voice down."

Holding his stare, Nick wound around a side chair and sat. "What are we gonna do?"

"Nothing."

"He's made the connection already."

"So what, son? We do business all the time with Cole's Seismic. We're in the oil and gas business. Besides, you have all the data and models secured. Right?"

"Yeah. We have them. But that kid is a problem. He's telling Rossi whatever he knows, and he was close to Cole."

"Rossi's fishing. He's got nothing. In a week, the trial is over."

"We need to get our hands on that kid."

"You mean your nephew? My grandson?"

The crimson rush retuned to Nick's face. "Call him whatever you want, Dad. He can put me away."

"Calm down. And I told you to keep your voice down. Look, we don't know if Jack knows anything, and Brooks assured me we'll have visitation by the weekend. I'll talk to the boy. He won't be a problem."

"What about Rossi? I hear he's a bulldog. He won't let this go."

This was a more difficult question. Any meddling by Joseph would link him to the problem—the problem that would end his marriage to Erin if she found out. While he loved his son, he loved Erin, too. If push came to shove, he'd choose her. It would kill him to do it, even after what Nick had done. Still, he needed deniability. He needed to put the ball in Nick's court.

"Have any ideas?"

Nick looked like a dog eyeing a piece of steak. "You bet I do. I can—"

Joseph thrust his palm into Nick's face. "I don't want to hear it. Just handle him."

Nick smiled, his confidence fortified by having control. Over the years, Joseph had seen that look many times. And every time his son delivered. "I'll get it—done."

A knock interrupted them.

"Yes?" Joseph said, looking to the door.

The door cracked open and Erin peeked in.

"Come in, dear. Nick and I were done."

Nick slammed his hands onto the arms of his chair and stood. "Guess we are."

Joseph knew that the contempt in Nick's voice wasn't targeted at him. Erin and Nick were like matches and gasoline, and Joseph was regularly blasted by each of them about the other. He'd confronted Nick and made it clear he wouldn't tolerate his disrespect for Erin. That stopped the frontal attacks, but the war simmered beneath the thin blanket of decorum.

Nick stepped around Erin as she entered. "Afternoon, Erin."

"Hi, Nick," she said, keeping her eyes on Joseph. "Honey, I want to talk about Jack."

Nick froze in the doorway.

"What about him, dear?" Joseph said.

"I think we should do what's best for our grandson. And this battle with his aunt can't be good. She's a good person and a good mother. I'm sure we could work something out after the trial."

Nick reentered the office. "You're kidding me, right?"

Erin didn't turn to face Nick. She held her gaze on Joseph. "It's none of your business." Her eyes looked for Joseph's support.

The alarms were sounding in his gut. He was squarely in the middle. "Let me speak with Erin about this, Nick."

"She doesn't know what she's talking about. The kid belongs with us. You know that as well as I do."

Joseph launched from his chair. "That's enough, son."

Shannon rushed in and stood between her mother and Nick. "What's going on here? I can hear you shouting across the hall. Now leave her alone, Nick."

She cut her eyes at Joseph.

He'd had enough. "Damn it. Nick, get out of here."

Nick tensed, apparently weighing whether to challenge Joseph. He cursed under his breath and left.

"Joseph, he's too much for me right now," Erin said. "He's getting worse."

Joseph could see a glaze of tears in her eyes. Patrick's death just eight months ago had nearly destroyed her, and none of them had recovered from it. "I'll talk to him." She didn't deserve that from anyone.

"And I think we should drop this custody thing until the trial is over."

"We're done, sweetheart. The judge rules tomorrow."

"He's our grandson. Just keep that in mind," she said, taking Shannon's arm.

"I'll see you both at home," he said as they left his office arm and arm.

Erin stopped. "And I'll be there, dear."

He got the message. That was her home. Their home. And she wanted it to be happy and safe. Nick didn't fit into that formula in the flesh or in spirit. They'd had that discussion before.

Erin turned back and left with Shannon. A storm surge of regret and sadness engulfed Joseph for a few seconds. He shoved it into a black hole and refocused. He had much bigger problems. This little family moment would be a walk in the park compared with what might be coming. With calculated clarity, Joseph now knew the risks. He'd face them head-on with an overwhelming force and end this threat—no matter what it cost.

CHAPTER 21

SHANNON FALZONE HAD felt a seismic shift in her family ever since her brother Patrick tragically died eight months ago. At the epicenter was her half brother, and the vibrations he created were shaking the people she loved for a reason she had yet to uncover.

As her mother cried in her arms behind Shannon's closed office door, Shannon chided herself for letting it happen. After all, she was a strong woman, just like her mother.

But she got another trait from her father: the ability to detach and assess a situation without emotional entanglements. She fortified her talents with a degree in communications from Pitt and an MBA from Wharton at Penn. She'd graduated early from both programs, and at twenty-six, she had five years of experience battling the tide of doubt and prejudice in the business against a woman blessed with her mother's good looks.

As always, her mom's breakdown was short—just a release of the poison injected by Nick. She'd never let anyone get to her, but since Patrick's death she'd been a bucketful of emotions. Shannon didn't judge her. She'd lost her only son. The unspoken rule was to never bring it up unless her mother did.

After fishing a Kleenex from her purse, her mother pulled back, sat in a side chair, and dabbed her eyes. A deep sigh signaled she was back.

Shannon couldn't maintain the façade of unity requested by her mom. "He's just an asshole, Mom." She rubbed her mother's back.

"You know I don't like that language against family members," her mom said, standing and slipping the tissue into the wastebasket and returning to the chair.

"I don't understand why you think you have to respect him."

"It's not respect for him." Her mom's look finished the sentence. *It's for your father.*

Shannon had heard that party line all her life. *Blended or not, this is a family. And we support each other no matter what.* It was a mantra spoken by her dad at every family meeting from the time she could talk. Usually, it was in response to some petty crime Nick had committed against Shannon or Patrick. As she got older, she realized Nick's actions were driven by a deep scar, probably from being sold off by his mother in his parents' divorce. But it went deeper. Shannon was sure Nick envied her and Patrick and the unbreakable bond they shared with each other and their mother. That bond that was driven by bloodlines and birth. A bond he never formed. And now there was something much more than that driving his actions.

"I hear you, Mom, but something's going on. Why do you think Nick is so adamant about getting visitation with Jack? He never spent any time with him or showed any interest in him."

"He may just be supporting your father. Your father wants time with his grandson, especially not knowing what will happen with the trial."

Shannon decided to let it lie. Her mother always supported her father, and while Shannon didn't buy it at all, it would be a losing argument that would only hurt her mother.

"Do you have everything you need for the benefit at the Duquesne Club?"

Her mother pulled out of her sadness and perked up at the prospect of helping the foundation. "I do. You've done a wonderful job, and I have no idea how you got the HUD secretary to speak before the auction. That will pull in all the old money."

"It was easy, Mom. I just dropped your name."

Her mother smiled, but it was the truth. One mention of the woman who had single-handedly throttled Pittsburgh's elite to clean up the Northside, feed every hungry child in the city, and bring affordable housing to struggling families crushed by low wages and soaring costs commanded the attention of every politician looking for funding and an endorsement.

"I'll have the final draft of your remarks proofed and fact-checked this afternoon," Shannon said, guiding her mother to the door. They said their good-byes, punctuated with a long hug and an air kiss to the cheek. She watched her mother walk down the long hallway toward the executive elevator. Then she spotted Nick, loitering in his doorway after her mother passed.

After the elevator doors closed, she marched to his office, her heels announcing her mood with every step. Nick heard her approach and retreated inside his office. She stepped in and deliberately eased the door shut. Nick's eyes simmered like a brewing volcano. But she'd had enough.

"You owe my mother an apology. She may be your stepmother, but you owe her the respect she's earned."

Nick leaned back and locked his hands behind his head. "Why do you think she's earned my respect, sister?"

The sister slight. Shannon hated that she shared her father's DNA with this slug. "Because she put up with your bullshit."

"Is that so? The way I see it is that she saw the gravy train and stuck her head in the trough. As a result, you and Patrick popped out."

Shannon imagined charging the desk and jamming the gold letter opener into his eye. But she calmed herself with a deep breath and took aim. "My brother was ten times the man you'll ever be. You bring him up again and I'll start digging until you're buried. I know about your little club you had going with Tanner. I don't know what you were doing, but I sure as hell can find out."

That revelation launched Nick to attention. She'd seen the same expression on his face for years, every time he got caught. It had hit home more than she'd expected. Until now, she'd thought his time with Tanner was about some arrangement to serve Nick's sadistic view of entertainment. But there was something more—something he wanted to conceal. He caught himself and struck a confident posture.

"There's nothing there. You can dig, but while you're digging, I'll be guiding Dad through this mess and making more money in the process. I assure you, I'll make you look petty and vindictive, and you know how that will play with him."

She knew he was right. While he was an ass, he was cunning, razor-sharp, and capable of delivering on his promise. She'd built a strong reputation, but with the table slanted against her, any sliver of doubt or family squabbling could sink her ambitions.

"Tell me this, Nick, why are you so interested in getting your hands on Jack?"

His slippery grin surely prefaced a lie. "He's my sister's son and my nephew."

"You hate Brenda and probably facilitated her coke-fueled spiral."

"He's also our father's grandson. I'm sure dear old Dad would enjoy hearing that you don't want us to do all we can to get him."

"Your threats don't scare me. You're up to something, and you'll leave Mom alone if you know what's good for you."

Nick chuckled as Shannon turned and headed back to her office. Deep in her heart, she knew this wasn't the last of it. And while she thought she could find Nick's secret, she hoped no one would find hers.

CHAPTER 22

IKE KNEW HE was running out of time. At three p.m. on Wednesday, he entered the Prices' law office and grabbed a cup of coffee on the way to the conference room. He passed through the door, then stopped.

It looked like a paper recycling plant gone wrong. Stacks of files and papers covered the table in an unrecognizable pattern. Both Ed and Jenna were hunched over their laptops attempting to read through their tired, bloodshot eyes. Jenna lifted her head, spotted Ike, and stretched against her chair back, blowing out as much tension as she could with one long sigh.

"Is it three already?" she said.

Ike looped around the conference table and took the seat facing Jenna, pushed a stack of papers away, and tossed his file in front of him. "You ready to do this?"

"Sure. Dad and I need a break anyway."

Ed raised his head and nodded at Ike. "Hi, Ike."

"Hi, Ed. How's business?"

"Less and less since we've taken this case." Ike was sorry he'd asked. Ed looked like shit and about ten years older than he did yesterday. Ike made a mental note to jump off a bridge if he ever thought of going to law school.

He took a sip and winced as the coffee seared his upper lip. "Any progress?"

Jenna and Ed shared an expression of consternation. *Which one of us gets to tell Rossi?*

Jenna apparently drew the short straw.

"We're running through the case law on the mental incapacity defense."

Ike wanted to punch someone. "You'll ruin Jack with that bull-shit."

Jenna stiffened and locked her eyes on Ike. "We'll save his life, Ike. It's all we've got unless you somehow come up with evidence that Tanner killed Jack's father. You'll have to do something in four days that two detectives and two pretty damn good lawyers couldn't do in six months."

"Whoa there. Someone needs a break," Ike said.

Jenna deflated into her chair. "I'm sorry, Ike. I had two hours of sleep. And by sleep, I mean closing my eyes and going through every angle in this case." She offered a weak smile. "Look, we do have to have this alternate defense. What do you have?"

"I talked to Shannon Falzone today."

"You talked to a Falzone?" Jenna glanced at her father and both looked suddenly energized.

"Yes, I did. At their office."

"Shannon Falzone met with you?"

"I wouldn't call it a meeting. It was more like an exchange."

Jenna's tall frame stretched halfway across the table. "Well, what did she say?"

"She basically scolded me. Told me that no Falzone would talk to me. And then I told her a bit of what I know to pressure them into a mistake."

"But she's a Falzone?" Ed said.

"Bingo. Something big is going on there. Something they want to hide. I think it has something to do with the seismic interpretation Tom did for Falzone before he died."

"Seismic?"

"Yeah, seismic. They send sound waves into the ground to image the geology thousands of feet deep."

"Forgive me, Ike. What does that have to do with proving self-defense?"

"Not sure yet. But look at this." Ike slipped a handwritten time line from his file. Ed waddled around and looked over Jenna's shoulder.

"If you work backward, we're in September here. At the trial. Tom Cole died in late March. Patrick Falzone died in late January."

"He died in a car accident," Jenna said.

"A one-car accident, no witnesses."

"You're saying he was killed?"

"Not yet. But keep moving down. In December, Tom Cole's company did an interpretation of seismic data for Falzone Energy. His partner said it was top secret. He'd never seen Tom keep something so tight." Ike let the information soak in before moving further down the page.

Jenna caught up and nodded for him to proceed.

"Then I pulled the press releases from Falzone's website. Looks like they were the high bidder for three offshore blocks in that sale off Virginia."

Ed looked up. "The first one on the East Coast?"

"Exactly. I could guess that the seismic covered that area. Falzone Energy kept it tight. They've taken more security measures to conceal that data than I've ever seen."

Ike moved his finger to the last line on the page. "Here in January, Tom Cole filed for divorce and won full legal and physical custody of Jack."

Jenna took the paper and leaned back. Ike could see her mind working through the options. Finally, she set the paper down. "So, you think some conspiracy centered around—" She hesitated and looked down at the paper. "This *seismic* is the key?" Her disbelief was across her face.

"Like I said. They're hiding something. They met with me because they wanted to see what I knew. What their exposure might be. That's the only explanation. Otherwise they didn't have to do anything. Just let the case run."

"A big conspiracy is exciting. But we need evidence that Tanner somehow was involved in Jack's father's death."

"I agree. But I'm telling you I can smell it. Something's not right here. And Tanner could be in the middle of it."

"How so?"

"Why did the Falzones wait until a few weeks before the trial to file for a custody change? The ruling was in January. Why not file then?"

"When they realized their grandson might not see the light of day for the rest of their lives, they had a change of heart," Jenna said.

"I'm not buying it. Then in a three-month period, a son and son-in-law both die?"

Jenna rocked back in her chair. "One by suicide and one by a car accident—according to the law. It's tragic but it happens."

"Maybe, but my gut says otherwise."

Jenna leaned forward and shifted back to her dark mood. "Look, Ike, I can't put your gut on the stand. We need evidence. Proof in a court of law. You have any of that?"

Ike understood Jenna's frustration. He shared it. "I'm working on it. I have the information on the seismic, and Cole's partner, Bobby Scott, will testify."

"Testify to what?"

"Hang on." Ike was losing his patience. "I'm going to talk to Cassidy about the evidence here surrounding Tom Cole's death. Then I'll dig into Tanner and the Coles' divorce. I'll do both today. Then, if I don't come up with hard evidence there, I'll go to plan B."

"What's plan B?"

"Not sure you want to know."

He knew she didn't want to know. But Ike was not going to fail because of legal restraints. He'd prevail no matter what it took. He'd not leave Jack stuck in a cell for the rest of his youth and probably for the rest of his life. He'd been there. Hell, he was there.

Ed leaned on his elbows. "Ike. We need this by the book. Anything tainted or illegal is useless to us."

"Ed, I'll get that if I can. But if I can't, I'm not going to let these people put Jack away. I'm just not."

A blanket of silence covered the room.

"I got another e-mail," Ike said.

"From Tom Cole?" Jenna said.

"Yes. It could be nothing. Just someone trying to screw with me."

"What did it say?"

Ike wrote the mathematical expression on the bottom of the page: $4+3-53+8+74$.

"Thirty-six," Jenna said. "Do you know what it means?"

Ike explained the analysis of the two messages he'd done that had led nowhere. "I'll keep working on it. You do the same as you can. But this bothers me. Someone has gone to some trouble to send this to me. If it's a distraction, then what are they distracting me from? If it's some coded message, who's sending it and what does it mean and why the hell is it from Tom Cole?"

"I'm sure you considered the possibility that Tom Cole set this up himself and had it delayed. He was a technical genius."

"Exactly," Ike said, picking up the paper and stuffing it back into his file. "And I've got four days to see if Tom Cole is sending me a message from his grave to save his son." Ike walked to the door. "I'll let you know what I find out."

CHAPTER 23

IKE MADE HIS way through North Shore and passed Heinz Field. The Steelers opener was days away, and despite the schizophrenic preseason, he and the other gritty fans were confidently looking forward to a seventh Super Bowl victory. He wished he shared that optimism about the meeting at police headquarters.

Mac had used his leverage and influence to force another interview with Cassidy. While Mac seemed to have banked an unending reservoir of goodwill during his tenure, Ike knew this might be the last shot he had at Cassidy. As he negotiated the rush-hour backup, exited on the West End Bridge, and wound down to Western Avenue, the abyss inside opened wider. Despite his determination to keep them buried, the dark sticky feelings resurfaced as he remembered driving to police headquarters to hear the gruesome details of his parents' murder. He hated this place and what it represented. But Jack needed this, and in some ways Ike needed this, too

As he entered the building, the sadness and anger coated him like heavy tar. Luckily, he spotted Mac surrounded by a half dozen detectives trading the things that detectives do and occasionally laughing at a zinger delivered by Mac. Mac spotted Ike, shook the detectives' hands, and headed over.

"How you doing?" Mac seemed to sense the residuals from the past.

"Good." Ike lifted the thick file containing Tom Cole's suicide report. "I went through this in detail. Lots of questions."

Mac rested his hand on Ike's shoulder. "You're a good man for doing this, Ike. I know it's not easy."

"My mother always said, 'Do the right thing—not the easy thing. The work will be more rewarding.' I hope in this case she's right."

Mac nodded. "Let's go. He's waiting in the conference room."

"Thanks for pulling these strings again."

"Like your mom said, it's the right thing to do."

Mac's presence and support fortified Ike's determination. They headed down a short hall and walked into the room.

Cassidy was sitting at the table, checking his phone, wearing another five hundred-dollar sport coat. Ike made a mental note to check that out if he got the chance. Cassidy was getting money somewhere.

"Have a seat, you two," Cassidy said without looking up. "I've got fifteen minutes."

Mac pulled out a chair and sat across from Cassidy. "I can go down the hall to the assistant chief and get you some more time?"

Cassidy stuffed the phone into his sport coat and leaned his elbows on the table. "Have a seat, Ike. This should be fun."

Ike slapped the thick file on the table next to Mac and sat. He wished he could get Cassidy into the ring—now. Then, as Ike opened the file and remembered the tabs he'd added to the key pages, he decided this might be almost as fun. He flipped to the first tab.

"These crime-scene photos from Tom Cole's garage show a three-quarter-inch garden hose sloppily duct-taped to the tailpipe and pinched in the driver's-side window."

"Glad you can read and look at pictures. I don't think they make picture books for junior detectives, though."

Ike wanted to take the bait. The time in the tank for assaulting a detective would be well worth it. But he thought about Jack and let it pass.

"Well, apparently, you didn't read your copies. Otherwise you would have questioned why an obsessive neatnik like Tom Cole would have been so sloppy."

"Christ, you idiot, he was getting ready to off himself. His prints were on the tape and the hose."

"The report also showed Tom was found in the seat with the keys on the console and not in his pocket. The radio was on to a rock station. His sister said he didn't like rock." Ike looked directly at Cassidy. "What I'm wondering is why you ruled it a suicide so quickly?"

"Here's why. I had the presence of a means of death, a body with no other signs of trauma, and a suicide note verifying the subject's intent to take his own life. The guy had a shitty divorce on top of that. The examiner's report verified the cause of death as carbon monoxide asphyxiation."

Ike flipped to the tab marking the ME's report. "He also said he found a puncture wound in the bottom of his foot."

"So what? If you read on, it says we found a broken thumbtack and a sock with traces of blood that fit the same location on his foot in the master. He stepped on a tack."

Ike ignored Cassidy and kept going to the next tab.

"It says here that the suicide note was composed on a computer. Not handwritten."

Cassidy leaned back and folded his arms. "Surprise, surprise. A dead techie used a computer. It had his prints on it."

"Did you check the house for other prints?" Mac said.

"You know better than that, Mac."

"So you didn't investigate any alternative scenarios?"

"I don't know if your mentor here explained how detectives work, but we don't have the time to waste the taxpayers' money."

"Did you check out the neighbors' security cameras?"

Cassidy shoved his chair back and stood. "This is bullshit. There was no evidence of homicide, an accident, or a natural death. He killed himself, end of story."

"So you didn't check the neighbors' cameras?" Ike knew the answer. He just wanted to fuel Cassidy's temper. Cassidy seemed to catch on and sat back down. "No, Mr. Magoo, I didn't. It was unnecessary."

Ike flipped to another tab. "It says here you talked to his sister and his son."

"You can read that in the report."

"I did. But did you talk to his crazy ex-wife or her attorney?"

"Again, unnecessary."

Ike found the last tab. It was a photo of Tom in the passenger seat. His head was tilted back, and his thick, curly dark-brown hair was against the headrest. Ike turned the file to face Cassidy and pointed to the photo. "Did you see this?"

"I was there when they took it, and I filed the report. Of course I've seen it."

"No," Ike said, moving his finger closer to the photo. "This." It was a minuscule fiber in Tom Cole's hair.

For the first time, Cassidy was speechless. Ike continued.

"But here, in the ME's report, there was no mention of fibers in Tom's hair."

Cassidy leaned back from the file. "It was a suicide."

Ike closed the file. "What if that fiber was the same color as the carpet in his house?"

Cassidy pushed the file at Ike and launched himself out of the chair, shoving the conference table into Ike's gut. "Up yours, you asshole. You're sitting here second-guessing good detective work? It fits. It makes sense that a washed-up jock would be comfortable be-ing a Monday-morning quarterback. You can't handle the fact that the guy committed suicide, the kid is a killer, and your parents' mur-der will never be solved. Get the hell out of here."

In one movement, Ike sprang over the table and had Cassidy by the throat against the wall. He pinned his forehead against Cassidy's. "I'll choke you out if you say that again."

"Ike. Ike!"

Ike could feel Mac pulling at his shoulders.

"You okay, Mac?" another voice said behind them.

"We're fine," Mac said. He squeezed Ike's shoulders again. "Ike?"

Ike realized where he was and released Cassidy. Cassidy's de-meanor shifted from anger to detachment when he saw the other detectives in the doorway, and he straightened his jacket. He walked around the table and stopped at the door. "It was a suicide." Then he left.

"You okay?" Mac asked.

Ike blew out a breath, pulled his shirt down, and gathered the file from the table. He knew he'd lost it, but Cassidy had it coming.

He grinned at Mac. "That was interesting."

"Somehow I thought you enjoyed that."

Ike had to admit it had felt great. "Looks like I've got some work to do."

"Let me help," Mac said. "I'll talk to the neighbors and see if they even had cameras. There's a big difference between questions and having hard evidence."

"Thanks, Mac. I could use the help."

Mac's comment hit home. Ike had no evidence to show a homi-cide. Just a little shabby detective work. Ike needed more. He needed motive. And motive started with a dead guy.

CHAPTER 24

IKE WAITED AT a table in the corner of the Fairmont Hotel bar on Fifth Avenue. Tucked behind the last plate-glass window, he watched throngs of workers pulsing along the streets, evacuating downtown in favor of the surrounding suburbs. With the threat of rain, the post-work Market Square crowd would be pushed home or inside.

Ike checked his watch. It was 5:05 p.m. Donna Martin was late, but she could unlock the inner life of Franklin Tanner. At least that was what she'd told Mac. Mac had known Donna for years, being a regular in Judge Palmeri's courtroom, but his senior clerk was connected. Connected to the unspoken network of clerks that ran the courthouse. She was especially tight with another senior clerk in the Family Division of the Court of Common Pleas, housed in the old jail.

Ike checked the time again. The one thing he didn't have time for was being stood up. He was close—close to the truth. And he'd blast through a brick wall to find it. The wild animal surging inside was fed by a mix of confidence, eagerness, and determination. He'd felt this way before, except it was fourth and long in a late-season snowstorm with 1:48 left in the game, on his own twenty. Back then, he didn't look at the score, he didn't hear the crowd, and he didn't see the jittery wide eyes of his teammates in the huddle. He focused on just the play and what the defense was giving him. Each snap felt the same. Play after play, they ate up the field. One chunk at a time. Then, with the state championship on the line, he called *the play.*

It was as if he was in that exact moment now but Donna Martin had the play call. He could execute it, but she needed to deliver.

He looked up and saw Donna enter through the back side of the bar. With her short dark hair parted to the right, wide smile and olive skin, she looked exactly like the picture Mac had provided. She stopped, spotted Ike, then scanned the bar patronage that spilled into the lobby. Apparently comfortable that no threat was present, she walked to Ike's table.

She offered her hand. "Donna Martin, Mr. Rossi."

"Ike," he said, shaking it.

She gently folded her raincoat on the seat between them and sat facing him.

"Let me first say how sorry I am about the inability to get justice for your parents."

"Thanks, Donna. I don't know if it's inability or not."

"I lost my dad to a criminal. I know what it's like to get closure."

Ike didn't want to say any more on the subject. "Thanks. And thanks for coming to talk to me."

"When Mac told me about what you were doing, I thought I might be able to help."

"What can you tell me about Franklin Tanner?"

Dislike spread across her face like she'd just swallowed sour milk. "Tanner was arrogant and rude. He was ruthless."

"Did you deal with him?"

"Not directly. But a good friend of mine in Judge Kelly's court did all the time. He was always causing problems. Not for the court but for the clients. He'd antagonize, accuse, and flat out lie to get the couples going at each other. He was sanctioned more than once."

"Did he do this in the Cole case?"

The corners of her mouth stretched down as if she'd stepped on a nail. "As clerks, we're not supposed to talk about our cases. I don't want my friend to get in trouble."

"I understand. If you know Mac, he's probably told you that you can trust me. I'll only use what you tell me to get my own information. You or your friend will never be involved, mentioned, or implicated. I'll guarantee that. I need to help that boy if I can."

Her discomfort melted into the appearance of a mother's concern. Ike guessed she was in her mid-forties and had children of her own at home.

"Yes. Tanner pulled out all his nasty tricks on Tom Cole. He accused him of affairs and abuse and even called his partner and made up lies about him. That move cost Tanner two thousand in sanctions."

"What about the attorney on the other side?"

"Mr. Cole's attorney? I think he's okay. He's not part of that group."

Ike's gut sounded an alarm. "That group?"

Based on her expression, Donna didn't realize what she'd let slip.

"Ike, I'm not sure I can say anything else."

"I promised you the court would never know."

Donna shifted in her chair and silently weighed her next words. She scanned the bar, then lowered her voice. "It's not the court I'm worried about. I have a family."

"You're afraid for your safety?"

Donna dipped her head as she nodded.

This smelled like pay dirt. Whatever she was afraid of might just be what Jack needed. "I don't want anyone to get hurt, but you can trust me. Whoever you're worried about will never know."

She looked around again. "Someone could be here that I don't know."

Ike examined the crowd. They were all more worried about each other than either of them. He wanted to tell her, *You're already here—the damage is already done.* Instead he said, "Trust me and tell me about the group. It might help Jack."

She swallowed hard. "There's a group of family law attorneys," she whispered, "maybe a few judges and others. Rumors are they have a club. They call it a poker club. But they do deals there."

"Deals? What kind of deals?"

"It's only rumors, but they preplan their arguments."

"Their cases?"

"Yes. They create as much conflict as they can. Conflict between the parties is a way to increase their billings."

"If it's known, why hasn't someone turned them in to the court?"

"Because the court is them, in some cases, but we don't know which judges."

"Just go to the *Post-Gazette*."

"The rumors say it goes beyond the Family Law Division. Maybe beyond the court."

The beast inside was breaking free. The anger warmed Ike's face. The system, again. "The police?"

"And maybe then some."

"Why am I just hearing this?"

"There are only three people that know outside the group. Me, my friend, and now you."

Ike leaned back and weighed the news. It had conspiracy written all over it. And Tanner was involved.

"Anything else?"

She waited as if chewing on her words to make them digestible. Without warning, she rose and reached for her raincoat. "Poker night is Friday." Then she disappeared into the crowd.

Ike threw a twenty on the table. He would have paid a hundred times that for what Donna Martin had told him for free.

CHAPTER 25

HER RECORD WAS easy to find. Brenda Falzone Cole had left a trail: a possession arrest and a divorce, followed by another drug charge. When Ike read the report, his thoughts went to Jack. For a kid, he hid the pain well. It was one of the traits that he and Jack shared. But Ike knew that with a mother like this, the pain was there for Jack, simmering somewhere below the surface. The file said the court mandated treatment followed by community service at a well-known shelter in Lawrenceville. Her parole officer had his doubts about her recovery.

Ike sat in his car at the end of the tree-lined street in an exclusive enclave of higher-end townhomes on the edge of Frick Park in Squirrel Hill. Tom Cole's revolutionary seismic processing technique had been developed during their marriage and the divorce settlement had served her well.

The parole officer's report said her work hours were from eight a.m. to five p.m. Ike had arrived just before six with no sign of Brenda. While the units had garages, street parking was common and Ike's car blended well with the others.

Thirty minutes after arriving, Ike spotted a white Lexus pulling to the curb in front of Brenda's unit. He waited for the driver to exit, then made a beeline for the walkway, intercepting Brenda before she reached the front door. She looked more aggravated than surprised. Her bleached-blond hair twisted onto her shoulders and frazzled at the ends. The dark roots said she'd given up on the ruse. She'd been relatively attractive at one point, but time had taken its toll along with an obvious lack of sleep. She'd made no attempt to cover it with makeup. Her eyes were pitch-black, and despite the waning sunlight, her pupils were wide and dilated—she was still using.

"Whatever you're selling, I don't want it," she said as she pushed past Ike to the door

"I'm here to help Jack, your son."

Brenda hesitated with the key inserted into her front door. She didn't turn but said, "Why in the hell would you be doing that?"

The question was an invitation, not a rejection. Ike pressed on.

"He's going to jail. He's being tried as an adult. They'll destroy his life."

Some fuel deep inside her ignited as she turned to face him. No motherly regret, no compassion, just seething anger. Oddly, she calmed. "He's getting what he deserves. Maybe he shouldn't have sided with his father."

The words weren't as telling as their delivery. In an instant, her cunning and disdain for the men in her life surfaced like a water moccasin readying to strike.

Despite her demeanor, Ike held his ground. "Can I ask you a few questions?"

"That depends. Who are you?"

"Ike Rossi. I'm working for Jack."

She turned back to the door and unlocked it. "Suit yourself," she said as she entered and left the door open.

Ike followed her in. The townhome was well-decorated and pristine—almost too much so. She tossed her purse onto the kitchen table and laid her coat over the chair. "I get it. He's my son. But his father turned him against me," she said.

Ike stepped closer. "He's a good kid."

She hesitated, obviously weighing Ike's words. "I raised him well. Then his father took over, and look what happened."

Ike avoided arguing with her. They had built some weird connection around Jack, and she was talking. She stepped to the counter and began making a pot of coffee. Her hands shook in tight, nearly imperceptible tremors. It was all she could do to cover them.

"He did do me one favor—killing that attorney of mine."

"You didn't like him?"

She jammed the coffee pot into its slot and stopped. "My"—she mimed air quotes— "*father* had hired him for me. I can't complain. I agreed, as long as *Daddy*"—more air quotes—"opened his wallet for me. But Tanner was an asshole. He was more interested in that shitty husband of mine than he was in me."

"Yeah. I heard Tanner could be that way."

She turned and pulled two mugs from the cabinet. "He let those two run me into the ground. Drug tests, psychologists … He did nothing for me, other than get me a shitload of cash that I deserved anyway."

Ike was shocked. She had no idea who he was. He decided to bring up the Falzones.

"So you're Nick's twin."

She placed the mugs on the counter. "Only on the birth certificate. I'm nothing like that shithead. Do you know I think he was actually the one behind Daddy hiring Tanner?" She was getting more animated—more confident. She must have used on the way home.

"Did you know Patrick very well?"

"That poor bastard. It's no surprise he's gone. Nick hated him. What's your name again?"

"Ike Rossi. Do you think Nick had something to do with Patrick's accident?"

She shrugged. "Rossi, Rossi ... You look familiar. You play football back in the day?"

"Yes, I did."

She snapped her fingers and pointed at him. "I knew it." Pleased with herself, she added, "You said you're helping Jack?"

"Yes. Did you think your ex would kill himself?"

Leaning on the counter, she dipped her head as if to tell a secret. "No. Can you believe that? What bad timing."

"What do you mean?"

"If he'd done it three months earlier, it would've been perfect. But then again, I've gotta give my asshole attorney credit. His bullshit pushed Tom over the edge."

"Is that why you think Jack did it?"

"Killed Tanner? Sure." As if being enlightened, Brenda said, "There's a part of me that wishes he didn't do that. I'd like to think I had a chance to be his mom again." Her face instantly saddened. She remained still. She looked fragile, staring at the kitchen floor.

"Brenda?"

She slowly lifted her head, and Ike saw a mix of anger and sadness in her eyes.

"We're done," she said. "Please leave."

"Can I ask one more question?"

She pushed off the counter and corralled him toward the door. "On your way out."

"Why do you think Nick and your dad were so interested in your divorce and Jack?"

She opened the door and pointed outside. Wanting to avoid a scene, Ike walked through the doorway and looked over his shoulder. Brenda was clearly considering the question.

"They're hiding something," she said and slammed the door.

CHAPTER 26

IKE HAD CALLED immediately upon leaving Brenda's. After experiencing Jack's mother, Ike needed to connect with Jack. Only God knew what gremlins she'd created in Jack's soul, and Ike wanted to be the counterbalance that neutralized them.

Lauren had answered and sounded somewhere between surprised and pleased. Ike explained his need to see Jack, and in an inviting tone, Lauren had said now was a good time. Jimmy had gone to hockey practice and wouldn't be back until after eight thirty. Jack was finishing homework and they'd both be happy to see him.

Using the address Lauren had provided, he made the trip to Shadyside in minutes. The homes were old red brick but remodeled and adorned with large trees and spacious porches. Ike arrived at the two-story home with white trim, pulled to the curb, and bounded up the stairs to the front door. Jack answered

"Hi, Mr. Rossi." Jack proudly stuck out his hand.

Ike shook it. "It's so good to see you, Jack."

Jack smiled and glanced over his shoulder at Lauren, who was standing at the edge of the entry giving her approval.

Jack seemed elated to share his home with Ike, oblivious to the fact that he'd be on trial for murder in five days. "Please come in,"

Jack said and led Ike into the entry. The home was beautiful. Polished hardwood floors accented with colorful area rugs. The furniture gave Ike more insight into Lauren—bright but comfortable.

Lauren stepped into the soft lamplight in the entry. She glowed with an aura Ike hadn't seen before. Her face lit up as she pushed her black hair back and looped it over her ear. "Welcome to our home, Ike." She offered her hand, and Ike wrapped it in his. She was soft, warm, and relaxed. She was on her home turf and this was a social visit. While Ike was here to see Jack, he was glad to see Lauren. The smell of fresh-baked chocolate-chip cookies pulled his attention toward the kitchen.

"Jack's idea," she said, gently stroking Jack's head.

"They'll be done in ten minutes and twenty seconds," Jack said, looking at the oversize watch on his skinny wrist.

"Jack, why don't you see if Mr. Rossi would like something to drink before we sit?"

Jack robotically faced Ike. "Can I offer you something to drink?"

Ike tried not to chuckle. Jack was trying so hard. Ike leaned in the direction of the kitchen. "I'll have what you're having with those cookies."

Jack's face lit up. "I'm having milk."

"That's what I figured," Ike said, sharing a smile with Lauren.

Jack's face turned serious. "But we can't have it until the cookies are done. The milk is at 39 degrees in the fridge and I put three glasses in there, too. That way the glass won't immediately conduct heat into the milk and warm it up."

Ike appreciated the science. He kept a glass in the fridge for the same reason. "That's a great idea."

Jack raised an eyebrow in Lauren's direction. "Can I show him now?"

"You need to ask Mr. Rossi."

"You know what, Jack? I think you and I are becoming friends, so you can call me Ike."

Jack's eyes widened and he glanced back at Lauren. She nodded.

"Okay, Ike. Would you like to play a game with me?"

"Sure."

Jack latched on to his hand and towed Ike past Lauren.

"I'll watch the cookies," she said as she chuckled and turned back to the kitchen.

Jack led Ike to a den off the hallway, ran to the coffee table, and grabbed an iPad. He quickly opened an app and shoved the iPad at Ike. "Here, try this." He touched the screen and the program started. There was a question: *Which is greater?* Then a series of equations flashed on the screen. Ike could barely keep up. He kept answering as he moved over and sat on the sofa. Jack sat next to him, monitoring every move and grunting when Ike missed one. They took turns with different games and reveled in the fun. That is, until Jack's watch alarm went off and he bolted to the kitchen, leaving Ike in the den. Ike followed him down the hall. Before he reached the kitchen he heard Lauren say, "Where's Ike, honey?"

Not wanting to embarrass Jack, Ike stepped in and said, "He's just a lot faster than me."

Lauren gave him an *I don't believe you* grin. "Offer Ike a seat."

Jack pulled out a kitchen chair facing the white cabinets. Ike took a seat, and Jack stood guard over the cookies cooling on the island.

"How are you doing, Jack?" Ike asked.

Jack glanced away from the cookies. "Fine."

Ike shrugged at Lauren and she returned the gesture. They sat in silence until Jack's alarm sounded again. After asking Lauren, he scooped two cookies onto each plate, removed the chilled glasses, and filled them with milk. He served Ike first, then Lauren, who took the chair across from Ike. Then he settled in his chair and waited with his hands in his lap, looking at Ike. His eyes were begging again, and Ike got the message. Looking at Jack, Ike slowly picked up the cookie, torturing Jack with each second, then grinned, dipped it in his milk, and took a bite. Jack grinned back and attacked his first cookie, sloshing it into the milk then into his mouth. Lauren just shook her head.

"Do you have a brother or sister?" Jack said after swallowing the remnants of the cookie

"Sure do. I have a sister," Ike said.

"What's her name?"

"Maria."

"Did you play with Maria when you were a kid?'

This is where it got complicated. "I did."

"Were your mom and dad gone then?"

Ike could see where Jack was headed. The playfulness left, re-placed by sadness and sympathy. "Not at first. Maria was younger than I was, but we still played when we got the chance."

"What about after?"

Ike knew what he meant. Maybe it was Jack's way of processing the loneliness he felt. Ike glanced at Lauren. "I was in college when my parents died. I was nineteen, but my sister was nine."

Jack's jaw dropped. "Only nine? That's younger than me."

For some reason that fact seemed to give Jack comfort.

"That's right. I came home and took care of her, along with help from my friend Mac and his wife."

"Were they like Aunt Lauren is for me?"

Ike looked directly at Lauren. "Yes. Like that. But probably not as pretty."

Lauren blushed and Jack let out a devilish grin. Then they all shared a laugh.

"Is your sister okay now?"

"Yes she is." Ike wanted to say *Just like you will be.* But he couldn't. "She runs our restaurant."

"You have a restaurant?"

"I do. It's called Rossi's. I'll have to take you there sometime with your Aunt Lauren."

Jack dipped his last cookie and stuffed it into his mouth. He finished it quickly, then asked Lauren, "Can I be excused?"

"We still have Ike here, honey."

"I'd like to work on my project."

"What project is that, Jack?" Ike asked.

"I'm building a game for the science fair. It's not ready yet, so I can't show it to you."

Lauren silently checked with Ike and he nodded in agreement.

"Okay," she said. "Please put the dishes in the sink before you go."

Jack cleared the dishes, then stopped next to Ike. He leaned over and hugged him. "Thanks for coming to see me."

Ike hugged back, hard. He tried to hug the memory of Jack's mother out of him, but Ike knew it would never leave.

Jack released him, hugged Lauren, and left. Ike watched the doorway even after he left.

"So you met Jack's mother?"

"What a piece of work."

"I can't stand the woman after what she's done."

"I can understand why."

"Did she tell you anything?"

"Surprisingly, she did."

Ike relayed the conversation to Lauren while she commented and groaned. When he finished, Lauren asked, "So you're after the Falzones and this poker group?"

Ike saw the concern leaking back into Lauren's mind.

"Don't worry. I'll get to the bottom of this. He's a great kid and doesn't deserve what he's facing." Ike stood. "Thanks for letting me come over."

"I think it was great for him. I can only do so much. He's talked to you more than anyone I've seen him with. I think he needed this." Lauren rose and they walked to the door.

"You know, I needed this," Ike said.

Lauren hugged him and kissed his cheek. Ike leaned in to return the kiss on her cheek but at the last second she turned and they were face-to-face, their lips nearly touching. He could feel her breath, and for a split second he wanted to kiss her, hard. But he needed to stay focused. He pulled away. "Thanks again," he said as he opened the door and walked across the porch and down the stairs.

Then he heard Lauren. "Ike?"

He turned and saw her standing in the doorway.

"Promise me one thing," she said.

"What's that?"

"Promise you'll be back."

Ike gently smiled and waved. "See you at the Prices'."

CHAPTER 27

IKE KNEW IT wasn't enough. Despite the fact that the revelations of the last twenty-four hours had raised doubts about suicide and the specter of a conspiracy, it still wasn't enough to save Jack. Ike rolled down the windows and accelerated onto I-279. Sleep was limited and elusive and he needed the fresh air. The warm September morning felt like summer, and the green rolling hills, just minutes north of the city, reminded him of his family's trips to Moraine State Park. But it was already Thursday morning, and as the evidence stood now, Jack would never experience that joy.

The trip to the Prices' office had seemed long, probably due to Ike's impatience and his burning desire to get the meeting over so he could nail down his leads. Stepping out of the Shelby, he pulled out his phone and checked his e-mail. A few e-mails with morning news from the *Oil & Gas Journal*, *Energy Intelligence* and *The Wall Street Journal* popped into his in-box. The iPhone continued to cycle, downloading another e-mail from his personal account. His mind coiled like a spring under load, anticipating another e-mail from a dead man. Sure enough, *Tom Cole* appeared in his in-box. He opened the e-mail.

9+13+30–7+8+7+99

"Shit," he said. A third e-mail. This was becoming more than a distraction. Someone was trying to tell him something. He thrust the phone back into his jeans and headed inside.

Almost immediately, Jack rushed up. "Hi, Ike," Jack said.

Ike extended his palm and Jack slapped it. "How you doing, big guy?" Ike said.

Jack pulled back. "I'm not a big guy. I'm in the twentieth percentile on size for my age."

Ike gently laughed and gave him quick hug. "I gotta get to work. See you when I come out."

Ike noted that the Prices' assistant looked as if she had less sleep than he did. "Hi Kristin, they inside already?"

"They started early."

Ike headed in and found Jenna, Ed and Lauren in a heated discussion that stopped upon his arrival. Lauren looked the unhappiest of the trio.

"What's up?" he said.

Lauren was the first to respond. "Hi, Ike." She stood from the table and hugged him, longer than before.

"You okay?" he asked.

"I think so." She threw a nod at the Prices at the end of the table. "Alternate defense."

"You won't need that." Ike sat next to Lauren.

"Hey, Ike," Ed said with his usual easy style.

"Good morning, Ike," Jenna said with a smile she'd probably reserved for the handshake with opposing teams after she'd crushed them. "You have something for us?"

Ike wasn't sure if their competitive nature was a natural thing since they were both athletes who'd competed at the highest levels for most of their youth or if it was just a way to keep each other sharp. He liked Jenna and, after thinking about it, liked the challenge. It raised his game. Hers, too. Maybe she knew what she was doing.

"Here's what I got," Ike said with renewed energy. "I've found several oddities in Tom's suicide investigation." Ike ran down the list of issues he'd reviewed with Cassidy.

"That's good," Jenna said as if Ike had outperformed her expectations. "That might go to reasonable doubt and help generate an alternate scenario."

Lauren placed her hand on Ike's forearm and looked as if some of the load had been lifted.

Ed raised his pen in the air. "Based on what Ike's shared about Detective Cassidy, they'd argue it was just sloppy detective work."

Ike glanced at Lauren. Uncertainty returned to her face. Ed was always the voice of reason. His job was to play the role of the prosecutor and he was doing it well.

"I've got more," Ike said. "As I'm sure Lauren told you, I talked to Brenda Falzone yesterday." Jenna acknowledged she had. "She had a lot to say about Tanner. All of it bad. She hated the guy and the only reason she had him represent her was that her father paid her to do it."

"He paid her?" Jenna said.

"Yes. She also said she thought he did it because of her brother, Nick. Said they were hiding something."

Jenna and Ed shared a questioning glance. "Back to the seismic?"

"Maybe. Or something worse."

"Worse?" Jenna said.

"Brenda gave me the feeling that Nick could've had something to do with his half brother's death."

"She said that?"

"No. She implied she wouldn't be surprised."

"Too weak," Ed said.

"Still, I might be able to use it," Jenna said, writing something down.

"I don't think you'd ever get Nick Falzone on the stand," Ed said.

"Can you subpoena the seismic?" Ike asked.

"The judge would never sign it," Jenna said. "If he did, they'd quash it."

Ike caught Lauren looking at him. He could feel her looking deeper inside him. He pushed the sensation from his mind. "I'll have more after today. I'm going back to Cole's Seismic Services. Scott has arranged for me to meet the party chief from the seismic crew that acquired the shoot across the Virginia blocks."

"Can you do that?" Jenna said.

"Sure. I'm not asking for the data. Just asking a few questions offline. I also have a lead on Tanner I have to run down."

Jenna set her pen down. "Tanner?"

"Yes. A source told me about a poker group he was in. Something didn't add up."

Jenna scrunched her nose. "A poker group?"

"I can't say any more right now. Let me check it out."

"Okay." Jenna picked her pen back up and started writing again.

Ike pulled his phone out. "I have one more thing," he said, opening his e-mail. He showed the phone to Lauren, then passed it to Jenna and Ed. After reading the e-mail, Ed offered it back to Ike. Ike took the phone and stepped to the whiteboard on the wall. He wrote down the three expressions:

$$3-53+8x2+19$$
$$4+3-53+8+74$$
$$9+13+30-7+8+7+99$$

"Three e-mails, so far untraceable. They're coming regularly. Not exactly the same time every day. They're not phone numbers, combinations, or some alphabet-number sequence. I haven't been able to figure these out, but my gut says these mean something. More than minus 15, 36, and 159, their mathematical results. Because Tom was a math expert, I e-mailed the head of the Department of Mathematics at Pitt. Didn't tell him where it came from. He came up with nothing."

Ike set the marker back in the tray. "These may hold the key to what I'm looking for. Then again, they may not. Any ideas?"

Jenna cradled her chin in her hand. "Cryptologist?"

"You know one?" Ike asked.

"No," Jenna said, writing again, "but I can find one."

"Let Mac know if you find one," Ike said.

Lauren's lip quivered. "You think these are from Tom?"

Ike walked over and sat next to her, covering her shaking hand. "Either it's him or someone helping him. I don't think it's a distraction." He squeezed her hand. "But we'll figure this out. I promise." He looked around. "Anything else?"

"Good work, Ike," Ed said.

Jenna glanced up from making a note. "Yes. Thanks, Ike."

"Enough to stop working on the mental incapacity bullshit?" Ike said.

Jenna looked at Ed, who shook his head. Then she looked at Lauren, then Ike. "Afraid not."

"I'm not done yet," Ike said, standing.

Lauren rose with him. "I'll see you out."

They walked out together. Ike felt Lauren close to him. She was strong and kept it together, but the pain was still there. She knew, just as Ike did, that making Jack feel as if there were something wrong with him would end the boy they knew. They passed Kristin's desk and saw Jack pecking away on his iPad. His face looked dour, as if missing someone.

"Ike, Aunt Lauren," he said weakly.

"What's up, Jack?" Ike said.

Jack showed the screen of the iPad to Ike. "Can you take me here?"

Ike's internal alarm sounded when he saw the image. The demons in his gut dragged his heart down. It was a map of Homewood Cemetery.

CHAPTER 28

IKE YANKED THE shifter into fourth and watched Jack smile as they accelerated down the ramp and onto the interstate toward Pittsburgh. Ike imagined he'd had the same smile the time a friend's older brother gave them a ride in his SS 396 when he was about the same age. Lauren was ahead as they made their way back to the city and Homewood Cemetery. The Shelby growled and Jack's hair parted in the wind from the open window. They both needed the distraction.

"How much horsepower?" Jack yelled above the wind and engine noise.

"Five hundred twenty-six," Ike said.

"Does it go any faster?"

Ike checked his mirrors, then ahead. No traffic in the southbound lanes. He downshifted to fourth and floored it, then hit fifth and sixth. Jack's head was pinned against the headrest, grinning ear to ear. Ike slowed before they passed Lauren.

"That was awesome," Jack said.

Ike found himself grinning. "Yes it was."

For the rest of the ride they talked about cars and growing up. But the conversation stopped when they pulled through the old stone-framed gate of the cemetery. Ike had been here many times, alone and with Maria or Mac. It was both a reverent place and a gateway to the past, both good and bad. But being here with Jack had a different feel: protective, insightful, even helpful.

Ike parked next to Lauren's SUV and he and Jack jumped out of the Mustang and climbed into her grocery boat.

"You boys have fun?" she said with one eyebrow raised.

"Uh, yeah," Jack said.

"Uh, yeah," Ike said, giving Jack a high five from the front seat.

Lauren sighed quietly and shifted into "drive." She wound along the narrow old pavement, weaving between gravestones and mausoleums that marked the past for both the ultra-rich and those without wealth or ego. As they wound deeper into the cemetery, the old trees formed a canopy covering the road. The cemetery had been there for well over a hundred years. For Ike, it never seemed to change.

Lauren took another turn and Ike could see her watching Jack in the back. No one spoke until Ike asked, "You doing okay, buddy?"

"Yes. Aunt Lauren, it's just down there," Jack said pointing down the hill to the right.

Lauren stopped the car and unbuckled. Jack unbuckled, then said, "Can Ike take me down this time?"

Ike gave Lauren a nod. Maybe he could help Jack. Anything for Jack.

"Sure, honey."

Ike got out and met Jack on the other side of the car. They started down the hill, Jack guiding Ike through the maze of gravestones. The trees provided welcome shade, and beams of morning sunlight streamed between the leaves. The air was fresh and crisp, and a light breeze toyed with the leaves and provided a majestic soundtrack.

They broke into an opening in the trees and Ike spotted the newer grave.

"This is where my dad is buried," Jack said, pointing to the headstone. "Aunt Lauren says he's in heaven."

"I'm sure he is. Your dad was a great man."

Jack nodded. "I miss him."

Ike could see a glimmer in Jack's eyes. "I can see you do."

Jack looked up at Ike. "I think he would have liked you."

"I know I would have liked him."

Tears escaped from Jack's eyes. "Do you think he would have left me?"

Ike knelt down and mustered all the love he had in his heart. He gently cradled Jack by his shoulders. "No way. No way, no how. He'd never leave you. You're such a great boy."

"I know I'm different," he said.

"So am I." Ike sat in the grass facing Tom's grave. "Let me tell you what I was like when I was young like you."

Jack sat against Ike and rested his elbow on Ike's knee

"When I was even younger than you, my dad gave me a train set."

"With a train?"

"Yes. A miniature one. It had a metal track, cars, even little people and houses. We hooked it all up and played with it for hours."

"That sounds like fun."

"It was for a while. But my dad knew I liked science and math, so then he gave me an Erector set."

"A what?"

"It was pieces of metal and screws that you could put together and build things, like buildings, robots, and stuff."

"That sounds fun, too."

"It was. Then he gave me a shortwave radio kit. He and I put it together."

"Oh. I'd really like that."

"I know. I did. We put that together and it worked and I talked to people all over the country. But then you know what I did?"

Jack's eyes widened. "What?"

"Well, I'd seen western movies where they used a telegraph."

"My dad and I watched some westerns. He liked them. Me, too."

"Me, too. I knew the transformer for the train provided power—electricity."

"Okay."

"Then I knew the headphones worked by picking up electrical impulses, so I took the Erector set and built a key—the thing they tap on in the movies."

"Cool."

"Then I hooked the transformer to the key and the headphone to a wire from the base of the key."

"And it worked?"

"Just like in the movies. My dad came in and saw it and smiled. He said 'Good job.' Then he explained that it might not be safe and I could be electrocuted. We both laughed as we took it apart."

Jack looked at the headstone. "My dad used to tell me 'Good job.'"

"I bet he did. Anyway, I went to school and told the other kids what I did and they looked at me like I was different. Some even made fun of me."

"They did?"

"Yes."

"You were different like me." It was a statement, not a question.

"I sure was, thank God."

"And you were a star quarterback."

"And the man you see now."

Jack smiled and wiped his eyes. "My dad would have liked you a lot." Jack looked at the gravestone. "Do you miss your dad?"

"Every day."

"Are you sad?"

"Sometimes."

"Do you talk to him?"

"Sometimes."

Jack looked around. "Is he buried here like my dad?"

Jack's question caught Ike off guard. "Yes. He and my mom are in another section."

"Can we go there?"

Ike would normally have declined. He never went with anyone except Maria or Mac. But the abyss didn't look as dark for some reason.

"Okay," Ike said, standing. "Let's go get Lauren."

Ike walked with Jack and they returned to the car. Lauren was leaning against the hood with an inquisitive look. Ike smiled. "One more stop."

Surprise spread across Lauren's face.

"We're going to see Ike's parents' grave," Jack said.

"We are?" she said.

"I'll show you how to get there," Ike said as they all got into the car.

Ike guided them back to the entrance and then around to the south side of the cemetery. They pulled up in front of four huge mausoleums.

"They're in there?" Jack said, pointing to the gigantic stone tombs

"Jack," Lauren said in a scolding tone.

"It's okay," Ike said. "No, Jack, they're down here." Ike pointed down the open hillside to their right. Ike got out and Lauren and Jack joined him. The hillside was grass and the size of a football field. A lone tree stood halfway down.

"I don't see any headstones," Jack said.

"They're markers," Ike said, pointing down. "You see, when Mom and Dad died, I was only nineteen and in college. My little sister was only nine."

"Nine. I remember," Jack said.

Lauren stepped close to Ike.

"Yes. I had to come home and take care of her."

"Like Aunt Lauren and me," Jack said.

Ike looked at Lauren. He hadn't thought of it that way. "Yes," he said, nodding. "Like you and your Aunt Lauren. But I didn't have any money, so we saved all the insurance money to take care of Maria and me. I could only afford to put them here."

Ike remembered the decision like it was yesterday. He was young, scared, and alone. But with Jack next to him, the memory didn't seem as intense.

Ike put his arm over Jack's shoulder. "Let's go, buddy."

"I'll stay here, boys."

Ike wanted Lauren to come, but he also understood. This was between him and Jack.

They walked a quarter of the way down the hill and stopped. Ike bent over and swept the mowed grass from the two stones.

The sun was warm and the breeze picked up. Jack studied the stones. He looked up at Ike, squinting in the sunlight. "Do you think your mom and dad would have liked me?"

"They would have loved you."

"I bet they were a good mom and dad."

"The best."

Jack looked at the stones, then at Ike. "You're a good son," he said.

Ike felt the moisture coming to his eyes but held it back. "I did the best I could."

Jack studied the markers again. "They died a long time ago."

"Twenty-two years."

Jack looked at his feet and kicked the loose grass. "Will you ever find out who did this?"

Ike waited for the anger, but it didn't come. "To tell you the truth, I don't know. But I'll never give up."

Jack faced Ike. "You need any help?"

Ike put his arm around Jack. "You'll be the first I'll call if I do." Ike looked up the hill to Lauren. "Time to go." As they walked up the hill, Ike felt lighter, focused and ready to find the truth—no matter where it took him.

CHAPTER 29

WHEN IKE STEPPED through the doors of Cole's Seismic for the second time, the reception was much warmer. Bobby Scott's assistant met him in the lobby and whisked him to the fifth-floor conference room. As he waited, he stood at the floor-to-ceiling window, looked over the rolling hills of the Southpointe Office Park, and thought about his time with Jack. That morning, his belief in him had solidified like cooling steel. A kid like that would never shoot Tanner unless he had a very good reason—only one reason: to save himself and his aunt. But Ike's belief was worthless in court. He needed proof. He needed to find whatever the Falzones were hiding. This was the last quasi-legal step toward doing that.

After a late-night phone call to Scott, explaining what he needed to help Jack, Scott had flown in from Houston that morning the head of the seismic crew that had acquired the seismic data on behalf of Falzone Energy. Because the data was acquired by another company and then processed by Cole's, Ike thought Scott had gone above and beyond to help find the truth about Tom's death. With the unusual nature of the request, the seismic company's president insisted on coming with its chief counsel. The executives would certainly gum up the conversation with legal constraints and cover-your-ass corporate speak, but Ike had confidence he could manage them—he'd seen it all before.

Ike heard steps behind him in the hallway and Scott led three other men into the conference room. The president and the chief counsel were easily identified by their dark suits and stern faces. The third man wore a tie like a hangman's noose and looked as if he'd been dressed at gunpoint. Scott made a beeline for Ike and shook his hand.

"I got them here as quickly as I could." He leaned in and pulled Ike closer. "Sorry about the suits," he whispered.

Ike patted Scott on the shoulder. "Thanks, Bobby. Looks like it was a package deal."

The two executives introduced themselves. Jeff Franz was president of ITR Seismic. Based on his pale skin and thick waistline, Ike pegged him as mid-forties and chained to his desk. Anton Keller seemed pleasant and young for a chief counsel. Franz introduced Pete Boudreaux, party chief for the shoot in question. Boudreaux had a thick Cajun accent and an energetic grip.

He gave a wide smile and loudly said, "I just watched your thirty for thirty."

Both executives looked at each other.

"On ESPN," Boudreaux said, glancing at his bosses.

"Thanks. That was a long time ago," Ike said, guiding Boudreaux into the seat next to him. The execs looked lost for a moment, until Scott stopped at the head of the table and offered them the seats facing Ike.

Keller pulled a single sheet of paper from his briefcase. "We have a confidentiality agreement with Falzone Energy surrounding this shoot. We understand the importance of this conversation, but we can't share coordinates, data interpretation, or the area of the shoot. The location of the OCS blocks is public record and is already in the public domain. I'll ask that Pete pause before answering any of your questions to allow me time to ensure it is within the boundaries of our agreement with Falzone Energy."

Ike thought it would take less time to recite the Gettysburg Address.

"As far as we're concerned, this meeting never happened," Franz said. "The only reason we're here is all the years of business we've done with Tom and Bobby."

Ike had carefully planned his opening remark to set the tone. "Thanks, gentlemen. I'm representing Tom Cole's *son*."

Boudreaux dropped his head. "Sorry about Tom."

"Did you know Tom?"

Boudreaux looked at Keller and waited for a nod. "Yes. We'd done several shoots with Tom in the Gulf. This was the fifth or sixth time we worked with him."

"He was on the boat?"

Another nod. "This time. But the other times he came out only for the planning meetings."

"Why this time?"

"He had very specific requirements for this shoot. There was a thick layer of salt above the target reservoirs and no 3D shot in the area. We used a special streamer he'd help us design specifically for this job. You know what streamers are?"

"Sure. You tow those behind your boat to pick up the seismic reflections. They contain hydrophones and motion sensors to detect reflections of the seismic waves from the air guns."

Boudreaux seemed impressed.

"I was on a boat in the Gulf a few times," Ike said.

"Okay. Just wanted to be sure."

"Besides being there for the shoot, anything else unusual about this job?"

Keller interrupted, ensuring he was worth the airfare to Pittsburgh. "Pete. Remember, nothing about the data acquired or its interpretation."

"Can I talk about how we handled the data?"

Keller nodded.

"We all were required to sign riders to the confidentiality agreement that said we wouldn't retain any of the data. Tom transmitted the data directly to his office after it was checked by the processor on board and okayed. We had a third party board the vessel and ensure that all drives and computers were clean."

Ike looked at Scott. "You said the data was deleted here?"

"Yes. The information went to a special server that was only connected to workstations in a secured room. Only Tom had access. If he needed another geophysicist he'd personally let them in and watch them work. But he did most of the work. Once the processed images were transmitted to Falzone Energy, the same third party swept the server and the workstations. They took everything else. Never saw anything like it."

"I'll say," Pete said. "Tom wouldn't discuss anything with us other than the necessary specs for the shoot. At the end, he seemed worried."

"When did you acquire the data and send it off? Complete the job?"

Pete glanced at Keller again. "November twenty-ninth. I'll never forget that day. An early winter storm was coming up the coast. I remember thinking that was the coldest I'd ever been. Glad we got the hell out of there."

Ike made a note of the date. It was two months before Patrick Falzone's accident. Ike turned to Scott. "How long to process something like this and get a 3D image of the reservoirs they were looking at?"

"It used to take a month or two, depending on the iterations around the salt layer, but Tom's process cut that to around three weeks."

"So the image would have been received by Falzone Energy the third week in December?"

"That's right. But they would have worked it further for the specific targets. Tom helped with that, but all the rest of the work was done at Falzone Center."

Ike wanted to ask another question but decided to wait until the others left.

"Anything else, Pete?"

Boudreaux tilted his head as if scouring his memory. Then he gave a sidelong glance at Keller before turning back to Ike. "I think he saw something."

"Saw what?"

"Something that excited him but something he couldn't talk about—in the data."

Keller stiffened. "Nothing about the data." He glared at Boudreaux, who yanked his tie loose as he eyed Keller, then winked at Ike.

Franz stood. "We've said all we can here, Mr. Rossi. We have a plane to catch."

"I'll walk you out," Bobby said.

Boudreaux stood and gripped Ike's hand again with a gleam in his eyes. "Do what you can for Jack. Tom loved that boy." He followed the suits out.

"Bobby," Ike said. "After you see them out I need to speak with you."

"Sure," Bobby said as he corralled the group down the hall.

Five minutes later, Bobby came back in and sat next to Ike.

"You have another question for me?"

"A question and a request."

"Okay. I'll do what I can."

"You said when we last met that Tom seemed different, yet you didn't think he was depressed?"

"I remember our conversation."

"If I were to ask you to speculate on the reason for the change, what would you say it was?"

Scott carefully weighed his reply. "I'd agree with Pete. I think he saw something in that data."

Ike let the reply hang in the air for a few seconds. "Now my request."

Scott half-frowned, but his eyes widened as he stood up. "Hang on—don't say a word."

He disappeared down the hallway and returned with an accordion file. "I think it's best we end here," he said, shaking Ike's hand. "My assistant is waiting for you at the elevator." He turned and rushed toward the door, sticking the file upside down under his arm.

"Bobby. I didn't ask my—" Ike heard something hit the floor. He walked to the doorway and picked up a security card with a small yellow Post-it attached to it. On the key card was printed *Falzone Energy Contractor* and a grainy pixilated photo of a bearded man and the name Mark Smith. Ike looked closer at the Post-it note. It said *Twelfth floor, third door to the right. User Name: Gongle21, PW: Oru12#4017, file folder: Minuteman.*

So much for the legal options.

CHAPTER 30

WITH THE ACCESS card tucked into his shirt pocket, Ike dashed into the parking lot as the noontime thunderstorm did its best to soak through his clothes. The air smelled clean and refreshed, but with the card he felt like he was handling nuclear waste and the pure rainwater couldn't wash away its effect. The longer he kept the card, the more it polluted his sense of fairness and self-respect.

He reached his car and ducked inside, wiping the water from his eyes. This was not the way he did things. Even in the most difficult cases, he'd always stayed within the limits of the law. He knew the value of his reputation with both clients, and law enforcement opened many doors. His father's advice echoed in his head. *Money earned with ethics and character buys more than that earned with unscrupulous acts*. He'd honored his father by following that code throughout his career.

He started the Shelby and saw his eyes in the rearview mirror. Staring at himself, he felt the shame planted by his father's memory. He leaned back and pulled the damp card from his pocket and rolled down his window. He turned the card between his index finger and thumb and cocked his wrist to toss it into the storm.

A flash of lighting in the distance grabbed his attention, and then the image of Jack's tearstained face surfaced like a drowning man fighting for life. The system was screwing Jack, even worse than it had screwed Ike. A heavy helplessness filled his heart, and for a moment he shared Jack's certain terror. It morphed into the bottomless well of sadness and guilt he'd battled since his parents' death. Failing Jack wasn't an option. The system's rules had been molested by the Falzones and their lawyers, so why not use their own tactics against them?

Ike rolled the card into his fist and rammed it into his thigh. "Shit." He powered the window up and shoved the card back into his shirt. After slamming the Shelby into first, he spun from the space and fishtailed out onto Southpointe Boulevard.

The dark clouds had blacked out the sun and the driving rain gave the windshield a molten look. Lightning alternated with heavy thunderclaps and Ike could feel the wind buffeting the Shelby. He barely saw the traffic light ahead and slid to a stop. He calmed himself. When the light turned green, he slowly accelerated. Through the blurry rear window, he noticed a black Jeep Cherokee closing fast—too fast. The front grille was reinforced with a black tubular deer catcher.

The Jeep was closing faster—accelerating now—and Ike downshifted and floored the pedal. There was no doubt, someone was coming after him. He'd expected it at some point, but not in broad daylight.

The Jeep slammed into Ike's rear bumper. Fishtailing on the wet asphalt, he quickly matched the Jeep's speed, leaving his assailant a car length behind.

The rain thinned and Ike spotted the golf course on the right, but a thick grove of trees quickly approached. Traffic was light, but not light enough for this. He looked down—already at seventy. The four-lane road provided some room, but there was no divider and any mistake to the right would end in a fatal head-on. A slip to the left and one of the hundreds of thick oaks would split the Shelby in half. Still, he slipped around the gentle curve and shifted into fifth.

The Cherokee was still on his bumper. *Probably a Hemi.* Two slower cars, one passing the other in the right two lanes, suddenly appeared ahead. Ike had no choice: he veered into the oncoming lanes and found himself head-on with a UPS truck. He accelerated and darted back into the right lanes.

The next curve was much sharper and he downshifted. The back wheels slid through the turn. When he recovered, the Cherokee slammed into the back, this time hard enough to snap Ike's head against the headrest.

Ahead, all four lanes were occupied at a red-light intersection. The forest on the right gave way to a thin sidewalk and another rolling hole on the narrow golf course. He yanked the wheel to the right and the car leaped over the curb, taking out a small hotel sign, and slid sideways on the wet grass. Ike accelerated and fought the car out of the skid. The Cherokee followed, but its tires dug deep and it faded back. Ike jerked the Shelby back to the road with a thud, and he felt the tires bite on the wet road.

With the Cherokee still behind him, he couldn't see the driver. Who the hell was he or she? Maybe this whole thing was backward? Ike didn't want to be the prey. He rounded another turn and accelerated onto a short straightaway. The sidewalk remained on the right, but the next hole of the golf course had a water hazard next to the road. The shore of the man-made lake sloped down to the road, just a few football fields ahead.

Ike slowed, and the Cherokee rammed the Shelby again. Ike accelerated with the bump. Jumping the curb, he raced down the sidewalk with his left two wheels on the walk and the right two on the slick grass. The Cherokee didn't have time to follow and paralleled Ike, staying on the road. Ike swerved from the sidewalk to the cart path along the narrow fairway. Ahead, a foursome waiting out the rain abandoned their cart and scurried away.

The lake was closing fast and Ike knew this was his chance. He slammed the brakes and the clutch at the same time, and the Shelby's tires clawed at the cart path. The Cherokee shot ahead on the boulevard. Ike slammed the shifter to third and turned back across the grass toward the road. He lost traction on the sliver of grass and the Shelby went sideways. He could see the rise of the small earthen dam topped by a tee box just ahead. He turned into the skid and pointed the nose of the Shelby at the Cherokee. The car leaped the curb and he skidded back into the lane two lengths behind the Jeep.

The windows were blacked out, but now Ike could see the desperation in the Cherokee driver's reaction. It was now about their survival, not his. Ike's anger about Jack was like a beast unchained. He wanted to get inside that Cherokee.

The boulevard had narrowed to one lane in each direction, and when the Cherokee pulled out to pass a slower car, Ike went with him. The Cherokee shot back into the lane, leaving Ike facing a head-on with a pickup. Ike yanked the Shelby's wheel to the right, missing the truck by less than a foot.

Back in the right lane, Ike moved the Shelby close and tapped the Cherokee's bumper. The Cherokee swerved but then pulled away. *Definitely a Hemi.* The road opened back to two lanes each way with a tree-lined divider. They ran through two more red lights and raced down the long hill to I-79. Ike closed to the Cherokee's bumper again as they approached the on-ramp. Ike wanted to be sure they couldn't slow for the interstate ramp. Too many cars and the state patrol might just get in the way.

They raced under the overpass and up the long hill, passing both the northbound and southbound ramps. This would all end soon, with the T intersection approaching at the top of the hill. Two cars were in the right lane, waiting at the light. The Cherokee skidded to the right and jumped the sidewalk, ripping the park-and-ride-lot fence out of the ground. Tangled in the deer catcher, the fence ran under the Cherokee. The undercarriage digested the posts and fencing. Ike threw the Shelby to the left, downshifting and hitting the brake. Sliding into the oncoming lane, he passed the two stunned drivers in a four-wheel drift and skidded around them. Then he accelerated hard to the right and back on the tail of the Cherokee as it barreled down Morganzer Road.

The Jeep was still dragging a section of fence, and Ike easily reached its bumper. Just as he clipped it, the Cherokee suddenly skidded and took a hairpin right onto a side road. The Cherokee nearly rolled but somehow made the turn and raced down the road that doubled back the other way. Then Ike pulled a one-eighty and barely made the turn. The car spun onto the shoulder and stopped. Ike floored it and roared down the road behind the Cherokee.

The road was narrow, with woods on both sides, but Ike wanted to end this. He saw a break in the woods just ahead. With the Cherokee slowed by the fencing, Ike closed quickly, then yanked the wheel right, hitting the Cherokee's left rear quarter panel. The Cherokee skidded, but so did Ike. Ike fought to keep control as the Shelby slipped sideways and onto the right shoulder. The Cherokee shot left across the roadway and catapulted off a small embankment, landing upright in a small pond.

In seconds, the only audible sound was that of both engines running. Ike opened the glove box and pulled out his Glock. He could see the Cherokee idling in the water, its wheels nearly covered. The passenger's side faced him, but the windows were black. If the driver was targeting him, he'd never see it.

He opened the door to forty-five degrees and used it as a shield. He slipped out, leading with the Glock. The Cherokee's window exploded and Ike heard three rounds hit his car. He ducked behind the door and returned fire. The Cherokee's engine roared, and Ike walked steadily forward and fired as the Cherokee climbed out of the pond. Without a passenger's window, Ike could see the driver. Black mask, large frame. Ike could see the whites of his eyes and black pupils. The driver fired two more shots—not at Ike, at his car—then pulled onto the roadway and raced away.

Ike ran toward his car until he saw the two flat tires. Watching the Cherokee pull away, he spotted the plates. Paper and temporary. He slipped the Glock into his belt and pulled out his cell phone. His pulse was racing but not from the chase. Ike was certain the only people who'd have enough at stake to attack in broad daylight were the Falzones.

He called AAA for a tow, then noticed that his phone's e-mail app showed three new e-mails. Another message from Tom Cole would confirm that they were more than just numbers; they were clues being sent from the grave. He opened the app and his eyes locked on the sender of the first message.

Tom Cole

53+25–7+47+10–7

CHAPTER 31

THIS HAD NEVER been Jenna's first choice. She'd planned to win. But as time was running out, so were her options. She could make Jack's behavior fit the profile. But every word she spoke would slice a piece of her soul away. He'd be forced into years of evaluation and treatment that would condemn his sense of self and destroy the hope that he radiated each day. She'd convinced herself that it was better than life without parole, but the dark hands of doubt were pulling her back into the realization that Jack Cole was dead either way. And that was the easy part.

They'd been in the conference room since ten a.m. and Jenna had covered the key points for tomorrow's custody hearing with Lauren. The judge would allow Mayer and the Falzones to call her to the stand. That, she explained, would be their only move. Showing her as unfit was their only chance at full custody. With the outstanding psych evaluation the judge now had, they'd attack her about Jack's killing Tanner.

Visitation, however, was more certain. As grandparents, they only had to prove that it was in Jack's best interest. Ike could quash that with proof of his theory that the Falzones were behind Tom's death, but it was Thursday and he'd found little in the form of hard evidence. Jenna had watched the stress etch Lauren's once-smooth face over the past two months, but the past three hours seemed to accelerate the process. Now she'd have to endure Jenna's discussion about the mental-impairment strategy in the criminal trial. Even with her father there for support, Jenna never hated herself more.

"Lauren, we need to talk about the criminal trial."

Lauren dropped her head as if anticipating the pain. Then she looked up. "Okay. We've been all through it. And Ike has promised he'll find what we need. What is there left to do?"

"I know. And God knows Ike's record speaks for itself. But it's Thursday afternoon and we still don't have any new evidence. We've had two detectives look under every rock for the last six months. We have to face the possibility that Ike won't do any better."

"You heard what he said. They're hiding something."

"We can't risk Jack's life on a hunch. Dad and I have been over and over the facts and there's a significant risk that we lose and Jack gets life." Jenna didn't want to imagine what those words felt like as they attacked Lauren's heart. They'd shared enough bottles of wine to get past each other's façades, and Jenna knew that losing Jack now would destroy her.

Jenna reached across the table and took Lauren's hand. She could see the tears welling in Lauren's eyes as Jenna readied to breach the subject. "I think we—"

Lauren cut her off with a glare. "Don't say it."

"But I—"

"I don't want to discuss any option about Jack's mental deficiencies."

"But we need to have that option ready and we need your consent."

Lauren stood. "I won't be a part of that." She gathered her folio. "I believe Ike will come through." She stopped at the door. "I'm going to take a break now." She left the room.

While Jenna understood Lauren's reaction, it filled her with frustration. She blamed herself for driving Lauren out of the room. She closed the file in front of her and cradled her forehead in her hand.

She looked at her father. "I don't blame her, but she puts us in a box, and maybe Jack in prison for life."

Ed slowly closed his file, leaned back, and rocked in his chair. He stayed silent, staring at the file in front of him. Then he stopped rocking. "I don't think you can change her mind. And she's the client, or at least his guardian."

"But that puts everything on a long shot. I'd be counting on Ike Rossi."

A wave of concern swept across her father's face, and for the first time he looked old and tired. "We're all counting on Ike."

Jenna could read him. She always could. This wasn't about the case, it was personal. It was about much more than the uncertainty of putting a decision into the hands of twelve strangers. "What is it, Dad?"

He folded his hands on the desk and eyed them as if he held a secret inside them. A few seconds passed, and he raised his head, locking his eyes on hers. "We're hemorrhaging. The firm is losing its client base, especially the few corporate and small-business clients we had."

"It's that bad?"

"At this rate, we're not covering costs. I've been supplementing the firm with my rainy-day fund."

Jenna had missed that. She'd been so absorbed by the custody hearing and the murder trial preparation she hadn't looked at the firm's finances since she took the case.

"Why? They love us."

"It's Falzone and Latham. They've been carefully planting veiled threats in the business community about dealing with us. Anyone that does will not be considered a strategic partner of Falzone Enterprises, including Falzone Energy. Everyone knows the political muscle they have, too. A few don't like the negative press about representing a murderer."

"They can't do that."

"They can. They're connected in ways you can't imagine."

The realization that they were in financial trouble crept in like an oozing, heavy tar. It wasn't the firm she was worried about. Her father had worked for forty years and built up enough of a cushion to enjoy a nice retirement. But he'd also built up enough of a reserve to help support her brother Michael for the rest of his life. He'd started when Michael was four years old. Michael had needed heart surgery so he could live a full life, not die in his youth. Their family had barely made it through. Jenna had worked in the evenings and on the weekends at a local bookstore and given every paycheck to her dad. Now the foundation they'd built to let Michael live in comfort was being eroded by her decision to take the case.

She didn't want to ask, but she had to know how bad it was. "So if we lose?"

"If we lose, we shut down. I have to start over." His hands were still locked but trembling, and his eyes turned glassy. "I'll have to find a firm to join and try to make as much as I can as long as I can."

Jenna let her father's pain become hers and soak in for a few seconds. She stood and moved next to him. She bent and hugged him. His trembling intensified until she heard a sob. A tear tickled her cheek and she wiped it away. "It will be okay, Dad. No matter what."

Deep down in the dark pit where her competitive fire lived, a storm began to spin into a hatred she'd never felt for anyone before. The Falzones had done this, and somehow she would find a way to stop them. She needed Ike to come through. To save Jack—and to save her family.

CHAPTER 32

IT WAS JUST after three p.m. and Ike had walked to Rossi's after the tow and tire replacement on the Shelby. Other than the sidelong glances and head shakes of the mechanic after he inspected the bullet holes, no one knew about the attempt to run Ike off the road. DeSantis Auto Repair was only two blocks from Rossi's, and Ike had known the family. He was close to the two sons, Vinny and Danny, since he started driving. The steady flow of business from his car addiction, along with a small incentive payment, would keep the secret in the family. Since the shooter had targeted Ike's tires and not his head, he assured himself this was just a warning. But that warning meant he was getting warmer and someone, probably with the last name Falzone, didn't like it.

Sitting on his barstool, Ike stared at the chalkboard and applied his best inductive reasoning. Normally, the board held the specials each evening, but with the lunch crowd gone and two hours to go before the Thursday night dinner menu, it held four expressions and their mathematical solutions:

$$3-53+8x2+19 = -15$$

$$4+3-53+8+74 = 36$$

$$9+13+30-7+8+7+99 = 159$$
$$53+25-7+47+10-7 = 121$$

Ike carefully thought of them as solutions and not what he needed most: answers. Since he'd received the fourth one, his gut told him the expressions represented clues. Clues that could lead to answers—answers that could free Jack. Ike had recruited Mac and Maria to brainstorm the possibilities, and they'd been gaping at the board for five minutes as if it were an alien spaceship. Rossi's was empty, a typical afternoon lull, but the silence was unsettling. They had no easy answers.

"What did the cryptologist from Pitt say?" Ike asked.

Mac didn't look away from the board. "He said they didn't fit any of the known cryptographic algorithms. As far as he was concerned, they're mathematical expressions."

"You know," Maria said pointing at the board, "could the solutions be the clues?"

"I thought about that," Ike said. "But the expressions didn't come with a solution, and the solution is easy. Something that obvious provides no encryption value at all."

"Then we need the key," Maria said.

"That's right," Mac said. "The cryptologist mentioned that was part of the process of decryption. But he was baffled." He took a long draw on his beer.

That made sense to Ike. "All right then, what key can we think of that would cover the range of numbers from two to ninety-nine?"

Still, nothing but silence.

"Some of the numbers repeat: three, seven, eight and fifty-three," Mac said.

Ike began to sense some pattern to the numbers. "That makes me think this is some kind of code. Numeric to alpha."

"That's the first thing I tried with the alphabet while you were gone. I simply substituted the letter corresponding to the numbers. If it was larger than twenty-six, I left the number." Mac pulled a bar napkin from his pocket and walked to the board. He wrote out his translation below the expressions:

C53HBS

DC53H74

IM30GHG99

53YG47JG

"Serial numbers?" Maria guessed.

"Maybe. But to what?" Ike said as he checked his watch.

"Too long for plate numbers," Mac said.

Ike looked at his watch again. "Can you two keep working on this?" He stood and pushed his stool to the bar.

Mac threw a disgusted look at Ike, took another drink, and set the mug down hard. "You're still going through with it?"

Ike had shown the access card to Mac when he'd arrived. "I'm running out of options. These things are gibberish right now, even though I think they hold the key to what we're looking for. I can't take the time here. The hearing starts Monday and I have no hard evidence."

"If you steal what you're looking for, you still won't have hard evidence," Mac said.

"It will be admissible."

"It's not its admissibility I'd be worried about. It's the weight the court and the jury will give it. It will be evidence stolen by an unscrupulous investigator from the oil business."

Ike found it hard to argue. "That may be the case, but it may lead to something much bigger."

"You don't know that. What you do know is that it will lead to losing all the reputational capital you've built up over the years with your clients and law enforcement. You'll be just like those two-bit PIs that live in the sewer with the rest of the scum."

"Mac." Maria touched his arm.

"No. Ike needs to hear this. It's a slippery slope. I've seen it a hundred times. Break the law a little here and a little there and pretty soon you're on the wrong side."

Ike felt as if he were back at the station at nineteen on his first days with Mac. One warning Mac had drilled into him had stayed with him all these years. *Most people have good and bad inside. It's the little steps that take them one way or the other.* This was definitely a step in the wrong direction. To argue any further would be pointless—Mac was right. But the powerful force inside wanted to free Jack no matter what virtue or vice prevailed.

"I need to get ready."

Maria called to the corner where one of the waiters was taking a break watching *Ellen* and asked him to take over for a few minutes. As she looped around the bar, Ike heard Mac's mug hit the bar again.

"And you, young lady. You're going to help him?"

Maria looked like a scolded puppy. "He's my brother and he needs me. I've done this before."

Mac held his disapproving gaze on her. But just like a puppy, she ignored his warning and followed Ike upstairs to his office. He walked to the closet and pulled out the kit. He'd used it many times when he'd gone undercover for his clients. It was one of the pitfalls of having your face plastered all over the sports pages in every publication in the country. Maria's artistic side was perfect for the task. The makeup and facial-hair work she'd done should have hung in the Louvre.

As she started, Ike reached over and kissed her on the forehead. He didn't say anything, but he didn't have to. The love they had for each other was a bond that had carried them through the terrible times of the past. As he leaned back and felt the soft brush stroke his face, he remembered Mac's warning—and hoped it wasn't a prophecy.

CHAPTER 33

MARIA HADN'T SAID a word. She didn't have to. Ike could see the building dissent in her eyes. It clawed away at his resolve, which held back a reservoir of guilt about disappointing her. At his core, he knew she was right, but she knew little of the abyss and how failure here would swallow him up. Ike sensed they were at a silent stalemate. A brother who'd become a surrogate father who was loved and respected by his little sister, versus an adoring sister who now was afraid to tell him he was wrong. As the soft brush stroked his face for the final time, it seemed as if she were covering up the face that was letting her down.

Ike checked the ID wedged into the corner of the mirror with the image staring back at him. If he didn't know the truth, he'd clear himself through a TSA checkpoint as Mark Smith. His iPhone rang and Maria stepped back as he answered.

"Rossi."

"Ike, this is Jenna. Is this a good time?"

Ike detected an accommodating tone that was uncharacteristic of her hard-driving spirit. He'd seen teammates do the same thing when their performance on the field fell far short of their own confident expectations. "Any time is good for you, Counselor."

"Great. I wanted to touch base—see how things are going."

That meant either she was coming to his point of view on the mental-impairment strategy, or Lauren simply said no. "I've got several avenues I'm pursuing. One is the seismic shoot. I think there's something there that the Falzones are hiding, and since Tom Cole was involved, this could be the break we need."

"I can subpoena them. It's not too late."

"I think all that would do is give them the signal to hide or destroy it."

"How else can we get it?"

Ike was in deep water here. He'd read Jenna as a straight shooter. Unlike some defense attorneys he'd dealt with, she wore her ethics like a jersey with her name on it.

"I'm working on an angle through Cole's seismic company."

Jenna hesitated long enough for Ike to know she suspected something on the dark edge. Maybe she'd handled a case or two on the theft of confidential information or she remembered what he'd said about the confidentiality of seismic interpretations.

"Don't do anything we'll regret. Keep the subpoena in mind anyway. What about Tanner?"

"I've got a great lead on him. I'm following up tomorrow."

"So no hard evidence yet?"

Ike got a whiff of desperation in her question.

"I'll have it soon. Just be ready."

"Okay. We only have a few days left to prepare any new strategy … and please remember the rule of evidence and maintaining its value." A polite rebuke, for sure.

Ike didn't want desperation to convince Jenna and Lauren to sell out Jack.

"Got it. Talk to you soon." Ike ended the call.

Maria kept her back turned as she returned the brushes and makeup to the kit. When she finished, she turned and faced Ike. Her eyes were wide and her voice soft. "I love you, Ike, and you know I support you no matter what you do, but ..." She gathered herself as if readying to stick her head in a lion's mouth. "But why are you taking such a chance? This isn't like you. You've never tried to steal something."

Ike had been challenged before by much more menacing opponents, but this one cut deep. He remembered carefully repeating all the lessons he'd learned from his parents to a nine-year-old Maria. He'd taken her to church and explained the differences between right and wrong. All in an effort to keep her from doing exactly the sort of thing he was about to do. "You have to believe me. There is no other way. I'm out of time and so is Jack. These people are hiding something that may prove what he did was self-defense. I can't fail. He'll be put away for life—and he's only ten years old."

Maria stepped closer. She reached out and touched his arm. "I've seen you struggle with trying to find Mom and Dad's killer. And this feels like that. You don't have to do this to prove anything—not to me, and not to yourself."

Ike stood and gave her a long hug. "I'm doing this for Jack. Maybe a little for me, too. Maybe if I can't get closure for us, I can get closure for him. And if I get closure for him, then maybe, in some way, it will give me a bit of closure, too."

Maria pulled back slowly, looked up at Ike, and nodded. She turned and pulled the access card from the mirror and handed it to him. "Be sure to stay out of the rain. Not sure that's all waterproof." She gave Ike the smile he'd seen any time they were about to color outside the lines on purpose.

Except this was not playtime. Someone could get hurt. Someone could get arrested, someone could get killed—but someone *had* to do it.

CHAPTER 34

IKE SHIELDED HIS eyes from the sun's reflection off the bronze upper floors of Falzone Center. It was warm again, and he could feel the sweat under the beard Maria had carefully tacked to his face. The feelings of guilt had faded. It was now all about executing the plan.

He'd parked at Forbes and Grant and walked a block, lingering on the corner of Grant and Fifth. Traffic was swelling in the city as the towers emptied their workers, all rushing to their cars to make the congested slog to the suburbs. The fumes from the cars filled Ike's nostrils, but that wasn't anything compared with the dark clouds of coal soot that must have had blanketed the city over the first half of the last century and stained the granite exterior of the corner of the courthouse he leaned against now.

The migrating workers clogging the sidewalks provided good cover, and he watched the front doors of Falzone Center as four fifteen approached. They worked from seven to quarter after four, their core hours. At least that's what the article in the *Post-Gazette* said where the Falzones had bragged about their flex hours. He'd bet that the building would empty like a shaken hive, especially with the culture he imagined Nick Falzone set within his organization. No one would want to work late out of dedication or as a way to enhance their performance ratings. He read Falzone as a narcissistic taskmaster, viewing his people only as a means to an end—not as intelligent and committed human beings.

The doors flew open and the great employees of Falzone Energy began to flood the street. Ike moved quickly, toting a Swiss Army backpack and sporting Dockers and a button-down oxford shirt. He felt like a salmon swimming upstream against the crowd. He'd underestimated their zeal to escape. The lobby was packed, full of people flooding from the turnstiles. Two blazered security guards flanked the bank of turnstiles and looked as if they couldn't care less. One lane was open, and Ike swiped the access card and slipped into an elevator as soon as it emptied. He opened the timer on his iPhone and set it to thirty minutes. He didn't want to stay that long, but he was certain the guards would change to the evening shift at quarter to five, thirty minutes after the employees left.

He'd learned that while working under his boss at Abbysis Energy years ago. The ex-FBI agent knew Ike's family history. When he first interviewed Ike, he told Ike there was no room for vengeance in the job and doubted Ike would be a good fit. But after speaking to Mac and Ike's old supervisor at the Pittsburgh Police Department, he changed his mind. One of the first roles he'd given Ike was supervising building security. Ike quickly graduated to investigations and managing kidnap-and-abduction training. He'd been slated to take his retiring boss's job until Abbysis was swallowed up by Targon Energy and Ike refused to move to Houston. The severance allowed him to set up his own shop—a blessing in disguise.

As the elevator crept toward the twelfth floor, Ike slipped the backpack off his shoulder. With security tied up monitoring the lobby, he'd hoped he'd be unchallenged on the floor. Whether there were a few stragglers was another matter. They'd be more of a threat, especially since they might have known the real Mark Smith, if he even existed.

The doors opened on the twelfth floor and Ike settled the adrenaline surging through his body. The hallway was old. Frayed gray carpet covered the floor and thick faded wood trim outlined each doorway. Low ceilings and bad fluorescent lighting made it feel more like a cell block than an office. Evidently, the Falzones had spent all their money on the lobby and a few executive floors and left the rest the same since 1984. The hallway was empty and he headed to the third door on the right.

The frame that should hold the nameplate was empty; perhaps it had been removed. The card reader just below it had a small green light, still active. Ike pressed the access card flat against the pad and the door clicked.

Easing it open, he spotted lights on inside. Despite the warning bells ringing in his head, he was committed. Cautiously, he pushed the door open and stepped in. The room's walls were covered with large maps. Closest to Ike was a map of Virginia's coast showing the locations of the offshore blocks. Ike recognized the others quickly: isopachs, structure maps, and well log cross sections. While every open space on three of the walls was filled, a bare square on the far wall looked like a missing jigsaw puzzle piece. Something had been there. Ike could see the pins.

He walked deeper into the workspace and spotted a door to an adjoining room. As he peeked in, a face met his in the doorway. Instinctively, he dropped the backpack and raised both fists to deflect a blow.

The young redheaded woman dropped her backpack and raised her hands. "Whoa, dude. Lay off the Red Bull."

Ike quickly de-escalated his response and slipped back into character. "I'm so sorry. I thought I was alone." Ike picked up his backpack.

"Well, you're not." The woman shouldered her backpack and pushed past Ike. She stopped halfway to the door. "Hey. Who are you?"

He raised the access card. "I'm with Cole's Seismic."

She hesitated and squinted at the card. Ike didn't want to have to restrain her, but he shifted his weight forward, just in case.

She quit squinting. "Great. You can turn this all off before you leave." She turned back and started toward the door. "I'm tired of getting my ass chewed out." She slammed the door as she left.

Ike spotted the three workstations in the back corner. He moved quickly to them and pulled the Post-it note from his pocket. Two of the workstations were on with the log-in screens up. Ike took the one nearest the wall and farthest from the door. More reaction time if the woman got suspicious and returned with security. He entered the user ID and password Scott had written down, and then the screen disappeared and a Windows screen appeared. Ike spotted the File Explorer icon and clicked it. In the search bar, he typed the folder name: *Minuteman*. That name was on everything in the room. Standard practice dictated that someone on the team, or the whole exploration team, got to name the prospect. It was a perk of sorts because that name would appear on the documents and maps and would be referred to in public disclosures and permits.

The search results showed the folder name. He'd found it. Ike quickly checked his watch: 4:40 p.m. Enough time had passed that the woman was no longer a potential problem. Shift change was coming and he'd slip out as easily as he'd slipped in. As he clicked the folder, he envisioned Jack playing with his Rubik's Cube and enjoying his freedom.

Suddenly the screen turned red and a warning appeared telling him he was in violation of the code of conduct by this unauthorized access. A bolt of electricity surged into his muscles. The alert would be sent to IT, but also to every security member's smartphone. The response would be rapid.

Ike grabbed the backpack and pulled out a Pirates cap and a pair of thick-framed glasses. He killed the light on the way out the office door and headed away from the elevators and to the emergency exit sign. He heard the bell sound behind him announcing the arrival of the elevator. He ran to the exit door and slipped into the stairwell. Twelve floors, and every floor represented a hazard.

Taking three stairs at a time, he quickly made it to the ninth floor. He opened the stairwell door, checked the empty hallway, and headed to the elevator bank. The car came quickly and Ike hid to the side until it opened. It was empty. By now, someone would be stationed at the turnstiles, and the stairwell at the first floor. But he'd anticipated that possibility. Ike punched the second-floor button and the doors closed. The second floor had access to the annex, the annex had access to the health club, and the health club had access to the street. He quickly stripped, pulled the athletic gear from the bag, and changed.

As he left the elevator and looked down the hallway, he saw a few people filing through a set of glass double doors, using their access cards to exit the annex and enter the back entrance to the health club. He trotted to the doors to catch up with a woman rummaging through her bag. Just as he arrived, she found her card. He politely grabbed the door handle as she swiped her card. He followed her into the back lobby of the club. The kid at the desk tracked Ike as he approached. The scanner on the desk required a membership card, but through the gym behind the kid Ike could see the street.

He patted his sweatpants pockets. "Damn, I forgot my card. Left it in the car. I'll just walk through and get it."

The kid nodded and Ike made his way around the crowded equipment. As he approached the front double doors, he breathed deeply to relax a bit. He'd be outside in seconds. But when he pushed through the front door, the security goon he'd seen in the lobby when he'd met Shannon Falzone appeared and blocked the door to the street.

Ike casually turned and started back through the gym. Four Security guards appeared at the back-lobby desk. Ike turned back and decided he'd take his chances with the goon. He'd have him on his knees with the first punch. Ike dropped the backpack and ran to the doors with his fist clenched and jaw locked. Just beyond the doors, two Pittsburgh Police squad cars pulled up. Ike stopped in his tracks. All the fight left his body. He'd never take on the cops. He had developed too much respect for them. As they rushed through the front doors with their hands on their guns, Ike raised his hands and dropped to his knees. This wasn't what he'd had in mind.

CHAPTER 35

MARIA'S SAFETY WAS not negotiable. At least that's what Mac and Ike had told her when Ike asked her to run Rossi's after he bought it from the previous owners. Every night, Mac or Ike escorted her on the seven-block walk to her home. Tonight, the amber sunset lit the storefronts along Liberty Avenue, and Maria admired the golden hue it gave the old buildings. The early autumn air was fresh, aside from the aromatic smell of garlic and butter pouring out of the kitchen ventilation fan from Rossi's. Mac walked with her, regaling her with another hilarious story of chasing stupid criminals through the neighborhood.

Since it was Thursday, Maria and Mac had left before the dinner rush—another agreement with Ike and Mac. Despite having a solid assistant manager at the restaurant, Maria spent every night there, either tending bar or performing. Both roles were the safest form of human contact she could find. She had several offers a week for a drink or dinner from well-intended patrons, but for the last five years she'd politely refused them all.

After she'd shared her therapist's insight in a moment of weakness, Ike and Mac had stepped in and negotiated a deal. Maria would take one night off a week—a date night—and take some time for herself. It didn't feel like a negotiation—more like an ambush. But Maria knew they were right. She'd never do it on her own. Relationships were difficult for her. Over the years, she'd spot flaws in her dates before they said their first words. There was always something wrong with them. However, through her therapist, she'd learned that intimacy took vulnerability and trust, two things that had become hard for her nine-year-old self after her parents died. She still carried that with her, but she took the therapist's advice and pressed on anyway: fake it to make it, she'd said, and Ike and Mac had personal missions to make it happen.

Mac finished his story and Maria caught her breath after laughing for half a block.

"Got a date tonight?"

The question was predictable and usually came on the fifth block of the walk.

"Yes. He's picking me up at seven."

Mac seemed satisfied—his plan was working.

"Give the poor guy a chance."

"I will." Deciding to head off any further interrogation, she said, "I'm worried about Ike."

"Me, too. He shouldn't do it."

"I think he needs to do it. It's like he doesn't have a choice," Maria said.

"That's not what I'd hoped Doris and I taught you both. No matter what, always tell the truth and always obey the law. I've seen hundreds of people make either mistake. Then they make six more trying to cover up or correct the first."

"I know. We did learn that, Mac. You and Doris were great. I helped Ike because he's my brother. I trust him even if I don't agree with him."

With both hands in his pockets, Mac stopped at the curb a block from her house. Before stepping off, he looked over at Maria. "It's all about getting an answer for the kid, isn't it?"

Maria slipped her arm under his and locked her elbow in his, and they started across the street. "It's that, but there's something else. I see something in his eyes. It's like he's gone backward in time."

"Your mom and dad?"

"I think so. He said something about how getting closure for Jack might somehow get closure for us."

Mac shook his head as they stopped at the concrete steps that led up to the house. "He's not thinking this through. He's not himself."

Maria turned up the steps. Mac followed for two steps until his phone rang. He answered but said nothing else, just listened for thirty seconds or so. "I'm on my way," he said and hung up. He looked upset. "I gotta go. You okay from here?"

"Of course. Everything all right?"

Mac nodded. "Just a friend who needs my help."

She hugged Mac. "I hope it works out."

"Always does." Mac smiled and headed down the sidewalk.

Maria watched him walk away, sensing something wasn't quite right. She debated the possibilities as she walked up the steps and fished her keys from her backpack. The house was a two-story brick home built in 1925. After several renovations, her parents had purchased it in 1975. A year later Ike was born. Ten years and another remodel later, Maria arrived. The thick front door was the last thing added to the home, and the two deadbolts were the only security system her father had ever needed. "This is Bloomfield, where neighbors take care of each other," he'd said. He was right. She always felt safe here. She unlocked each deadbolt and opened the door with a welcoming creak.

The house had wood floors, wooden trim, and radiant heat, and the house always talked to her. Each step brought a familiar but nearly imperceptible squeak. Visitors rarely heard them, but Maria had ever since she could remember. They'd announced her father's arrival each night. He'd be amazed by her appearance before he'd left the entryway. Over the last twenty-two years the house had remained the same, other than upgrades to both bathrooms and the kitchen. Maria had wanted it that way.

She cleared the small entryway and walked down the hallway to the kitchen. While daylight still seeped in through the sheers, it was still shadowy inside. She reached for the light switch and heard the creak behind her.

Before she could turn, her upper body was locked down in what felt like a human clamp. She couldn't move her arms and her scream had been cut off by a thick leather glove across her mouth and face. The smell of the leather mixed with gasoline filled her nose. She fought hard to free herself, but her struggle was pointless. Dragging her backward and slamming her into the hallway wall, the intruder demonstrated his physical control. She decided to stop fighting and preserve her energy. He'd used no weapon and didn't seem interested in sexually assaulting her. As soon as she settled down, he spoke.

"I have a message for you. Are you listening?" He tightened his grip for effect. His deep voice had a painful rasp. He spoke with some kind of cowboy accent. She nodded as best she could and he released her mouth.

"Tell your brother to stop."

Maria immediately knew why Ike had decided to get into Falzone Center. He'd obviously got someone's attention. Maria wanted to keep the intruder talking.

"What if he won't listen to me?"

Her assailant grabbed her jaw and nearly crushed it, tightening the pressure around her chest like a boa constrictor. "Then he dies."

She went limp and let her knees buckle. When he loosened his grip, she spun and snapped a backhand at his nose. He caught it and crushed her fist. The pain buckled her knees for real this time. He pressed her wrist backward until she hit the floor. He lowered both knees onto her chest and grabbed her throat. She struggled to breathe. He was masked.

"If you tell him about this, I'll kill him first and then you." He choked off what little air she had left. Her vision faded; she was on the brink of passing out.

"Get him to stop or I'll be back." He shoved her body into the floor, and the pressure on her chest stopped. His steps faded down the hallway and across the kitchen, then out the kitchen door.

Maria rubbed her neck, trying to regain circulation and a little breath. She pressed herself up and stumbled to the kitchen door. The deadbolt locks were unlocked but not broken, and the door's window wasn't shattered. She shivered thinking how easily the intruder had got in. She relocked them anyway, but still she felt trapped and scared, like she had that dreadful night Mac and Ike had told her about her parents in this same kitchen. But this feeling was worse. She knew what would happen ahead of time—and she wasn't sure she could stop it.

CHAPTER 36

IKE HAD SAT alone in the interrogation room for the last hour. He'd been here before, on the other side of the mirror, and he knew the drill. Hand the perp off to the detectives and let him sweat.

The patrol officers had recognized him upon removing his disguise and apologized for leaving him there on orders from their supervisor. Ike graciously told them not to worry. He had plenty to think through.

As he stared at the two-way mirror and the nicked white walls, the anger inside him burned white-hot. A tsunami of suspicion reinforced his determination. While this was a setback that might cost a few clients, he didn't care. Falzone's system had been scrubbed, and he was convinced they were hiding the seismic. But the seismic wasn't his only lead—he still had time to get to the truth.

The door eased open and Vic Cassidy appeared. The asshole had probably been watching through the mirror trying to sweat Ike. But Cassidy would be the one sweating. His shoddy detective work was decaying like origami in a rainstorm.

"Ah, the great Ike Rossi."

Ike didn't react as Cassidy circled the steel table, laid a new manila file folder between them, and sat in the chair facing Ike. He'd shed his sports coat, revealing an oversize white shirt that struggled to stay tucked into his black slacks. His maroon tie rested on his belly. Ike wanted to slap the grin off Cassidy's face, but the assault charges would take him off the playing field. He needed to stay in the game.

Cassidy opened the file and lifted the single sheet of paper. "Looks like attempted theft of trade secrets. That's a nice felony to add to your bio."

Ike said nothing.

"What were you looking for?"

Cassidy asked the question as if he already knew the answer. Ike just stared at the slug who'd dragged his feet on Ike's parents' case for the last eight years. Ike knew the Falzones wouldn't want press about the seismic. That was the last thing they needed—especially, if for whatever reason, the image was somehow linked to Tom Cole's death. Cassidy was bluffing.

"I wasn't looking for anything," Ike said, his expression unchanged.

Cassidy's grin faded and he leaned across the table. Ike could smell his stale coffee breath. "This is why you never found your parents' killer."

Ike scrambled around the table, grabbed Cassidy by the throat and pinned him to the mirror. "You know something about that, detective?"

Cassidy struggled to free himself, but Ike drove his lower body into him. "You know, Detective, I'll eventually find who killed them. And when I do, your luck will run out. I'll find out who's backing you, and that will be the end."

Two uniformed officers stormed in and pulled Ike away.

"Get him out of here," Cassidy yelled, pulling his rumpled shirt from his neck.

"Hang on." Ike was stunned as Jenna stepped into the room with Mac just behind her. "Unless you're charging him with something other than trespassing, we're done here."

Cassidy gathered himself and snatched the file folder off the floor. "He's all yours. Falzones aren't pressing any charges."

Ike realized Jenna's anger wasn't directed only at Cassidy. She turned and headed down the hall, ignoring Ike. Mac took Ike by the arm and led him out of the room.

Jenna beat Mac and Ike out of the station, her long strides building a rapid lead. Ike trotted up to thank her, but she spun at the curb and her eyes flashed like lightning.

"I can't believe you did this. You put the entire case at risk—and maybe the custody hearing tomorrow."

"I'll fix this."

"No, you won't." She pivoted to walk away but then stopped and turned back. "Do you know the worst thing? That boy and his aunt believed in you. They thought you could ride in and save the day. Hell, even I thought you'd help us. Now we only have one choice."

"No—no. You can't do that to Jack."

Jenna closed to within inches of Ike's face. "I have no choice now. Anything you might possibly uncover will be tainted by your attempted theft. Your action reflects on all of us. Jack, Lauren, me, and my father's firm."

Ike saw Jenna's eyes drop their intensity.

"I'm sorry. There's much more to find. I'll make it good."

Jenna stepped back, took a deep breath, and spoke calmly. "No, you won't. I talked to Lauren on the way here—you're out."

A darkness swept over Ike and sent his mind reeling. He'd never been fired before. The fact that he'd been working for free didn't help cushion the blow. Lauren had lost faith—and he'd let Jack down. As Jenna walked to her car, he wanted to stop her. Tell her it didn't matter if she fired him, he'd still get to the bottom of this. But he gauged the words as hollow, and he knew when to cut bait.

He walked back to where Mac had been waiting at a respectful distance.

"You don't have to say it," Ike said.

"I know I don't. Sometimes we have to put our own footprints in the snow to know we're headed nowhere."

That was Mac's way of saying Ike didn't listen. Ike couldn't remember Mac's ever telling him, *I told you so.* He'd always had some little metaphor or fable to make his point.

"I can't stop. I can't leave this unfinished."

Mac wrapped his arm around Ike and they headed to Mac's car. "I know. I wouldn't expect any less."

CHAPTER 37

JOSEPH STARED AT the lights outside his office window and held his worst fears at bay. Instead, he focused on a retaliatory strike of such scale and impact that it would overwhelm his grandson's keepers. Rossi's attempt this afternoon was both a blessing and a curse. He could use it tomorrow morning in the custody hearing to give cover to the judge's ruling in their favor. Then again, using the incident could unravel the family he'd painstakingly stitched together over the last thirty years. Circumstances had dictated that he let Rossi go, but he'd ensure that one way or the other, Rossi would pay the cost for putting him in this position. A call to the station had released Rossi from custody, but not from Joseph's powerful reach.

He'd dealt with Rossi, but now he'd have to deal with Nick, who waited in his outer suite. Like it or not, he'd accepted Nick as his only son and the only one capable of carrying on the Falzone name. He'd had his shortfalls for sure, and those shortfalls had cost Joseph dearly. While Nick was all Joseph wanted in terms of a great business mind, his temper and lack of people skills were fatal flaws unless corrected.

But Joseph put those problems on his own ledger because of Nick's motherless childhood. He'd done everything he could to save

Nick from his mother. She'd revealed a cunning narcissism once Nick and his sister Brenda were born. The wild accusations, bizarre behavior, and two a.m. expeditions were destroying the family Joseph had always wanted. After Joseph had begged her for months to attend counseling, she'd finally agreed, but she'd never fully participated. His therapist had said she never would.

He'd tried to get both children away from her, but she'd refused to budge with Brenda. She'd been willing to surrender Nick for the right ransom, however, and Joseph had done the only thing he could have to save him. Brenda had adopted her mother's personality flaws, and she suffered irreversible damage. Now, Joseph was committed to saving Nick again, an effort to hold on to the last thread of hope for his son. Nick's recent actions had made Joseph question that commitment; still, he realized he didn't have a choice. Save Nick, and save the family.

Joseph called his assistant. "Send him in."

Nick rushed in red-faced and slammed the door. "He knows. The kid told him. That kid knows."

"Sit down, son."

Nick crossed his arms in protest, but Joseph kept his stare on him and waited. Sometimes the same tactics he'd learned from their dog trainer worked on Nick. One command, then expect compliance. Finally, Nick dropped into the chair.

"Let's assume Rossi knows something," Joseph said. "It's only that the seismic represents a tie between us and Tom Cole. The data is secured, I assume?"

Nick nodded.

"Then he'll never see it."

Nick's face hardened. "But he's dangerous. We have to assume he knows."

"Agreed. I assume you can handle that?"

"Already working on it."

Joseph had kept deniability. Nick had handled a similar matter a few years back, but the risk had escalated with his recent poor decisions. "Be careful—no blowback."

"There won't be." Nick stood. "We need to get that kid."

"The hearing is tomorrow. I'll have Mayer mention the other side's transgressions by Rossi. That should get us visitation, at least."

"That's not enough."

"It will have to be. And don't forget, that's my grandson and the only other male left in this family."

Nick's expression showed little recognition and an alarm sounded somewhere in Joseph's head. "You'll keep your hands off him. Understand?"

Nick stuck out his lower lip and nodded.

The desk phone beeped and Joseph picked it up.

"She's here."

"Send her in."

Nick started to leave.

"Stay put. We must convince Shannon that the break-in was nothing. She said it's already on Twitter."

Nick did an about-face and rolled his eyes skyward. Shannon knocked, then entered. She stopped short of Nick and silently waited for Joseph to speak. Nick and Shannon's relationship had been a disappointment, to say the least. Joseph had wanted a unified family, supportive and protective of each other. But years of reading every book on blended families and hours of family therapy had yielded nothing. The pair couldn't stand each other. Still, Joseph forced them to work together, hoping they'd eventually tire of the battles. It wasn't working.

"How's the media?" he asked her.

"Just a few bursts on Twitter about a crazy man at Falzone Center. But security said it was Rossi. Is that true?"

"Oh, Christ," Nick said. "We need to shut them up."

Shannon looked at Nick, then Joseph. "So it was him?"

"Yes," Joseph said. "But we need to keep that quiet."

"Why? What was he after?"

"None of your business," Nick said.

Shannon ignored him and gave Joseph a questioning look.

Joseph was ready. "We don't know. He accessed the computer system and it stopped him."

"Where was he?"

"Twelfth floor."

"That's the Minuteman team," she said. She surveyed Nick and waited. He silently stared back. "Why would he be there, of all places?"

"Like Dad said, we don't know."

Joseph could see Shannon's mind grinding. She couldn't know about the seismic. "Look, Shannon. For the company, it's best this doesn't get out. No mention of Rossi. He'll be a lightning rod and we don't need that attention before the hearing."

"Wouldn't revealing that help us?"

"No. I don't want the publicity. We're on firm ground on the custody hearing tomorrow and I don't want any more publicity around Minuteman until we get a well drilled."

Shannon carefully weighed Joseph's words. "I can call it a random trespass."

"Perfect," Joseph said. "Let me know if y—"

The desk phone pinged again and Joseph spotted the time on the display. He remembered his dinner with Erin, and a sickening dread spread over him as he answered.

"Mrs. Falzone is here."

Joseph never made her wait. He respected her too much. Despite his certainty of a pending storm, he said, "Send her right in." A warning to Nick was in order. "Your mother's here and we're headed to the veterans' dinner. Be nice to her. She's been through a lot and this will be her first time out since Patrick's accident."

Erin opened the door and hesitated when she spotted Nick. Like a sheepdog herding a lamb away from a wolf, Shannon intercepted her with a hug and gently moved her to her side of the office. Joseph rose and gave Erin a hug, too. Nick watched them and waited for a glance from Erin.

"Erin," was all he said.

"Nick," she replied.

If looks were daggers, Joseph's walls would have looked like a knife thrower's backboard.

Erin looked back at Shannon and Joseph. "I heard there was a break-in?"

The question rattled Joseph. If Erin found out about the seismic, she'd be one step away from the truth, and her response would be nuclear. Erin's intelligence was the trait that had sealed Joseph's decision to marry again. Just a crack in the veil hiding their secret and she'd walk right through. "It was nothing, dear, just a trespasser."

"How did he get in?"

As Joseph took a millisecond to weigh his reply, Shannon jumped right in. "He used a stolen access card. We think someone lost it somewhere outside the building."

It appeared Shannon was protecting her mother, but for another reason. They were close and Shannon had been protective of Erin since Patrick's death. But it also felt as if Shannon had rescued Joseph, and a seed of suspicion was planted in Joseph's mind. Shannon had been pressing lately—pressing Joseph and Nick about the operations. Her challenges to Nick had become more frequent. Joseph had written it off as more sibling competition now that Patrick was gone, but he wasn't so sure.

Erin smiled at Shannon, "That's a bit of bad luck. Did the thief just happen to look like that person?"

"Yes," Nick said.

Shannon cut her eyes to Joseph, as if asking for confirmation.

Joseph knew Erin had a great bullshit detector. "He actually wore a fake beard to look like the contractor."

Erin's brow furrowed. "That's a lot of effort for a trespasser."

"You ready, dear?" Joseph said, cutting off the questioning.

"I need to speak with you about the hearing tomorrow before we go," she said.

Shannon kissed her mother's cheek. "I'll leave you two to it." She kissed her father's cheek

Before she could clear the door, Nick said, "I'd like to hear any new information. We need to be sure we prevail."

Erin locked her eyes on Nick. "That's none of your business."

Nick's cheeks turned crimson, but Joseph warned him with a look.

"Erin, that's your opinion. But he's my nephew."

"He's never been your nephew. Three weeks ago, you called him your sister's crack baby." She turned to Nick again. "This is between my husband and me. We are the grandparents and we are the plaintiffs in the case."

"Nick, let's go." Shannon moved to the door.

Nick ignored her. "I don't care—"

"That's enough," Joseph said. "Leave us, Nick."

"So that's it. You're going to take her side?"

"Go."

Nick stood there, but Joseph nodded toward the door. Nick was playing with fire and couldn't see it. Finally, he bumped past Shannon and left. Shannon waved, smiled, and followed him out.

Erin directed her ire at Joseph. "You need to do something. You always let him treat me like that. He's not right. He's mean and he doesn't like me. He never did. But you just keep giving him more of the company."

"He's under a lot of stress."

"Those are just excuses. He didn't have a mother. He had a difficult childhood. You could have done better when he was younger.
It's all just manipulation on his part. He's using your guilt." Erin's
eyes welled with tears. "Do you know how that makes me feel, to
have your son talk to me that way?"

Joseph evaluated his options. Nothing short of kicking Nick out,
just as he'd done to Brenda, would appease Erin. He just needed to
let her unload.

"I'll talk to him."

Erin pulled a Kleenex from her purse and dabbed her eyes.
"That won't do any good." She dropped the Kleenex into the wastebasket next to the desk and let out a deep sigh. "Let's just go home."

Joseph allowed his heart to feel Erin's pain for only a moment,
and another stitch ripped away from the family ties. And while he
knew he should have directed his anger at Nick, he couldn't do it.
Instead, he buttoned up his heart and took aim at Ike Rossi.

CHAPTER 38

AS IKE APPROACHED the back door of the bar at Rossi's, his senses surveyed his surroundings like sonar probing the depths of the dark sea. Maria had texted last night to check on him after getting the news of his detainment. But her principal concern was her request that he meet her at eight a.m. at Rossi's. The text had ignited his protective instincts. He knew his sister, and her failure to provide a reason alerted his suspicion. Normally he'd be probing like a TSA Labrador, but this was Maria and his unease tempered his aggression.

The first cold front of the year had raced through Pittsburgh, chasing the last remnants of summer into hibernation. A few stray newspaper pages fluttered past and were pinned against the dumpster. Despite his frigid nose, he could smell coffee brewing as he entered through the alley door. The bar was always immaculate in the morning, no stale beer or garlic in the air.

His eyes swept the bar. The Naugahyde booths and thick brown tables formed a fairway to the stage. The Takamine six-string was still in its place where Ike had left it Sunday night. The lights were dimmed, other than those above the bar. He could hear the copper clock on the wall ticking down the seconds until eight thirty, when he'd head to the courthouse to slip into Jack's hearing.

As he approached the bar, he heard Maria's footsteps cascading down the stairs. She popped into the hallway, and before he could see her face through the darkness, she rushed over and hugged him.

"Hey, sis, what's going on?" he said.

She released him and moved briskly behind the bar, then stopped, facing him. She placed two mugs on the bar and filled them with coffee. "What? Can't a sister miss her brother? I was worried about you after I heard they had you at the station."

Ike grabbed the mug but kept his attention on Maria as he took a seat. "It wasn't as bad as it sounded."

"Because they didn't press charges?"

"They didn't. I'm shocked, but I suspect the Falzones didn't want the publicity and they didn't want the cops sniffing around for what I was looking for."

Maria let go of her mug and put both hands on the bar. "You're smiling. That was stupid, Ike. If that gets out, your career is over."

"It won't get out. They won't let it."

"You could've gotten hurt."

"By who? The twelve dollar-an-hour rent-a-cops? Come on, what are you not telling me?"

Maria looked away for a few seconds, then turned back, eyes welling. "I'm worried about you. The Falzones are powerful in this town. I'm worried something could happen to you and I couldn't live with that. Can't you just stop?"

The question was like a flaming arrow that ignited a firestorm of guilt and anger. On one hand, he'd do anything for her, and to see her this way made him feel a little selfish. But he was doing this for *them.* Not helping Jack wasn't an option. The force that held Ike was too strong. He didn't fully understand it, but something told him he didn't need to.

He reached across the bar and gently wrapped his hand around hers. "I'll be careful. That boy has no one else. If I don't turn something up they're going to plead mental incapacity. And chances are it won't work. He could get life without parole. I can't let that happen." Ike slipped into parental mode. "And weren't you the one pushing me to do this? What changed?"

Maria pulled back and rolled her eyes a bit. "I just got worried about you."

Ike remembered the nine-year-old who had knocked over his WPIAL MVP trophy, breaking the figure from the top. On the rare occasions when she lied, she didn't do it well. "Tell me what happened, Maria."

Maria started crying and yelled, "I just don't want anything to happen to you, you dumb jock." She threw her mug into the sink and it shattered. Then she ran for the stairs. "Don't follow me. Just leave me alone. I'll be fine."

A few seconds later he heard the upstairs door slam. She was hiding something. She'd responded like a trapped animal. Ike had seen it in other reluctant witnesses. Usually in those cases, the truth might harm someone close to the witness. In this case, the someone close must be him.

CHAPTER 39

IKE HAD TO time this perfectly. While the conversation with Maria was troubling, being discovered here, by Lauren or Jenna, would be painful. He'd driven downtown and parked in the garage just up Fifth Avenue. The cold wind cut at his cheeks and he pulled his black Penguins hat low over his eyes. It would provide some concealment until he reached Judge Kelly's courtroom. Many judges didn't allow hats to be worn in their courtroom, but he'd arrived late and the hearing would be well underway. The room would be packed, with all attention on Lauren and the Falzones, and Ike planned to slip in undetected.

As he turned the corner at Fifth and Ross, he couldn't help but look up. The Family Law Court was housed in the old prison and connected to the county courthouse by the Bridge of Sighs, which spanned Ross Street. Designed after the famous Bridge of Sighs in Venice, the structure, built in 1888 and made of rough-cut granite, looked weathered and stained. The brownish hue of the stone, with only one small window centered on the span, made it look as heavy and draconian as its history. In the old days, prisoners would be dragged from their cells and across the bridge to hear their fate, then dragged back to the prison.

But Ike would learn one piece of Jack's fate in the old prison this morning: he'd stay either with Lauren or with his grandparents, or something in between. Based on the experience of some of his friends at Rossi's, the family court's rulings never completely satisfied either party. So Ike expected the worst. Despite some rough patches, he was thankful his parents had never split.

Looming in the back of his mind was Monday, when the venue would move across the Bridge of Sighs to the county courthouse. He imagined Jack being convicted and dragged across the span to the holding cell still located there, and he had to look away.

Ike entered the building, cleared security and made his way to Judge Kelly's fifth-floor courtroom. As he'd imagined, the room was packed. Looking through the window of the thick wooden court-room door, Ike spotted Lauren on the stand. She appeared to be holding her own as Jenna read questions from a yellow tablet she held in her hand. Jenna's father watched calmly from the table. Ike cracked the door open and slipped inside. Each row of the gallery was full all the way to the wooden railing that separated the specta-tors from the court. Ike quickly eyed the wall on either side of the door and wedged into a space between two reporters, feverishly typ-ing notes onto their small tablets. The gallery was quiet and Ike could hear Lauren and Jenna clearly.

Ike had read Judge Kelly's courtroom rules published next to his name on the Allegheny County Family Court website. He ran a tight ship and expected punctuality and decorum from all parties, and si-lence and proper attire from the gallery. Still, a sadness hung in the air as if everyone in the room mourned Jack's loss of a supportive and loving family.

Jenna described the glowing report of the court-appointed psy-chologist and ran Lauren through a series of questions outlining her daily routine with Jack and her son. When she finished, Ike thought there was no one in the courtroom who wouldn't vote Lauren mother of the year. Jenna returned to her seat and Lauren stiffened in the witness chair and braced for the assault she seemed to already dread.

At the table on the right, Ike spotted the white hair of Brooks Latham, who sat next to Joseph and Erin Falzone on one side and a slickly dressed fortyish attorney who Ike assumed was Mayer on the other. After conversing with Latham briefly, Mayer rose and began his questioning.

"Mrs. Bottaro, you have quite a detailed account of your day with your son and Jack. Do you agree that their safety is one of the most important roles of a parent?"

"Of course."

"A 'yes' or 'no' answer will be sufficient."

"Yes."

"And would you say you are personally responsible for Jack Cole's safety?"

Lauren and everyone in the courtroom could see where this was going. Her eyes narrowed on Mayer. "Yes."

"So if safety is one of the primary roles of a parent, can you explain how you allowed a ten-year-old boy in your care and under your daily supervision to get his dead father's rifle and kill a man?"

"Jack had hidden the rifle the day his father died. Tom had several guns he used for hunting. I don't know how Jack got access to them. They were always locked in a gun safe."

"You're saying Jack had a rifle and you didn't know it?"

"Objection, your honor. Asked and answered," Jenna said as she stood.

"Overruled. Mrs. Bottaro, answer the question."

Ike could see that Lauren was cutting her eyes to Jenna, begging her for help. But it wasn't coming.

"Jack's a good boy," Lauren said.

"Yes or no, Mrs. Bottaro." Judge Kelly's attention cut to Latham and back in a millisecond. The judge's look went undetected by the gallery as far as Ike could tell, but from where he stood, it sought Latham's approval.

Lauren paused and looked directly at Ike. She'd spotted him. She seemed to gain strength, holding her gaze on Ike. But Ike could see that the answer she had to give would break her. He wanted to rush to the stand and protect her from Mayer's humiliating questions. Finally, Lauren's voice broke as she looked at Mayer and answered, "Yes." Then she began to cry.

Mayer stepped to the side of the table, closer to Lauren but not crossing into the no-man's-land that would trigger the ire of the judge. "I'm wondering, Mrs. Bottaro, if you think that such a parent should be trying to keep one of the pillars of this community from his grandson?"

Jenna rocketed up. "Objection, you—"

"Withdrawn. No further questions, your honor." Mayer took his seat and Latham patted him on the back.

The judge excused Lauren and she made her way back to the table with Jenna. She leaned in and whispered to Jenna. Jenna's head snapped around and she eyed Ike.

"Ms. Price, anything else?"

Jenna turned back to the judge. "No, your honor."

"Okay," Judge Kelly said. "Normally, I'd adjourn and we'd reconvene, but nothing about this proceeding is normal." He picked up a small stack of papers. "I've heard both sides, read the psychologist's report and considered all the information provided in the previous hearing. It is, in my judgment, in the best interest of the boy that the grandparents be granted unsupervised visitation. That visitation will be every other weekend. However, considering the upcoming trial, the child will be with the grandparents this weekend, Saturday at nine a.m. until Sunday at noon, unless otherwise agreed by the parties."

Ike dropped his head. Jack would be in the Falzones' hands. He'd be in danger.

The judge adjourned the proceeding and disappeared into his chambers. Ike got caught up in the rush to get out the door. As he was shoved toward the door, he pushed back against the crowd and looked over their heads to Lauren's table. She stood there, tears running down her face, staring at Ike. Jenna shamed him with one wag of her head and she gathered Lauren in her arms. Ike surrendered to the pressure of the crowd and moved out the door.

But the pressure he felt the most came from inside. Jack would spend time with the very people who had killed his father, and Ike was on the outside looking in. He reminded himself that if he solved the clues and found the evidence that would exonerate Jack, they'd still use it. For a moment, a flicker of hope sparked in his heart. Then the shared look between Judge Kelly and Latham reemerged in Ike's mind, and he remembered this was Friday.

And Friday was poker night.

CHAPTER 40

IKE FELT THE minutes slipping through his hands like water. He'd spent what was left of the morning at the courthouse reviewing family court records, then sending the data to Mac, who was holed up back at Ike's office. Ike had driven to Rossi's and entered through the alleyway again. It was nearing noon and the Friday lunch crowd had been trimmed by the nasty cold front ripping through the city.

He'd spotted Maria behind the bar and she'd conveyed a look that said nothing had changed between them. While he wanted to convince her he'd be fine, he couldn't take the time. Jack was in danger, and Ike had put him there. Like an anchor dragging behind a speedboat, that burden attached itself to every thought Ike had. But this was no time to get bogged down. Ike knew finding concrete evidence that proved Jack's story was the only thing that could save him, and as he entered his office, he was happy to see Mac hard at work.

Mac sat in one of the wooden side chairs with his eyes glued to the only windowless wall. He'd taken a page from the flip chart and tacked it to the corkboard that Ike had hung when he moved in. On the page, he'd written all the expressions Ike had received from Tom Cole's mystery account with their operators missing, just as Ike had asked on the phone.

3 53 8 2 19

4 3 53 8 74

9 13 30 7 8 7 99

53 25 7 47 10 7

Mac looked up at Ike. "Tough morning?"

Ike shrugged off his jacket and tossed it onto the other side chair. "He's going to be sent to the Falzones. There's nothing good about that." Ike pointed to the sheet of paper on the wall. "I'm now convinced this means something. I think it's the key to the whole thing."

Mac looked at Ike like his father had when Ike was caught drag racing across the Fortieth Street bridge. "You know anything about a car chase through Southpointe yesterday?"

Ike remained silent for a moment. He never lied to Mac and wasn't about to start now. "I had a little problem."

"Well, that little problem could have killed you, from what I heard."

"I'm fine."

"I know you're fine. But I spent half an hour this morning calming your sister down."

"You told her about that?"

"No. That's the problem. I didn't say a word. But she's convinced this case will be the end of you."

"Look. I talked to her early this morning. She wanted me to quit. Just fold it up and go home. She was the one who pushed for me to get involved. Now that I am, she wants me to quit."

"You were fired."

"I don't care about that. I was doing this for Jack."

Mac walked over to Ike and put his hand on Ike's shoulder. "Be careful. She can't go through losing you, too."

Ike returned the gesture, his hand on Mac's shoulder. "I will. You know this means I'm on the right track."

"I do. Just be careful."

Both men paused, silently connecting like father and son, and then Mac broke away. He returned his attention to the flip chart and dropped into the side chair.

"I've been looking at it since I put them up there," he said. "Why remove the pluses, minuses, and multiplication symbols?"

Ike circled around next to Mac and leaned on the chair back. "The expressions were taking us nowhere. Even your cryptologist said so. I thought that if we only focused on the numbers we might get another perspective."

Mac wagged his head. "All I get is that two of the four expressions have five numbers. One had six and the other had seven."

Ike thought about that. If the two oddballs were thrown out, it would look like a matrix. But tossing some the clues didn't make sense. If Tom Cole was anything, he was logical. "The recurring numbers tell me each of these numbers means something. The recurrence could be repeated symbols from a key. That key has to convey a message."

"He could have made up his own key. A special decoder," Mac said.

"If that's the case, there are more e-mails coming. But they're not coming fast enough. And why wait until the end to provide a key? If he suspected his life was in danger, he should have suspected that Jack's life was at risk, too. I think he'd get to the point quickly."

"Then we're back to a known key."

Ike stood and took a deep cleansing breath. He absorbed the numbers with no preconceived idea of what they were. He'd done this with evidence in other cases that appeared to be dead ends. The inductive thinking that followed was usually quite productive.

His mind drifted to a trivia question he'd once heard on the number of languages in the world. The answer was more than 6,900, but Tom would most likely favor the major European languages first. That meant Spanish, French, German and Italian, and Ike threw in Greek and Latin for good measure.

"Hey. Earth to Ike. What are you thinking?" Mac's words shook Ike from his trance.

"Sorry. I'm thinking about other languages."

"I'd think the cryptologist would have run that to ground."

"Maybe not," Ike said, pulling his iPhone from his pocket. He searched for the letter count for each of the languages.

Greek had twenty-four characters, Latin had twenty-three, and the others ranged from twenty-three to twenty-seven. He then shifted his thinking to the other major languages in the Eastern Hemisphere. Chinese had three thousand, India's Devanagari had forty-seven, Russian had thirty-three, and Japanese Kanji symbols could go as high as fifty thousand. But none of the languages matched the range of the numbers in the expressions, two to ninety-nine. If the clues were simply meant to distract him, they were doing their job.

Ike quickly decided to prioritize his time. "Can you send this over to a linguistics expert?"

"Sure. We used one before I left the force. She's at Pitt, too."

"Great. This could be a waste of time, and there are two areas I've got to run to the ground. The first is Tanner and his past. If Jack's right, there'll be a trail of some sort. Did you get the files I sent you?"

"Sure did. Printed them all out, just as you asked." Mac stood and walked to the printer stuffed in the office closet. He pulled out a thick stack of papers.

"I had the clerk help me pull all the family court documents for the past year. But the last pages I sent you were all the cases Tanner had before the court."

"Saw that. Looks like he really liked Judge Kelly." Mac pulled the first sheets from the stack and spread them across Ike's desk. "And it looks like he usually faced off with the same six opposing attorneys."

"Exactly," Ike said. "I think that's the poker-night club."

Mac snapped his attention to Ike. "Poker club?"

"Yeah. I found out that there's a group of lawyers and judges that get together every Friday night for poker."

"Poker?"

"That's what they call it. But apparently they script their cases to create as much conflict as possible between clients to increase their billings."

Mac dropped the stack of papers. "You're kidding me."

"Afraid not."

"The judges are in on it?"

"Some of them."

"Let's just shut that down now. I still know the editors at the *Post-Gazette*."

"No go. My source said it may go farther than the Family Law Court. And before we blow this up, I need to get the evidence that will free Jack."

Mac picked the papers up again and raised them in his hand. "You think this bunch had something to do with his dad's death?"

"It makes sense. Build up the case so the pressure appears to be nearly unbearable for Tom Cole."

"Was Cole's attorney on this list?"

"Sure was."

"And Kelly?"

"I bet he was there, too."

Mac paused and Ike could see him grinding on the information. "You'll need more than just this conspiracy. With Cassidy's holes in the suicide report, you might have enough for reasonable doubt."

"Not enough," Ike said. He wasn't about to risk leaving it up to a jury to find Jack not guilty. "I need to show self-defense."

"You'll need to show the premeditated plan to kill Tom Cole and his son."

"That's right. I'll need the Falzones and their motive, their connection to this group, and Tanner's complicity."

"You're not going back for that seismic again?"

Ike felt a grin come across his face. The same one he'd show the defense when he knew he'd called the perfect play. "Not yet. But you and I are going to poker night."

CHAPTER 41

IKE KNEW HE'D only have one chance to do this. He kept his eyes on Brooks Latham's Caddy, maintaining a cushion of at least three cars between them. The veil of dusk was dropping and helped conceal Mac's old Buick. The wind had died down at sunset and the leaves on the trees lining Washington Boulevard were still. Behind the trees were Highland Park and eventually the Pittsburgh Zoo. Memories of warm summer days with his mother and father flooded his mind, back when they'd introduced him to the much larger world beyond his backyard.

Traffic slowed as he neared the intersection at Allegheny River Boulevard, and Ike forced the thoughts from his mind. This was no time for a trip down memory lane.

Mac sat in the passenger's seat and watched for any sign of another tail. He'd spotted one earlier, following them when they'd left Rossi's in Ike's Shelby. Ike had pulled to the curb across from the hospital on Liberty Avenue, and the tail, just four cars back, did the same. It was an amateur move, but nonetheless one that had warranted action. After a series of quick turns and then a sprint at ninety down Bigelow Boulevard, they'd lost the tail. From there, they'd parked the Shelby in Mac's garage and taken his ten-year-old Buick to stake out Latham's house. Now, Ike was sure Latham was leading them to poker night.

"He's going straight," Mac said as the light turned green.

Ike looked ahead. All the traffic was going left. There was no sign of a road straight ahead. Just a large opening in the trees and an area of broken pavement and gravel. Beyond the opening, Ike spotted what looked like dilapidated storage stalls half filled with gravel. "He's headed to the river?"

Mac pointed. "To the right along the river is the old water-and-sewer maintenance shop, then a small low-cost marina. To the left is the lock road to Lock 2 on the river. Halfway down, there's an old park that has some old stairs leading to a concrete dock, riverside. Before you get there, there's a bed-and-breakfast and an old house."

Mac's knowledge of the area he'd worked for forty years always impressed Ike.

He moved with the traffic, but the three cars insulating him from Latham followed the rest of the traffic to the left and he found himself entering the opening behind Latham.

"Go right, go right," Mac said. Ike turned right and Latham went left. Ahead, Ike spotted an old railroad trestle, stained black by the decades of coal soot that had soaked the area for the first seventy years of the previous century. Beneath it, he spotted a front loader just beyond the gravel bins and a two-story yellow corrugated-steel building he assumed was the water-and-sewer maintenance building. He slowed without hitting his brakes and eyed Latham's Caddy in the rearview mirror. It was going the other way, down what looked like a single-lane road. Then he saw Latham's brake lights illuminate.

"He's turning," Ike said.

"I got him," Mac said, stretching forward to get a view in the side mirror. "He's waiting. Now he's in."

Ike killed the lights and swung the Buick around, then stopped next to the gravel bins. The bins gave a little cover, but he and Mac could still see the point where Latham had left the road.

"He's in the house. It's an older place, large, with lots of river-front property. I think it was owned by some old Howard Hughes type. Made lots of money but no one ever saw him."

"Let's wait here and see if anyone else arrives," Ike said. He didn't expect to see anyone else. He'd seen guys like Latham before. They liked to make a grand entrance once all their minions were present.

They waited for fifteen minutes and watched the dark night sky chase away the last remnants of light. Ike suggested one pass by the house with lights on, as if they were a couple of mechanics headed to the lock. Mac agreed. One pass in. One pass out. Same speed. No delay.

The passes revealed a long faded eight-foot privacy fence, with a sliding security gate about a third of the way down. The entire complex stretched from the bed-and-breakfast to the decaying concrete steps that led from the abandoned park to the river. From the car, Ike had seen the rusted-out railing on the old dock below the stairway. The darkness was thick now and Ike slipped the car behind the last gravel bin, avoiding the few overhead lights closer to the water-and-sewer building.

"I'm going in," Ike said as he unbuckled and reached into the backseat for a duffel bag he pulled to his lap. He pulled out the flat black directional microphone and parabolic dish.

"You gotta get within a hundred yards unobstructed with that thing to pick up their conversations, and that fence goes all the way around," Mac said.

Ike jammed the battery pack and transmitter into their cases and slipped it over his shoulder. He handed the receiver to Mac. "Don't worry. I got it figured out. Just capture the recording." He yanked on the black Under Armour pullover he'd retrieved from the Shelby.

Mac assembled the small receiver and placed it on the dash. "Be careful. Don't know what they have in terms of security there."

Ike could see the message in Mac's eyes. He didn't agree with any of this. The crimes Ike would be committing soon were the very thing Mac had battled in his career to keep Pittsburgh livable. And while it wasn't assault or murder, he knew Mac understood that Ike's actions might lead to those outcomes. On the other hand, Mac was here and the depth of his involvement demonstrated that he knew Ike needed this—more than anything.

Ike reached across and patted Mac's shoulder. "Thanks, Mac. And sorry for pulling you into this."

Mac's eyes glistened for a moment, and then he faced forward. "Just get the bastards on this thing and get out."

Ike reached to the dash and turned off the dome light switch, opened the door, and slipped the strap of the black equipment bag over his head to the opposite shoulder. The colder air tightened his lungs and the smell of grease drifted from the front loader behind the car. He made his way alongside the rusted chain-link fence that lined the old road to the end of the city's property and crouched behind a lone evergreen that marked the beginning of the bed-and-breakfast.

Beyond that, the lock road began and the privacy fence for the bed-and-breakfast stretched about thirty yards on one side. Thick woods lined the other. The twenty yards between him and the lock road was a no-man's-land. The headlights of the cars coming down Washington Boulevard acted like searchlights that fired through the opening to the area and swept away when the cars made the left turn onto Allegheny Boulevard. The lights would easily nail him trying to enter the dark road. The intervals between the cars were unpredictable, other than when the lights turned red and the beams pointed straight at his path, so he waited for a green light and allowed traffic to clear. Then, with his eyes vacillating between Washington Avenue and the lock road, he darted across.

Scanning the fence, he noted that the bed-and-breakfast had no security cameras. He crossed the road and crept down the edge of the woods, then settled in a crouch just short of the recluse's estate. The faded stained fence was smooth and at least eight feet tall. There were no security cameras along the outside of the fence, but the entrance was recessed from the road and he suspected a camera and a call box were used to allow entry. With his plan formulated, he pressed ten yards deeper into the woods. Then he paralleled the road, pushing through the underbrush as it crackled under his feet and snagged at his pullover.

When he reached the beginning of the small abandoned river park, he dropped to one knee and surveyed the end of the estate across the street. The fence ended and reached through the thin line of brush to the river. To the left of the fence, he could see the bent and rusted rails to the stairs that led down to the old concrete dock Mac had mentioned. There were no signs of cameras or security, but he could see the light coming from the entrance to Lock 2 about three hundred yards down the narrow road. He hoped no emergency would arise that would require the arrival of Corp of Engineers personnel down the lock road.

With the speed he'd once reserved for eluding defensive ends, he raced to the stairs and bolted down them with the crumbled concrete crunching under his feet. Reaching the bottom, he tried to stop but slipped on decaying concrete and stopped just short of the edge. He peered over and saw the black water swirling against the dock, five feet down. He knew the Allegheny was about fifteen feet deep here, but the depth wasn't what bothered him; it was what lurked on the bottom. Over the years he'd heard about all the junk in the river. Cars, refrigerators, and old boats. One diver had even pulled up old wagon wheels from the 1800s. And with the dam only three hundred yards away, he didn't want to fall in.

Ike dropped to one knee and scanned the dock to the north. It appeared to narrow and terminate at the estate's fence that ran from the road to the river. Ike crept to the eight-foot fence and leaned over the river to look around it. Another chain-link fence was tied to it and blocked him from swinging around the privacy fence. It was attached at the top, then tapered down to four feet high about ten yards up the river. It was firmly mounted into a six-inch-thick retaining wall that dropped into the water.

He followed the fence line until it intersected an old dock in the river. Two large boats were moored there. To his right, through a line of maples, he could see lights from the house. But the yard was dark and anyone could be watching. Still, he had to get closer.

Ike checked the bag slung across his body and then flexed his hands. The cold night air had stiffened them and he warmed them with his breath. There was only one way in. He dropped onto all fours and backed toward the river. Ignoring the water rushing below, he dropped over the retaining wall, hanging by his fingers. His weight strained his fingers and he knew he'd have to move fast.

He moved sideways, checking his grip with each move, as he squinted to keep the pieces of crumbling concrete from dropping into his eyes. He moved closer and closer to the dock, pulling himself up every few feet to scan the yard for any threats. Halfway to the dock, his left hand reached for the wall and it crumbled. He fell against the wall. The bag was pinned against his body and the strap snapped. Suddenly, he was dangling by one hand above the dark water. If he fell, the current would sweep him to the dam. And if he went over, he'd be rolled in the undertow until he drowned. If he tried to pull himself up, the listening equipment would disappear into the river. He tried desperately to catch the bag with his knee, but his right hand was losing its grip. In one motion, he swung his left hand

and reached for the wall as the equipment splashed into the dark water below.

He looked down and shook his head. Mac wouldn't get any recordings tonight. Still, he eyed the dock and began to slide hand over hand. Reaching the dock, he grabbed the splintered wood and rolled onto the planks. Lying flat on his stomach, he scanned the boats first. Both were cabin cruisers that could easily hold ten to fifteen people. Ahead, he examined the walkway all the way to the house. A large bank of windows ran along most of the back of the old home. Ike could see motion inside, but he was still too far away. There was no motion in the lighted areas, but the shadows were still a problem.

Pressing himself up, he scampered to the first tree along the path. From there, he advanced, tree by tree, until he was ten yards from the house. The door to the house was closed and Ike moved to the other side of the tree and looked in the windows.

The large room was covered in knotted pine and spread across most of the back side of the house. Five poker tables were neatly spaced throughout the room. Ike's heart deflated when the chance that this was only a poker game crossed his mind. Four men sat at each poker table, but their attention wasn't on the cards in front of them; they all looked to the right end of the room. Ike crept to the next tree and scanned the last few windows.

Then he saw them. Brooks Latham stood next to Judge Kelly at the front of the room. Both looked to their left at three other men. Ike slipped over one more tree and peered into the last window. He easily recognized the three men: the DA, the assistant chief of investigations, and Nick Falzone. Ike dropped to his knee, trapped a yell inside his mouth, and pounded his thigh to stop it. He could go in right now and get enough satisfaction with his fists before they killed him. But then he thought about Maria and then he thought about Jack. He stopped punching his leg and held his head in his hand. He didn't trust anyone now. Not the police, not the DA, and not even the FBI.

Ike stood, pulled his iPhone from his pocket, and snapped a few pictures. They'd be useless against the men with their alibi of a poker game. But he'd have them just in case.

Suddenly, he heard applause inside. Everyone stood and began to make their way out of the room. The back door opened and Ike lunged for the shrubs against the house. Most of the crowd moved out the door and to the boats. In five minutes, the boats were loaded and gone. Ike heard cars starting on the far side of the house as the remainder of the conspirators headed out the front gate.

Ike waited thirty minutes and then made his way back through the park and down the lock road to Mac. When he got to the car, Ike opened the door and got in.

"Lost the equipment?"

Ike just nodded and pulled out his iPhone, opened it to the photos, and handed it to Mac.

"Holy shit," Mac said.

Ike started the Buick. "They're going down."

CHAPTER 42

JENNA ENTERED THE garage of her three-story townhome a mile north of the office just after nine p.m. She'd had a worse day than this—exactly one. That was the day her mother told her that her soon-to-be baby brother had Down syndrome. She was eight years old and didn't understand the term. What she had understood was the love in her mother's face.

She'd just spent the afternoon sitting with Lauren in the corner of the Capital Grill, comforting her client-turned-friend about turning Jack over to the very people she thought were trying to destroy him. Lunch, a bottle of Silver Oak cabernet, and three packs of Kleenex had resulted in a plan: Jenna agreed to go home with Lauren to explain to Jack that he'd be in his grandparents' house at nine the next morning.

The look on Jack's face had broken her heart and fueled the pile driver hammering guilt permanently into her soul. She'd comforted Lauren by reminding her that Joseph and Erin Falzone were very public figures, and at the end of the day, they were Jack's grandparents. They wouldn't do anything to hurt him while he was with them. They couldn't afford the negative publicity. She knew it sounded cold, but cold was necessary to quell the emotional firestorm Lauren was experiencing.

As the garage door rolled shut on another day in Jack's case, Jenna realized just how tired she was. She also realized she had only two days left before his trial. She dragged herself up the two steps into her condo. The hallway was dark and she spotted the digital clock's numbers glowing from the microwave. Another Friday night alone. The place seemed emptier on the weekend nights. Cranberry's nightlife was nonexistent, and she'd quickly grown tired of lonely dates arranged by her friends and family and the occasional foray into the online-dating world. But she'd never leave Cranberry and the company of her brother. At least once a week he'd fill the place with his joy and great sense of humor, usually targeted at her.

She moved into the kitchen, where she dropped her purse on the small island. Checking her phone for messages, she headed upstairs to change. As she reached the top of the stairs on the second floor, a ripple of hesitation moved through her. She stopped and scanned the small den and office space. Something *felt* out of place despite everything's appearing to be in order.

Convincing herself it was just fatigue, she made the turn, flipped on the hallway light, and headed up the last set of stairs to the bedroom.

Entering her bedroom, she could see the light from the streetlamps filtering through the sheers covering her bedroom window. She turned on the lamp next to her bed, pulled her jacket off, and tossed it onto her reading chair tucked in the corner. Rather than give Mr. Epperson, the peeping Tom across the street, a show, she pulled the heavy drapes shut. She stripped to her underwear, decorating the chair with the rest of her clothes, then moved to the closet and opened the door.

A masked face lunged from the darkness and crashed into her, driving her toward the bed. She knew from the contact it was a powerfully solid man. She used his momentum and spun away, hooking him high with an elbow to the head. She darted to the door, but he was too quick. Her head yanked back and she thought her scalp was on fire. Pulling her hair, he reeled her back to him and clamped his hand around her throat, the other arm clamped across her chest, locking her arms at her sides. Jenna felt him struggle to lift her from her feet, but she was too tall. Still, his grip was strong and she was using more air than she could take in. She stopped struggling, hoping he'd relax his grip on her throat. He didn't.

"I can see you like to fight," he said. "That's why you've been such a pain in the ass." He yanked his grip even tighter. "You need to listen. I'll say this just once. Tank the case with the kid, or your brother dies. Tell your father or the cops and I'll kill him, too." His voice was raspy, as if damaged somehow, and he sounded like a Texan.

At first, the words cut through her. She pictured the goon man-handling her brother. Then her protective anger rose and swallowed the words. She pulled to the right, then launched her left foot to his crotch. The move freed her left arm and she back-fisted him to the jaw. She twisted from his failing grip and threw a punch to his throat. She wanted to kill him now and end the threat. He reeled back but caught himself with one step back. He reset and spun, and she never saw what hit her jaw.

She awoke on the bed with a headache that reminded her of the concussion she'd had in her junior year at Pitt. She shot up, ready to face her attacker, but she was alone. The clock on the nightstand read 1:00 a.m. She'd been out for three hours.

She scrambled out of bed, found her phone on the floor, and dialed her parents' house.

Her mother answered in a half-frightened tone. "Hello?"

"Sorry, Mom. It's me. I know it's late."

"What's wrong, honey? Are you okay?"

"I'm fine." Jenna knew the truth could be deadly. "I had a nightmare, Mom. It was terrible. Dad and Michael, are they okay?"

"Of course. Michael is sleeping and your father is looking right at me."

"That's great, Mom. I'm so sorry. It was a really bad dream, but I'll be okay."

"Are you sure?"

"I think so. Just do me a favor. Be sure the doors are locked and the alarm is set. It will be easier for me to get back to sleep if you promise to do that."

"Okay, honey. Hang on ..." Jenna heard her father say something. "Your father wants to know if he should come over."

"Oh. No, Mom. Tell him thanks but I'm fine."

"You've both been working too hard on that case."

"I know, Mom. I've kept you guys up long enough. I love you. Good night."

"Love you, too. Good night, honey."

Her next call was to the detective sergeant of the Cranberry Township police who had been a family friend forever. She reported the break-in and assault, along with the threats to her brother and father, but asked that it be handled confidentially.

She then placed a call to her best friend from high school, whose parents had a place in Ocean City, Maryland. She made arrangements for her mother and brother to stay there starting the next day.

Finally, she called the personal security team she'd used once for a client. They'd start immediately, following her mother and brother to Maryland.

Jenna hung up the phone but couldn't shake the image of someone attacking Michael. He wouldn't stand a chance against the thug. He'd be terrified and Jenna couldn't live with that. The only way out of this was to win. Not only in court but with overwhelming evidence that would destroy the Falzones. She needed to think, she needed help—no, she needed a miracle. The image of *the play* entered her mind. She needed Ike Rossi.

CHAPTER 43

IKE ROSSI SAW the gunmetal pickup truck race from the curb
in front of Rossi's moments before the explosion. *Maria!* His sister's
face flashed before him and Ike floored the Buick, dodging the few
cars on Liberty Avenue at eleven o'clock at night. He had the car
door open before he slammed the brakes and shoved the car into
"park." It was still sliding when his feet hit the ground. He ran toward the door but was momentarily pushed back by the flames roaring from the front window.

"Ike. Here," Mac yelled as he bolted from the car, dropped his
shoulder, and blasted through the door like a fullback. Ike followed
and found Mac on the floor. He tugged at his arm, but Mac raised his
head and yelled, "Go, Go!"

The heat was searing and the smoke was thick and black, dropping from the ceiling like a curtain of death. The bar was splintered but
Ike grabbed a bar rag from the rippled floor and covered his mouth.
The blast had driven what was left of the bar to the back wall, blocking
the hallway to the stairs and the restrooms like a beaver's dam. Ike
quickly scanned the bar's rubble and didn't see his sister. The flames
were chasing him now, working through the fuel provided by the

tables, mahogany booths, and bar fragments. Ike's lungs burned and his eyes became worthless rivers of tears. The smell of gasoline filled his nose. Still, he ripped the jagged bar top from the doorway and started down the hall.

"Maria," he yelled as his vocal cords tightened from the heat and smoke. He kicked the ladies' room door open and yelled her name again with no reply, then started up the back stairs. He could see flames licking the second-floor ceiling. If she was here, she'd be in what was left of her office. Vaulting up the stairs, he kept yelling her name. At the top, a blast of heat hit him from the right, and he turned and saw a wall of flames blocking the hallway to her office. The smoke was much thicker, and his troubled breathing evolved to rapid-fire choking. He shielded his eyes from the heat, and the flames shoved him back.

He could feel Maria. She was here. She was behind the flames.

In that instant, he hurled himself down the hallway and into the flames. He crashed into something and hit the floor, his pullover flaming and melting into his arm. Ripping it off, he sprang to all fours and crawled through what had been the office doorway. Flames danced across every surface, and the smoke layer was so low he couldn't see the top of the desk chair.

"Maria!"

The desk chair moved. He scrambled around the flaming desk and found her, stunned and reaching for him. He sucked in a searing breath and scooped her up. Squatting, he stomped the bits of flame on the floor and headed to the small shattered window facing Liberty Avenue. Knocking out the shards of glass, he leaned out with Maria. Despite the waves of intensifying heat cooking his back, he sucked in as much air as he could, then looked down at Maria. She was limp and not breathing.

Ike scanned the sidewalk below. "Mac!" He heard the sirens in the distance. They wouldn't make it in time. "Mac!"

Suddenly Mac appeared from the doorway below and looked up, soot covering his face. Ike gently rotated Maria and slid her limp body through his arms and grabbed both wrists. "Take her, quick." Mac spread his feet wide and flexed his knees with his thick arms open. Ike let go, and Mac caught her. Mac's knees buckled and he fell backward on the concrete. Ike swung out, hung from the ledge, and dropped. Pain ripped through his legs as he hit the ground and rolled. Jumping to his feet, he took Maria from Mac's arms, moved her three doors down from the burning bar, and laid her flat on the sidewalk.

Maria looked blue and wasn't breathing. Her pulse was nonexistent, and he started CPR. Ignoring the wave of panic, he kept up with the compressions. "Maria. Don't leave me, Maria."

Suddenly, her body quivered and she sucked in a loud, deep breath. It was the sweetest sound Ike had ever heard.

"Hang on, Maria." Ike looked up and saw the paramedics running toward them, Mac leading the way. "They're coming."

In the distance, he saw the Rossi's sign crash to the ground as the fire engines flooded the flames. Steam and smoke disappeared into the dark sky above. When he looked down at Maria, she was watching it, too. After a moment, Ike saw the tears cutting through the black soot on her face.

"Ike," was all she said, crying.

They'd lost the place where their mother had found so much joy— the place that connected them to her. And they'd almost lost each other.

CHAPTER 44

JOSEPH NEVER EXPECTED to be in this position. As he
spied through the glazed panes of the living room window of their
Squirrel Hill home, he watched Jack hug his aunt and cling to her as
if she were his lifeline. Then they walked from the car and down the
winding, shrub-lined walkway to his wife and daughter. After several
minutes of tearful negotiation in the bright morning sun, his grandson hugged Lauren one last time and was embraced by Erin and
Shannon. They each placed a hand on a shoulder and led him to the
front door, with Jack looking back to Lauren like a prisoner walking
to his death.

Since Joseph had been the lead antagonist in Lauren Bottaro's
nightmare, Erin had decided he couldn't be present to greet his own
grandson. He'd asked Shannon to join his wife because Shannon and
Jack had developed a close relationship upon Brenda's departure. It
was a curious connection and Joseph sometimes wondered why, but
his gratitude for the connection always dwarfed his suspicions.

When he heard the front door open, he knew he'd need to strike
a delicate balance. On one hand, he needed to know what Jack knew.
That knowledge could kill his only remaining son, Nick, and destroy
the family he'd so painfully built. But on the other hand, if Erin

sensed any effort to interrogate Jack, her suspicions would over-flow—and with the ensuing explanation, he'd lose his family anyway.

Erin and Shannon led Jack to the large entry, and Joseph moved from the window and slowly walked to meet them. The smell of white-chocolate-chip macadamia-nut cookies—Jack's favorite—filled the air, and he could see that Jack's nose had found the trail.

"Hi, Jackie boy," Joseph said, extending a hand. Jack looked up and shook his hand. Joseph eyed the young boy. His dark-brown crew cut and bright blue eyes reminded him of Nick as a kid and trig-gered a touch of guilt he quickly discharged.

"Hi, Grandpa," Jack said. His sadness and unease were obvious.

"Did you have breakfast yet, honey?" Erin asked.

"Yes, ma'am. Aunt Lauren got me up early and we stopped at IHOP."

Shannon seemed to sense Erin's disappointment and reached out and touched Jack's arm. "You ready to try some of those cookies?"

Jack nodded and showed a bit of a smile.

"Can I take your backpack?" Shannon said.

Jack nodded again and slipped it off.

The cookies were a great idea, and as Joseph sat at the kitchen table, drinking tea and eating cookies, he began to enjoy himself and let the mission ahead drift into the background. They talked about what had happened since they'd last seen each other over Christmas. Erin and Shannon took turns waiting on Jack, and all seemed to en-joy their roles. Two hours later, after helping clean up, they lured Jack into his favorite card game with the promise of computer time. As each hand played out, Joseph felt the weight of anticipation growing. He needed time alone with his grandson. When Jack won for the third time in a row, Joseph saw his opening.

"Okay, young man. You're pretty good at this, but can you have the same success with the chessboard?"

Jack's face lit up. "Yes, Grandpa."

The chessboard had been a gift from a Russian oligarch, but most important, it was in Joseph's library. While Erin was always welcome, an unspoken respect for Joseph's work space had developed over the years.

"You boys go ahead," Erin said. "Shannon and I will clean up here. Just remember we have lunch plans in an hour."

Erin's encouragement made Joseph hate himself even more for deceiving her. She had a good heart and genuinely wanted her grandson to get to spend time alone with his grandfather. She never would have suspected that Joseph wanted to grill him over his reasoning for killing Tanner. But it had to be done.

Joseph excused himself and Jack followed him into the sprawling library. On previous visits, Jack had loved gawking at the shelves of books stretching to the twenty-foot ceiling and playing chess with the oversize hand-carved ivory chess pieces that depicted a czar, his family and his court. The Russian had jokingly said it was Ivan IV, better-known as Ivan the Terrible, who was said to have died playing chess. Joseph always went with the more generic description since his research showed that Ivan the Terrible had killed his oldest son in a fit of rage.

The board was mounted on a hand-carved table near one of the large windows. Jack moved next to the velvet seat and awaited his grandfather's permission to sit.

"Go ahead, Jack. You've been here before." Joseph took his usual seat.

As they began play, Joseph was impressed by Jack's level of improvement. He'd played chess masters who weren't at Jack's level. As they alternated moves, Joseph thought it was time.

"Jack, do you mind if I ask you a few questions about the trial coming up? I want to understand it from your view in case I can help you."

Jack stuck out his lower lip and gave a matter-of-fact nod.

"Okay, then. Do you mind if I ask you why you shot that man?"

Jack didn't look up from the board and contemplated his move as he spoke. "He was the reason my father died. And they were coming for me and Aunt Lauren next." He moved his piece and glanced at Joseph, then leaned back and awaited Joseph's move.

Joseph struggled with his focus on the game in the face of Jack's frankness. He contemplated his move, and as he positioned his piece, he said, "How do you know that?"

Jack quickly reached for his piece and moved it. "I heard my dad on the phone."

Joseph realized he'd made a mistake and Jack was pouncing. He liked Jack's instincts, but he was more concerned with his answer. If his grandson truly knew too much, letting him go to trial and then prison was the only outcome that would save the family. Sacrifice the boy for the family—it didn't seem fair. He made his next move and contemplated his next question.

Without warning, Nick appeared at the library door. Joseph knew why he was there.

"Hey there, boys. What's up?" Nick said as he closed the door and walked to the table, smiling. Something in his look changed when he came face-to-face with Jack.

"Hi, kid."

Jack ignored him and focused on the board.

"I said, 'Hi, kid.'"

"Nick," Joseph said, warning him.

Jack stayed quiet, and Joseph could see the anger flare in Nick's eyes. "You should answer your uncle when he talks to you," Nick said.

Joseph stood. "Nick, that's enough. Leave him alone."

"He needs to talk to me. I have a few questions for him."

"Not here. Not now."

"Why not now? He's here. And I need to know."

Jack was now watching the argument.

The door sprang open and Erin rushed in. "What are you doing?" she yelled at Nick.

"None of your business," Nick said.

Joseph took Nick by the arm and pushed him toward the door. When he was halfway there, Shannon stormed in. "Are you always an asshole?" she said as she passed Nick.

Nick lunged for her, but Joseph clamped down harder on his bicep and dragged him out the door. Joseph looked back and saw Erin and Shannon comforting Jack.

Joseph narrowed his glare on Nick. "With me, now."

Nick followed him to Erin's study and Joseph slammed the door closed.

"You need to get control of yourself."

"No. That kid can take us both down."

Joseph stepped toe-to-toe with Nick, looking down on him. "What you're doing will put you in prison faster than anything. I'll take care of it."

Nick looked away, then stepped back. "Fine. Have it your way." He left the room.

While Joseph had heard the words, he couldn't read his son's intent. Most of his life, his son had been a great liar. And if what Nick had just said was a lie, Joseph knew he was capable of anything to get his way.

Joseph had served his dues—done his time—and using his money and influence to guide the outcome of the trial didn't bother him. He controlled the odds, but he was losing control of his son— and that loss could cost him everything.

CHAPTER 45

JENNA WATCHED LAUREN collapse into the chair and eyed her from across the conference room. Waves of guilt rose up and engulfed her as she tangled with a decision she'd never thought she'd have to make. Michael had always come first. In high school, time with Michael was more important than time with friends. She'd chosen her college to stay close to him. And despite graduating at the top of her class and receiving offers from some of the most prestigious law firms in the country, Jenna chose to stay close to Michael and work for her father. This was supposed to be her chance to show her true worth—by beating one of those firms in open court. But now she'd chosen Michael again, trading her vindication and a ten-year-old's life for his.

They'd agreed to meet at ten a.m., after Lauren had dropped Jack at the Falzones. Lauren's face sagged and the bags around her red eyes signified the depth of her pain. Jenna poured a cup of coffee and delivered it to Lauren with as much sympathy as she could muster.

"You okay?" Jenna said.

Lauren nodded. "It's the first time since Jack's arrest that we've been apart like this." She clenched the cup with both hands and looked up at Jenna. "And it's with them—with *them*."

Jenna saw Lauren battling back tears and wrapped her arms around her.

"It's okay. He'll be okay." Jenna was disappointed that words of betrayal came so easily. She'd be leading Lauren to a decision she was certain would deliver a conviction in order to save Michael. The thick claws of self-loathing dug into her insides.

She wanted to save Jack *and* Michael, but these people were capable of anything. They'd entered her alarmed townhome and assaulted an officer of the court, then disappeared without a trace. She'd love to call the cops or even Judge Nowicki, but based on the photo Ike had texted last night, they were part of this.

Jenna circled back to her chair at the conference table and sat. She gathered herself and looked across the table to her father. She started, knowing this wouldn't be easy. "I was reviewing our defense plan last night and I'm worried about it. It has holes all through it."

Her dad threw a look of concern in Lauren's direction before he returned his attention to Jenna. "We've all been over this. It's the least destructive alternative for Jack. Incapacity gets him an evaluation and, perhaps at some point down the road, freedom."

Jenna had expected her father's retort. "Jack's a genius. Hell, the boy is ten times smarter than I ever was. How do we get around that?"

"Like we agreed to. He wasn't aware of the gravity of what he did. Our experts will testify to that." Her father gave her a stern look. "What's going on, Jen?"

Glancing at Lauren, she took her best shot. "Jack did this in self-defense. I know he did. And we still have two days to prove it."

"How Jen? How do we prove it? We haven't been able to do it over the past six months. What makes you think we can do it in less than forty-eight hours?"

Jenna faced Lauren. "We bring back Ike."

"Rossi?" her father said. "He has a credibility problem. Especially with anything involving the Falzones. The judge will punt anything he has so far out of sight we'll never see it again."

Lauren's coffee cup hit the table hard and her eyes ignited. "That's what I wanted all along. But you talked me out of it. You said it wouldn't work—it would blow up in our faces."

Jenna felt the vise around her tightening. Her conviction to her position waned until Michael's smile entered her mind. "Ike's made some progress without our sanctioning. I think he might actually pull it off."

"Are you seriously considering making that bet?" her father said, his bulging neck veins feeding his reddened face.

"Yes. Ike has evidence of collusion. If we turn him loose, he'll find more."

Her father tossed the yellow pad and pen onto the table and leaned back. "That's a long way from proving self-defense."

"Are you certain this could work?" Lauren said.

"Yes. If it were my life at stake, this is what I'd do."

Ed slowly shook his head.

"I've got to try to save Jack. I never liked the insanity plea. It would destroy him. I've always had a feeling about Ike." Lauren glared at Jenna. "But you talked me out of using him. You convinced me that was only way for Jack to survive. Now you change your mind?"

"All I can tell you is after going over everything last night, I got a text from Ike. Now I think this tactic could save him—save Jack." As Jenna listened to her deceitful words, a seed of hope sprouted among them. What if she was right? What if Rossi could pull it off? That option put both Michael and Jack at risk, but if Ike threaded that needle and exposed those behind this conspiracy, they'd be home free: Jack would be acquitted and Michael would be safe.

Then darkness drowned her hopes for Jack. Rossi's failure would end Jack's life, but despite the eternal damnation she'd live with, Michael would be safe.

Lauren leaned back in her chair. "He's a good man. He wouldn't let Jack down. He would've told me if he didn't think he could do this. I'm in."

Jenna's dad crossed his arms. "Did you forget? His bar blew up last night and his sister is in the hospital."

"No. Oh, no," Lauren said. "How bad is she?"

"Serious but stable," Ed said.

"I'll get him back." Jenna said. It was her best lie. Lauren seemed to believe it because she wanted to.

Her father's eyes were filled with suspicion, but she couldn't tell him about the threat—not yet. He was old-school, and he'd pick up the phone and call the FBI and Michael would be dead the next day. Jenna had no idea if she could get Ike back, but one thing was on her side. Ever since she'd met Ike Rossi, she'd use one word to describe him. Right or wrong, no matter what the consequence, he was always one thing. Determined.

CHAPTER 46

IT WAS NEARING eleven a.m. and Ike sat in the waiting room of West Penn Hospital thrumming his thumb against the seat. Maria had almost died, and he'd never felt this darkness before. He'd been in and out of Maria's room whenever staff members interrupted her periods of sleep as they ran a battery of tests to determine the degree of oxygen deprivation from the smoke. With Mac's help, he'd filled in the fire investigators and the bomb squad during the interims. The ATF had been called, and Ike fully expected to repeat himself again. Detective Cassidy arrived and tried to question them but left when Ike offered to rearrange his face.

Mac faced him in the opposing chair, asleep and covered in soot. Mac had been with him all night, refusing treatment to remain at Ike's side. Ike entered another debt in his ledger to Mac. He'd help save them both.

Over Mac's shoulder, Ike spotted the nurse assigned to Maria walking toward them. Ike had learned that her smile always preceded an invitation to reenter his sister's room.

"Mr. Rossi," she whispered. "She's awake and the breathing tube is out. The doctor says you're welcome to see her."

Ike stood and Mac opened his eyes.

Ike touched Mac's shoulder. "Going back in." Ike addressed the nurse. "Mac saved us both. Can he come in for just a moment?"

"Of course." She turned and led them through the double doors and into intensive care. As they entered Maria's room, Ike noticed the bank of monitors tethered to her by a network of cords. A clear IV bag hung at the right head of her bed and dripped into the tube connected to her hand. He tiptoed in with Mac trailing him. They stopped at the foot of her bed. She partially opened her eyes. When she recognized them, she smiled.

Ike moved to her bedside, knelt beside her, and stroked her forehead. It was the first time he'd seen her without the breathing tube and awake.

"Hey, sleepyhead," Ike said.

"Hey yourself."

Her reply was weak, but Ike sensed something else in her tone. For the first time in his life, he felt distance between them. He wanted to write it off to the injuries, but he couldn't

Maria's eyes drifted to Mac. "Mac. You look terrible."

"You should see the other guy," he said, smiling.

"I *am* the other guy," Maria said.

The doctor appeared at the door, glancing at Mac and then Ike. "Can we talk, Mr. Rossi?"

Ike nodded in Mac's direction. "It's okay. He's family."

The doctor stepped into the room. She was young, younger than Ike, but she'd earned Ike's confidence with her fact-based approach to Maria's care.

"She's had a rough go. Good thing you were just down the street. The EMTs and ER staff did a great job. I see no permanent damage to her lungs or her heart." She shifted her eyes to Maria. "Very lucky."

Ike squeezed Maria's hand and dropped his head in thanks to a greater power. He looked up and saw Maria smile back at the doctor.

While Ike had no time for guilt, he knew he was on the hook for this. "She'll be okay?"

"We need to keep her for a day, but it looks like she'll be fine."

Mac reached down and squeezed her toes through the blanket. "She's a tough one."

The lead weight on Ike's mind lifted. Maria would be all right. But the weight was replaced by a burning vengeance.

Ike rose and shook the doctor's hand. When he turned back to Maria, her smile disappeared.

"You need to end this." Maria's voice was raspy and weak.

"I'm sorry you were hurt."

"Not hurt. Almost killed. And the only real connection we had to Mom and Dad is destroyed."

"I'm helping Jack because he needs me. I need to do this."

"You're just fooling yourself. What you're doing won't bring Mom and Dad back. And it won't give you closure. You've destroyed everything—and for what? To help a kid who everyone knows is a murderer. He killed someone's father. Ever think about that?"

"Yes. And you wanted me to do this."

Tears streamed down Maria's face. "I didn't know it would cost us everything."

Ike was trapped. Jack or Maria. He glanced at Mac, hoping for a lifeline.

"You two can't live without each other," Mac said. "It's always been that way—always will be. I know this means a lot to you, but she's right."

Both Mac and Maria stared at Ike. The silence was like a thick concrete wall between them. Ike's phone vibrated in his pocket. He pulled it out and stole a glance. It was Jenna.

"I'll be right back."

"No. No, you won't. Get the hell out of here. I don't want you he—" Maria coughed hard and the nurse came in.

"Everybody out. Now," the nurse said.

As he turned to walk out, he heard Maria say, "He's kidding, right?"

He made it to the waiting area and took the call with Mac eyeing him.

"Jenna?"

"Yes. Ike. I wasn't sure if I'd get you. So sorry about your sister."

"You heard about that?"

"The entire country has heard about it. They're calling it a bombing. Is she okay?"

Ike hated talking to Jenna with Maria just down the hall. It felt like a betrayal. "No. But she will be."

"I hate to call you now, but the case is thirty-six hours away and we're in trouble."

Ike weighed dumping her right now. But Jack's gravity reeled him back, and the words eluded him. He decided he'd play Solomon and split the baby. "I have more information for you. Can I come out to your office?"

"Of course. You sure?"

"Never been surer." Ike ended the call.

Mac wagged his head and stared at Ike. Ike didn't yield and raised his eyebrows. "Can you meet me out front? I need to get to the Shelby."

"I'll meet you out front." Mac stomped out of the lobby.

Ike's world was ripping in half. He knew what he had to do. Maria meant everything to him. She was his responsibility—his alone. He hated what he'd have to do, but he'd do it. He pulled out his phone and scrolled to the contact for The Farm. Moretti answered on the first ring.

"It's me. Tonight."

He stuffed the phone into his jeans and headed for the front doors.

CHAPTER 47

JOSEPH NEEDED TO wrestle this story to the ground and kill it. It was the quicksand that could swallow his family and his business. Decisive action internally and silence outwardly was the only response. He closed the door to his library and faced his family.

Erin had left Jack in front of the TV in the den, Shannon had run in at the last minute and sat next to her mother on the sofa after doing damage control for the family, and Nick sat quietly in the side chair. The glib expression on Nick's face pushed Joseph past any guilt he'd had for causing Nick's behavior. It was just after four p.m. and the explosion at Rossi's had been the lead story on every cable news channel. These days, explosions always made the national wires, but it wasn't the fact that the story had gone national that troubled Joseph. He'd spotted the CNN banner on the flat screen mounted on the wall: "Falzones Linked to Explosion Victim."

Joseph pointed to the screen. "Does everybody see that? That's our name on the national news. This is what I've always talked about. It only takes a second to injure our reputation."

Shannon responded without hesitation. "I've talked to all the major media outlets and sent out a tweet saying the link was coincidental and we condemn the act and want the best for the Rossi family."

"Good," Joseph said. "Let that be the last thing we say publicly about this matter. Any response could lead to more difficult questions."

Nick stood and threw a disrespectful nod to the screen. "We have nothing to worry about, Dad. Any inquiries will hit a brick wall, and the things you may be worried about are safe. Besides, they got what they deserved."

Joseph scrutinized Erin's face and weighed his response. She was right there—he could see it in her face—on the edge of an issue that would end her marriage to Joseph. And Nick, with his stupidity, was leading her there. But the nuclear response he wanted to deliver would be confirmation of something big.

"While Ike Rossi was working against us, violence against him or his sister is unacceptable. Now sit down—I'm not done."

Erin tilted her head slightly. "Joseph, what's going on?"

Joseph used his rehearsed remarks. "Rossi was the investigator working for Lauren Bottaro and her attorney. We caught him in the office Thursday trying to access some three-dimensional seismic images on the Virginia blocks. We don't know why he wanted them, but as you can imagine, they're highly sensitive. We paid a lot of money for those blocks and that data. I had Nick secure it. It's nothing more than that." It was his first barefaced lie to Erin and he hoped she didn't detect it.

Erin appeared to be unsatisfied. "Okay then." She stood. "I need to check on Jack. Anything else?" Her tone said everything. Joseph dreaded the private conversation he knew was coming.

"No, dear. Just a few things for the kids about the PR strategy."

Erin didn't kiss his cheek on the way to the door. Shannon was deep in thought, putting the pieces together, it seemed.

"Okay, Nick. No more. No more of anything. Take some time off or do whatever you have to, but don't meddle in this." Joseph pointed his finger at Nick. "And leave Erin alone."

"Sure, Pops."

~~~~

Shannon hadn't seen that look in Joseph's eyes before. Nick had crossed the line, and she rarely avoided Joseph's wrath when that happened with her. But this was Nick—mister fair-haired, give-him-a-pass golden boy. She'd known about the seismic, but the intensity of her father's response caused her to think again. It was the first she'd heard of 3D images for the Minuteman prospect.

"Dad, what's going on?"

"Just what I said."

She could tell when her father wasn't truthful. He rarely kept anything from her, which was why this was so obvious.

"What's on the seismic?"

Joseph dropped his head. The truth was coming.

"It's an image of the largest structure we'd ever hoped for. And based on the work we've done, we think it's mostly oil."

He was still hiding something.

"What else?"

"Nothing. That's it."

Nick walked to Shannon. "It's none of your business. You do the PR and government affairs. That's your job. Running the company is mine, so just back off."

"I won't back off anything. I'm as much a part of this family as you are."

"Is that why they call you my half-sister?"

Shannon took a step, closing the distance between them to inches. "I want to know what you're hiding."

Nick smiled and wagged his head. "We all have our secrets, don't we, sis?"

Shannon felt the warm flush rising in her cheeks and fought it back. There was no way he knew her secret. They'd been too careful.

"That's enough, Nick."

Nick shot up. "Can I go now?"

"Get out of here," Joseph said. "And remember what I said."

Nick headed out the door.

Now it was just the two of them. "Father, I know there's something else. And I know you're protecting Nick. I guess that's your business. But I have a few questions to ask you."

"Sure, sweetie." He walked to the sofa and sat next to her.

"When did we acquire this seismic?"

"Why do you want to know that?"

"Just answer, Father."

"Okay. It was in November."

"And when was the data processed and the images delivered?"

"Just before Christmas."

She readied herself for the next question. She hadn't thought of it until Nick mentioned the things Joseph might be worried about. She wanted the answer, but she wasn't prepared for it. She felt her hands tremble. Still, she dived in.

"Patrick died in January. Is there any link to his death?"

There it was. It was as if she were accusing her father of murder. That shock registered on Joseph's face. But she saw a hint of something else. It wasn't obvious and she wasn't sure. She also didn't want it to be true. It was just the slightest hesitation before he answered. She committed to examining the flight logs for that night.

"No. Absolutely not. Why would you ask me such a thing?"

"I never believed Patrick would have crashed on that road. He was the best driver of all of us. He never drank either. And Nick had it out for him. He even said so at Christmas."

"Nick says a lot of things he doesn't mean."

"You have to quit protecting him, Father. We both know he's a loose cannon. And you have him running the company. I don't want you to go down with him."

"We all have problems. I won't take it anymore from him."

Shannon stood. She wanted to leave before she said something she regretted. Regardless of his need to protect Nick, she knew her father was a good man. And she'd protect him if she could. "At some point, you're going to have to decide whether you want a daughter like me or a son like Nick."

She headed to the door.

"Wait. Shannon, wait."

She didn't. Tears filled her eyes and a seed of doubt acidified her stomach. She needed to check the flight logs.

CHAPTER 48

IKE ARRIVED IN Cranberry just after four p.m. Taking the case file he'd worked on most of the afternoon, he left the Shelby and headed to the door. With each step, the overheated pressure cooker inside expanded a little more. He entered Price and Price, and Kristin greeted him and hurried him into the conference room. Jenna and Ed were huddled at the far end of the conference table and Lauren sat alone, staring at her phone. Her face was long and drawn, and her eyes sagged under the weight of what Ike imagined had been a terrible night. She looked up and the smile on her face weakened his resolve. He tossed the brown envelope onto the table.

Lauren rushed to him and enveloped him in a long hug. "Ike. So glad you're here."

He hugged her back hard. It was the best thing he'd experienced in two days. She pulled back. "We're going back to self-defense. We need your help."

Jenna approached and extended her hand with a smile. Ike instinctively shook it and noticed a bruise below her knuckles. "She's right," Jenna said. "We need you. I'm so sorry about that mess a few days ago."

Jenna's one-eighty and her repentant demeanor set off alarm bells. Ike wondered what had happened. Less than forty-eight hours ago, his credibility and usefulness had been worthless to her and Jack's case. Making matters worse, he could see hope written all over Ed's face.

"How's Jack?" Ike asked Lauren.

Her energy dissipated. "He's gone. At his grandparents."

"Sorry to hear that. Can I sit?"

Ike dropped into the nearest chair and Lauren sat next to him. Jenna returned to her spot across from Ed.

Ike opened the envelope and pulled out the contents. "I have some information I think you may be able to use."

"Yes," Jenna said. "Thanks for the text last night. Does it mean what I think it does?"

"It means the judge, the DA, the attorneys, and at least the assistant chief of investigations are colluding. Beyond that, I'd be careful."

Lauren's face ignited. "That will help Jack, right?"

Jenna looked like a cat trapped on a raft in the middle of the ocean. She wrestled for the right words. She eyed Ed, then focused on Ike. "The only thing that will help Jack is evidence that shows Tom was murdered, that Franklin Tanner was involved, and that they planned to kill Jack next."

Ike grabbed the stack of papers in front of him and held it up. "I think you'll find enough mistakes were made at the suicide scene to warrant reasonable doubt that Tom Cole's death was a suicide. You'll also see that you can call Tom's partner as a witness who will testify that he was working on a project for the Falzones. Tom's job was to take that seismic data and develop detailed three-dimensional images of the subsurface formations on the offshore blocks the Falzones were betting their company on. I think that's why he was killed."

"That's great, right?" Lauren said. "If we have evidence of that we can free Jack."

Ike felt all eyes on him.

"Do you have evidence to back that up, Ike?" Ed asked. His tone and face said he already knew the answer.

"No. I think the suicide scene can speak for itself. Tom was meticulous in everything he did. The scene was sloppy and rushed. He'd never do that."

"But what about evidence, Ike?" Jenna said. "We need evidence that Tom was murdered and that the Falzones and Tanner were involved."

Ike hesitated. Lauren was still smiling, but it faded with every millisecond of his delay.

"Ike?" Lauren said.

This was the moment he'd never wanted to happen, but for Maria, Ike had to press on. "Look. I think your investigator might be able to finish this and get you what you need."

"But you're our investigator, aren't you?" Lauren said.

Ike reached for her hand, but she yanked it away.

Ed read the expression on Ike's face. "Damn. You're done."

Ike didn't answer. He held Lauren's piercing stare.

"Ike, is he right?" Lauren said. "Are you refusing to help Jack?"

The words sent a wave of sadness through Ike. He imagined Jack being convicted. But even worse, he imagined Jack never knowing why his father died. "I can't anymore. They've destroyed our place and nearly killed my sister. I can't risk her. She's all I have."

Lauren slapped Ike. It stung worse than any punch he'd taken in the ring.

Lauren stood up. No tears, just contempt in her eyes. "You're going to abandon Jack after all that talk and all those promises?"

Ike remembered Lauren's definition of commitment as defined by her husband's death in Afghanistan. She was right. After keeping his word as his father had taught him all his life, Ike was breaking it for the second time in a week. His character was failing him. But he had no choice. Maria was his responsibility, and twenty-two years ago he'd promised himself and pledged to his parents' spirits that he'd protect her—no matter what.

Ike was still under Lauren's glare. "I'm sorry."

"Tell that to Jack," Lauren said.

"Hang on, Ike," Jenna said. "There has to be a way. We can't let these bastards get away with this. They've threatened me and my family, and we have to get them. The only way we do that is with you."

Ike slid the file across the table to Jenna and rose. He was with her in spirit, except his spirit wanted to rip the Falzones' guts out. They'd nearly killed Maria, and that alone warranted Ike's action. But he couldn't give them a second chance. Maria was right. He was kidding himself that if he somehow pulled off a miracle and saved Jack, he'd get closure. In the cost-benefit analysis, the cost was too high to take such a long shot. For the first time in his life, he'd quit—just walked away. He'd weighed his feelings about Jack and his feelings about Maria and run them through a meat grinder, and what came out was uglier than what had gone in. He took a last look at Lauren.

"I'm sorry. I'm done."

He left the office and drove north toward The Farm.

CHAPTER 49

IKE STEERED THE Shelby through the gates and drove along
the paved drive. The opposing forces in his conscience ground
against each other and generated a red-hot anger. Still, his anticipation felt different this time. He'd convinced himself he'd made the
right choice: save Maria, save himself, and protect what was left of
his family. But his promise to help Jack ground against that decision
like seismic plates pressurizing for an earthquake.

As he wound down the tree-lined road again, he spotted more
cars than he'd ever seen here. They spread beyond the white gravel
surrounding the corrugated-steel building and were at least six rows
deep into the grassy field beyond it. He pulled next to Moretti's
Lamborghini and stepped out. The giant double doors were open,
and Ike could see the empty ring in the center. Moretti's clientele
swarmed through any open space, sporting thousand-dollar sport
coats and more gold than Fort Knox. Ike retrieved his bag from the
trunk and headed through the doors.

Moretti raised both hands. "Here he is. The undefeated champ.
Get your bets in, gentlemen." He walked to Ike dragging what looked
like the offensive line of the Steelers with him.

"Ike, I'd like you to meet these gentlemen." Moretti said, extending his hand.

Ike shook it. "Not now." He pushed through the crowd and entered the makeshift dressing room. Alfredo was standing by the locker without gloves or tape. His old face was lined with worry, and he met Ike with both palms in front of him. "No, Ike. Not this one. No fight."

Ike didn't need this, even from his oldest friend. Ike dropped his bag and grabbed Alfredo by his shoulders. "I appreciate your concern, my friend. But this is going to happen."

"He's a killer," Alfredo said.

Ike reminded himself: *Size doesn't matter.*

Alfredo pushed Ike's arms from his shoulders. "No, no. This one mean. Like a snake. I heard he killed a man."

Ike bent down and ripped open his bag. He yanked out his trunks and held them in front of Alfredo's face. "I'm doing this. With or without you, my friend."

Alfredo's shoulders sagged and he dropped his hands to his sides. His face grew long, and he turned and grabbed the tape from his bag. Ike quickly dressed, and Alfredo taped his hands while he silently wagged his head. He slipped the thin gloves on and tied them off. Then he made the sign of the cross and rested his right palm over Ike's heart.

Ike slammed his gloves together. "Don't worry, Alfredo, I'll be back."

Alfredo forced a smile and Ike stormed out toward the ring. He reminded himself of the attack on Maria and the obliteration of their bar but then remembered her scolding in the hospital. He thought about the assailant who'd put two slugs into the Shelby. He imagined Jack in court getting his sentence, and the anger grew. He pounded his fists together harder and imagined them as made of lead. He envisioned an iron shield covering his body and burst through the door.

As he approached the ring, he saw his opponent waiting in the corner. He was tall and thick with shoulders as big as basketballs. His skin shone like polished ebony. His hair was black and close-cropped and continued into a beard that hugged tight to his skin. His eyes were darting and wild.

Ike slipped between the ropes and planted himself in the corner. One nickname came to mind as he eyed his opponent. *LeBron.*

Moretti stood on a box next to the ring with a hammer in his hand and silenced the crowd. "Gentlemen, betting is closed. Here we go." He struck the bell mounted on the pillar next to him and Ike and LeBron charged to the center of the ring. LeBron launched his right first and Ike blocked it with his left. But then LeBron's left crashed through and caught Ike in the cheek, rocking him back a step.

Ike countered with a right and caught him squarely on the jaw. LeBron ignored the blow and hammered Ike's midsection with a left that landed with a crack. Ike still had air, but he was down one rib. Ike circled to regroup and LeBron just plodded closer, his eyes blazing with sanitarium rage. Ike hammered him with a combination that slowed his advance. Then without warning, a fist crushed Ike's jaw and he felt his legs go. Halfway to the canvas, he extended his arm to soften his face's impact. He was down. For the first time in ten years, he'd been knocked down. Ike tasted the blood in his mouth as LeBron circled once and headed to the corner. At least he observed the knockdown rule.

Moretti started a count with the help of the crowd. With no referee, Ike knew to take his time getting up. Moretti reached five. Inhaling and then blowing out the cobwebs, Ike pushed himself off the canvas and raised his guard.

Smelling an upset, LeBron appeared instantly and threw a barrage that Ike slipped as he slid to his left and caught LeBron with another right. This one stood him up. Still, LeBron kept coming, huffing like a locomotive. Ike stepped to the left again and tagged him with an uppercut that dropped most opponents. LeBron shook his head and his eyes burned even hotter. They came together and LeBron bulled Ike into the corner. Ike covered, but a right drilled into his ear and everything went silent.

He awoke on the canvas again with Moretti hitting six. The bell rang, but as agreed, the bell saved no one. He pressed himself up as Moretti reached nine. His vision was blurred, but he found Alfredo in the corner—he'd never done that before. No fight had gone to the second round.

Alfredo wiped Ike's face and shoved a water bottle at him. Ike's mouth burned when the stream hit it. He spit blood into the bucket at his side. Alfredo raised the towel in his hand.

"It's enough. Like I say."

"No." Ike said as he stood. "We finish."

The bell sounded and Ike stormed toward LeBron. He'd end this now. Ike hesitated as they came together, then planted his right foot and threw a left that caught LeBron by surprise. Stunned, he lowered his guard enough for Ike to pummel him with a combination. LeBron wobbled backward, and Ike stepped in with his right cocked, ready to finish him. Ike launched it, but before it could reach LeBron's jaw, Ike's face ignited in pain. His legs collapsed and he hit the floor. The crowd was roaring—for LeBron. Ike heard Moretti at two, but the crowd noise faded.

An image of Jack kneeling before his father's grave flashed before Ike. Jack was older, maybe twenty and crying. Ike was standing in the distance, hiding like a coward.

Then, in an instant, it hit Ike. A way to save them all. The rage he felt electrified his body. The roar of the crowd returned and Moretti said "Eight." The surge of adrenaline lifted Ike off the floor and one word exploded out of his mouth. "No!"

He snapped his attention to LeBron, who had his arms raised. LeBron turned away from the crowd, and for the first time Ike saw doubt mixed with the crazy. Ike thought of Jack and charged LeBron, who responded by raising his iron fists and charging. Ike waited and LeBron led with his right. Ike hammered it down with his left and launched his body and every ounce of vengeance—for him, his family, and Jack—behind a right that caught LeBron square on the cheek. LeBron's head snapped to the left and he quivered and crashed face first into the canvas.

The crowd stormed the side of the ring in a near riot, and Ike couldn't hear Moretti's count. It didn't matter. Ike rushed to the ropes and a stunned Alfredo parted them. Ike shoved through the crowd, biting at the laces on his gloves. He reached the dressing room, grabbed his clothes, and shoved them into the bag. With his hands still taped, he fought his way to the Shelby. He opened the door, tossed the bag inside, and got in. He fired up the engine, then reached into his bag and pulled his iPhone out. He found a message. It was from Tom Cole.

He threw the phone onto the seat and slammed the car into first, spinning and slinging gravel at the crowd and their cars. He'd save them all or die trying. When he'd cleared Moretti's drive, his phone rang. He answered hands free. "This is Ike."

"Ike," Jenna said. "Jack is missing."

He fishtailed onto the two-lane road and raced toward I-79.

CHAPTER 50

JOSEPH HAD TRIED to avoid this all along. Now a piece of him was torn off and exposed. Nick had succumbed to his demons, and Joseph had to stop him.

The rain pelted steadily against the window as Joseph waited. He'd called the number Latham had given him, and they promised a quick response. Just in case, his second call went to his head of corporate security, who promised, Saturday night or not, he'd assemble a team to quietly hunt down Nick and Jack. Neither would be as hard as the explanation to Erin. She'd trusted him all along, just as he'd asked her. Now that trust was crumbling. He could hear Erin sobbing down the hall. At least Shannon was with her. They'd expect answers—answers Joseph didn't want to give.

Erin appeared in the doorway first. The shock had left her tear-streaked face, but she'd aged twenty years in fifteen minutes.

"Did you make the calls?" Erin asked as she entered the library.

"Yes. I'm so sorry about this."

She kept walking closer. "What did they say?"

"A detective will be here in minutes, and security is already out looking."

She reached his desk and stopped. "How could you let this happen?"

It wasn't a question. It was an accusation.

"I didn't know."

"Come on, Joseph. He's been a problem since before I arrived. And I did everything I could to make him a part of our family. I set aside everything for him, and all he did was shit all over me. No matter what I said, you told me he'd be fine. He'd had a rough time without a mother, but he'd be okay." She folded her arms. "Well, he's not. He's got our grandson and I want to know why. Why would he take him? What's going on? I know there's something going on." She pointed at him. "And you know, Joseph. You know." She refolded her arms and waited.

Joseph was on the defensive—a place he rarely was, especially with Erin. He read her face, and the chasm between them felt irreparable. It was as if he'd been dropped into the deepest, darkest part of the Atlantic with no sight of land.

He stood and walked around the desk. He reached for her, but she pulled back and stared at him.

"I hope you know, all I ever wanted was to build a loving family," Joseph said. He looked away and thought about Nick. "He was a good boy at the core. I know you can't see that now, but I did. I thought I'd stay with him—give him my love and support, and someday that boy would return. I had no idea it would turn into this."

Her eyes narrowed. "Why, Joseph? Why did he take Jack?"

There was no way to answer that question and not end the family right here. "I don't know. But I'll get him back. And Nick is done, I promise. He's out."

Erin quaked. Her eyes burned into him like lasers. "You're lying, Joseph. I never thought you'd lie to me. If you don't tell me the truth, I'm done."

Joseph was trapped now. He'd have to give her something. "He thinks Jack is after him. He thinks that's why he shot Franklin."

Erin furrowed her brow and ground through her own analysis. She was brilliant and not easily fooled. "Why would Nick think that?" Joseph saw her eyes widen. "Unless he had something to do with Tom's death? Joseph?"

Joseph remained silent a little too long.

Erin's eyes glazed and she pivoted and headed to the door. Shannon met her there and Erin pushed past her.

Shannon called after her. "Mom. Mom?"

"I'm going to look for Jack," Erin said over her shoulder and left the hallway for the garage

Shannon turned and eyed Joseph. "What did you tell her?"

Joseph wagged his head.

Shannon marched closer. "It's Nick. I know. I warned you about him. He's a—"

The doorbell interrupted her.

Joseph thanked God for the interruption. "That's the police."

"I'll let them in," she said. She left and returned with Vic Cassidy.

"You have him yet?" Joseph said.

"No," Cassidy said, "It won't be long, though."

"So no news?" Shannon said.

"No, ma'am."

Shannon cut Joseph's throat with one look and marched toward the office door, pushing past Cassidy. "I'm going with Mom to look for him."

Cassidy stepped into the library and strolled to Joseph.

"You know what's at risk here?"

Joseph always knew the risks. "I'm well aware, Detective Cassidy." He moved inches from Cassidy's face. "You get your ass out there and earn your money. I don't give a damn what's at stake. Find them. No matter what it takes. Then you call me, Detective."

Cassidy lingered.

"Now."

Cassidy grinned sickly and left.

Joseph knew he had to find Nick before he did something else stupid. At this point he was out. The disappointment and guilt over Nick's failures didn't matter now. There was no telling what Nick would say when he was caught. It was a risk Joseph had never wanted to take. His family was unraveling, and if he mishandled this, his fortune could be right behind it.

CHAPTER 51

IKE ROCKETED DOWN I-79 toward the city. He pushed the Shelby to 110 miles per hour and threaded through the thin Saturday-night traffic. He knew the longer Jack was with Nick, the more likely he'd be killed. He guessed either Nick wanted to know what Jack knew and who he'd told or he was looking for a place to kill him. Or both. Whatever the case, time was his enemy and Ike had no idea where they were, other than in the city. Jenna had said Jack was taken around nine—thirty minutes ago. She'd said Lauren had alerted both the Pittsburgh Police and the State Police. An AMBER Alert had been issued, but that wouldn't save Jack.

He remembered that Jack had an iPhone, and he gave the voice command to the hands-free system to call Lauren's cell phone.

Lauren answered on the first ring. "Ike. They have him. They have Jack."

"I know. I'm on it. Where are you?"

"Just getting into the car to head to the Falzones'."

"Go back inside and give me Jack's Apple ID and password."

"I know it. It's AppleJack. The password is Jac01Col04."

"Got it."

"Why do you need his log-in information?"

"Sorry, Lauren. I don't have time to explain. I gotta go."

"I'm so sorry about slapping you."

"No worries. I'll get him back."

He ended the call, downshifted, and skidded to a stop on the shoulder just before the I-279 ramp into Pittsburgh. He opened the iCloud website and entered the information. If this was a desperation move, Nick may not have deactivated Jack's phone.

The connection was slow and Ike chided the phone. "Come on."

The map appeared and Ike immediately recognized the location of the green dot: the old marina adjacent to the poker-night house. He slammed the car into first and ripped through each gear. Without police interference, he'd be there in fifteen minutes. He'd already decided he wasn't stopping even if the entire force was on his tail.

He raced down I-279 and along the Allegheny River on Highway 28. When he crossed the river on the Highland Park Bridge, he looked upriver for any boat traffic. The black water was smooth and undisturbed. Running the traffic light at Butler Street, he skidded hard through the intersection and turned north. He paralleled the river until he reached the entrance on the left.

Slowing, he killed his lights and made the turn. To his left was the lock road leading past the bed-and-breakfast and the poker-night house. To the right was the water-and-sewer maintenance facility, then the old marina. Ike checked his phone. The dot still hovered over the marina.

Ike coasted the Shelby past the long maintenance building and onto the narrow decaying road to the marina. Hugging the trailered boats for cover, Ike prowled closer to the river and stopped. Weak floodlights mounted on the dilapidated repair shop illuminated a black Hummer. Ike reached into the glove box, slipped out his gun, and slid one into the chamber.

He left the car and crept along the boats until he had a view of the old dock. Several speedboats sat quietly in the slips. He could hear the water lapping against the piers, and the cold air nipped at his hands. Leaning around the bow of the last trailered boat, he could see three larger cabin cruisers at the end of the dock. The dock lights were burned out and all three cabins were dark.

Then his eyes detected movement on the middle boat. It was an old wooden cabin cruiser with peeling paint and faded wood trim. A dark shadow moved to the stern and released a line, and the engine roared to life. Ike darted around the boat and sprinted down the dock. The figure turned and Ike caught a glimpse of a gun as it swung in his direction. He dropped to the dock as it fired. The wooden planks splintered in front of him. He rolled, then crawled over the gunwale into an uncovered speedboat.

A smaller figure darted onto the deck as the cruiser pulled from the slip. *Jack.* "Ike! That's Ike. Ike come help me. Please, Ike." Someone dragged Jack back into the cabin.

Ike yelled over the engine noise. "I'm coming, Jack."

The cruiser had cleared the slip and was heading upriver fast. Ike scrambled to the dash of the speedboat but found no key. He hammered the glove box open and threw the contents onto the deck. Still no key. The next boat was covered. He leaped onto the cover and ripped it from the boat's edge as if he were opening a sardine can. Slipping into the opening, he peeled the cover from the windshield. There was no key in the ignition. Ike cracked the glove box with the butt of his gun and it popped open. As he watched the cabin cruiser head upriver, his fingers found the keys. He jumped to the deck, untied the boat, and checked the cruiser's location again. It was nearly out of sight, heading around the bend in the river.

After leaping back in, he jammed the key into ignition and the Sea Ray roared to life. It was dark, but with the diffuse light from the city along the shoreline, he could see the heavy wake of the cruiser. Ike weighed his options and chose to keep the pressure on. Falzone was a coward and the boy was still his leverage. He'd keep him alive as long as Ike was close. As Ike traced the wake around the corner, the crack of a gunshot followed by splintering fiberglass made him slow and swerve. They raced upriver, Ike weaving between shots.

They passed the Fox Chapel Marina on the left and Ike continued to close. Ike knew this part of the river well. He'd been up and down it with the DeSantis brothers in their old man's ski boat every summer in high school. Sycamore and Nine Mile Islands bounded a narrowing of the channel ahead.

He swung away from shore as the dark outline of Sycamore Island loomed ahead. After the cruiser curled around the island, its engine was killed and it disappeared. Ike looped farther out and spotted the cruiser beached on the northeast side of the island. Beaching alongside would be deadly, but Ike was out of options and Jack was running out of time. Ike headed into the island and beached about fifty yards away, keeping his gun aimed at the cruiser

Ike jumped onto the muddy shoreline and waited. A faint light glowed from the cabin cruiser's windows, but there was no movement. Ike had spotted only one car back at the marina, but Nick might have help. He'd have to take his chances.

He weaved to the tree line that covered his advance to the cruiser. Beached, the bow towered over the shore by about ten feet. The stern still floated in the river and the swim deck was easily accessible, but the glow from the city lights on either side of the river would give anyone onboard a clear view of his advance.

He dashed to the bow and waded into the water, working his way down the side toward the stern. The river was cold and Ike could feel the current tugging at his legs. After reaching the swim deck, he swung a leg up and climbed aboard using the stern as cover. A round could easily pierce the thin, rotted wood. He had to move quickly.

Peeking over the stern, he spotted the door to the cabin. Leading with his gun, he worked his way there. Standing aside, he pushed the door open. He spotted Nick holding a gun to Jack's head and took aim, slowly descending the steps.

"Well, well. The great Ike Rossi in person."

Ike kept his aim at Nick's head. "You okay, Jack?"

Jack shook his head.

Ike watched Nick's eyes and aimed right between them. "You don't need him, Nick. Let him go."

"Ah, that's where you're wrong. This young lad could end my life."

"Your life's over anyway."

"That's the problem with you jocks. You always overestimate your abilities. My life has only just begun." He pulled Jack closer and shrank behind him. Ike lost his angle

Jack's eyes brimmed and shifted between Ike and the gun at his own head.

"It's gonna be okay, Jack."

But that didn't ease Jack's fear. Instead, Jack's gaze darted over Ike's shoulder and his eyes grew wide.

Nick seemed to relax. "What took you so long?"

Ike started to turn, but the blow to the back of his head dropped him to his knees. Then he hit the floor. In an instant, everything went white, then black.

CHAPTER 52

IKE GUESSED THIS was a dream with a terrible ending. He floated freely, defying the laws of gravity, while a growing dread made his flight more difficult. The first thing Ike heard was crying. It drifted through a thick gray fog and echoed somewhere in the distance. It was higher-pitched and beckoned Ike like a siren's call. He was supposed to be there—to do something.

As the crying grew loud, his head throbbed. His hands and feet were paralyzed. In seconds, he'd entered the no-man's-land between sleep and consciousness. He forced his eyes open and saw Jack, his hands behind him with his feet bound to a thick chain, crying. He followed Jack's gaze to Nick and the thug who'd tried to run him off the road.

"Glad you could join us," Nick said. He stood resting his foot on an upside-down bucket with his gun hand draped casually over his knee. Ike shook his head to clear it and noticed the pungent smell of gasoline. He spotted the red can in the thug's hand and it all came rushing back. The bar, the explosion, Maria. This was the asshole who destroyed Rossi's.

Ike's feet were bound to an anchor chain that connected him to Jack, and his arms were bound behind him. He yanked at the ties, trying to break free, to no avail.

Ike recognized the dilapidated cabin of the old Chris-Craft cruiser he'd chased to Sycamore Island. They were against the back wall of the rope locker under the bow, the farthest from the stairs. The locker door had been removed and Ike could see all the way to the cabin door. The window in the door had been broken out, and Ike could see into the darkness. The seating and tables had been ripped out, but the old rotting galley between them and the cabin door remained. Trash and rags covered the floor, and the anchor chain holding them was coiled in the corner facing the galley, atop a rusted anchor. He noticed that the boat gently swayed. They were afloat, not beached.

"Ike? Ike, are you okay?" Jack asked, his lips quivering.

"I'm good, Jack. Hang in there."

"Oh, how nice," Nick said, shoving the bucket from under his foot. "However, it's not going to be okay, Jack. You see, I can't have you around yapping away about what your father did or didn't do and trying to put me in the gas chamber. And Mr. Rossi here never should have stuck his nose in our business." He stepped past the thug and circled closer to Jack.

"So, you did kill Tom Cole," Ike said.

Nick twisted and faced Ike. "Not me," he said, grinning. He pointed to the thug. "Him." Nick faced the man. "Isn't that right, Roustabout?"

Jack's eyes hardened and he stopped sniffling. "You killed my dad?"

The big man just chuckled. He was thick, with eyes that shifted with discipline and precision. Ike had seen that look before, and with the thug's rigid posture and the fact that he'd handled explosives, Ike wondered if he was ex-military. Ike spotted a tattoo low under his neck that said he was an ex-con. It didn't matter. When Ike got free, he'd be sure he was ex-alive.

Nick paced back to Jack. "It wasn't hard, kid."

"No, it was brilliant," The Roustabout said. "An injection into the neck with succinylcholine and a cylinder of carbon monoxide masked to his face, and I had all day to set the sad scene in the garage."

Jack lunged at the man and the anchor chain snapped him back to the ground. "I'll kill you. I'll kill you!"

Ike worked hard on his wrists while Nick and The Roustabout enjoyed their taunting. The ties were tight and the material wasn't plastic. It felt like a smooth synthetic rope of some type. The technique he'd taught potential kidnapping victims would be useless.

Nick poked the nose of the gun into Jack's red face. "You're not gonna kill him, but he has a treat in store for you and mister football." Nick stood and paced back across the small cabin again. "And you know what the best part is?"

"Yeah," Ike said. "The best part is you're an asshole who can't do anything without your daddy's money."

Nick slammed the butt of the gun into Ike's cheek. The fragmenting pain was instant and the force knocked Ike backward on his arms. More time to work them—and it took Nick's attention off Jack. Ike could feel the blood running down his cheek, and still he couldn't get any slack in the rope.

"Now, where was I?" Nick said.

The Roustabout jiggled the gas can.

"Oh, yeah," Nick said. "We have an old wooden piece of shit, and we have two depressed souls tied to an anchor chain with PVA rope that will dissolve in the river water minutes after they drown. Their burned bodies may or may not be found after they're ground up in the boil and backwash on the downstream side of the lock's low-head dam. You'll either drown or burn—or hopefully a little of both. With a bit of help, they may even conclude that a washed-up football hero who failed to help a condemned boy decided to end it all for both of them."

Ike eyed Jack. Jack's anger had faded and his face turned pale. He began to shake. Ike hated that Jack was experiencing the terror of expecting death. He turned back to Nick but spoke to the boy. "Don't worry, Jack. They'll never get away with it."

Nick slowly handed his gun to The Roustabout, grinning. The Roustabout kept the gun on Ike. Nick deliberately turned his face to The Roustabout, who wound up and hammered Nick on the cheek. Nick turned back to Ike, grinning, with blood running down his face.

"We will now."

The Roustabout sloshed the can again and headed up on deck.

"Just on the deck. None in here," Nick said. "And set the timer for five minutes. I want our guests here to experience a slow burn before they drown." He laughed and followed the Roustabout onto the deck, slamming the door behind him.

Ike heard the gasoline hitting the deck as the footsteps creaked and then faded and stopped. The smell of gasoline intensified.

Jack was crying.

"Jack."

Jack ignored Ike.

"Jack! Look at me. Now!"

They both flinched when they heard a pop on deck. Then Ike heard the crackle of the flames.

"We'll get out of this, Jack," Ike said. "You have to stay with me here. I need your help."

Smoke seeped under the door. Ike scanned the narrow cabin for anything that could cut the poly rope. Jack stared at the flames coming through the cabin door, his eyes wide with terror. Ike could see the fire through the portholes. The entire deck was engulfed and their only exit would be through the fire.

"Jack. Kick the chain, Jack. Into the cabin."

Ike yanked the chain tied to his legs and pulled it into the doorway of the locker. Jack caught on and helped kick the chain into the threshold. There were about five feet of chain between them, and Ike wanted Jack to be behind him, farthest from the flames that were now devouring the yellowed lacquered walls of the cabin on all three sides. The thick acrid smoke dropped like a curtain. They had a minute or two—no more.

Ike coughed. "Get behind me," he said. With his hands bound behind him, Jack struggled to inchworm past Ike. Ike would not watch Jack die first. "Watch this."

Ike dragged his arms under his legs and cleared his ankles, lifting the chain bound to his legs. Now behind Ike, Jack slipped the chain beneath him, cleared his feet, and held the slacked chain in the rope binding his wrists. That would give Ike precious seconds if his plan worked.

The flames raced across the floor of the cabin and hit the chain. The boat groaned and Ike felt the floor quake. The boat was splitting. Ike kicked the chain farther into the fire.

"Yeah. That's it!" Jack yelled. "Manganese and iron. Mg and Fe. It's very conductive." The chain was galvanized and Jack recognized it. A true genius.

In that moment, Ike saw the periodic table.

"The key," he said. "The key to the clues."

"What?"

The thought energized him. The heat seared Ike's face and feet. Still, he leaned forward, gritting his teeth. Fire engulfed the distant part of the chain, and the boat lurched again. The links resting against the painted wall of the galley smoked, and Ike pushed his wrists against the chain. He smelled the hair on his hands burning. He growled in pain but kept the poly rope against the hot chain. He yanked his wrists apart, breaking the rope, and he pulled his blackened hands back. The boat heaved and the hull parted beneath them. Freezing water rushed in. Ike sucked in deep a breath. The water smothered him, and the anchor chain rocketed Ike toward the bottom of the river. Ike's mind locked on one thought. *Save Jack.*

CHAPTER 53

IKE HIT HARD on top of the anchor and the chain on the river bottom. He reached for his legs and clawed at the poly rope. He fought the current pushing him backward. The rope softened and he found the knot. His lungs burned as he untied his feet. Once he was freed from the chain the current ripped him away, but he caught a few chain links with his hand. Jack was at the other end of the chain and Ike was running out of breath.

Hand over hand he followed the chain in the dark water and collided with Jack's limp body. Finding Jack's hands, he tried to yank them apart. Pain ripped through his chest as he fought the urge to take a breath. He yanked Jack's hands again and felt the rope give. On the third try, he ripped Jack's hands free and grabbed for his body before the current could rip them apart.

Jack's body weather-vaned in the current, but Ike held him tight and moved hand over hand to Jack's feet. When he felt the rope, it was mush, but Ike was passing out. Rage fueled him and he tore Jack's ankles free. The current ripped them downstream, but Ike held on to Jack and kicked off the river bottom with his last shards of energy.

He wasn't sure how, but he found himself at the surface, gasping for air and holding Jack's limp body in one arm, flailing with the other. He sucked in the cold air and cleared his head. Ahead in the darkness, he saw the lock and dam racing closer. They were in the center of the river, and in the dim light he spotted the Highland Park Bridge just ahead. The bridge pylons were their only chance before the current swept them over the dam. He'd have to catch a pylon with one hand. Alive or dead, he was not letting go of Jack. Ahead, the flaming debris from the boat crashed into the dam.

Ike clawed at the water with a fury he'd reserved for the last twenty-two years. The current dragged him toward the center of the dam, but he fought back toward the dark pylon, still fifty yards away. Jack's body was still limp.

Ignoring his instinct that it was too late, Ike shoved down a lump in his throat. Now just ten yards from the pylon, he struggled to stay on a line that would get them there before the current swept them over the dam. He kicked hard and reached for the concrete base. His fingers caught a gritty edge and he pulled them both onto a narrow foundation just above the waterline. Ike cradled Jack, flipped him over, and, with three desperate thrusts, tried to clear his lungs. His lifeless body did nothing.

"No, God!"

Ike thrust his hands against Jack's back again. On the third try, Jack coughed and threw up. Tears flooded Ike's eyes. After flipping him over, he rubbed hard against his skin to warm him. Jack's eyes were glazed and his pupils dilated. He'd been at least four or five minutes without oxygen, and Ike hoped his brilliant mind hadn't been destroyed. Jack's body jerked and his eyes focused on Ike.

Ike smiled and wiped his eyes. "You made it. You made it."

Jack raised his head. "The periodic table?"

Ike was laughing and crying at the same time as he hugged Jack. For an instant, he let go the leaden revenge he harbored for Falzone.

In the distance, he spotted the River Rescue Patrol boat. It cleared the lock and headed their way. Ike knew from his time with the Pittsburgh Police that the boats were like floating ambulances. It would have an EMS team and one police officer on board. As the spotlight swept over them, Ike waved.

"You're going to be fine, Jack. You did great."

But Ike knew this wasn't the end. For him, it was just the beginning. As the boat approached, all he could think about was destroying Falzone and the Roustabout. When the boat pulled aside, two EMTs steadied the vessel against the pylon while a third reached for Jack.

Ike handed Jack to them. "Take care of him. He was underwater and without oxygen for at least four minutes."

Ike stepped onto the boat and they carried Jack into the cabin. The police officer driving asked one of the EMTs to take the helm. Then he pulled his gun and aimed at Ike's chest.

"On the deck."

Ike raised his hands. "What's the problem, Officer? I rescued the boy."

"On your knees."

Ike dropped to his knees, but he knew he couldn't waste time in custody. Falzone's next steps were unpredictable, and despite his confession to them, Ike would still need hard evidence to clear Jack.

"No. No. He saved me," Jack said from the cabin.

"I'm Ike Rossi. I—"

"I recognize you. We just got a report from the boy's grandparents that you beat his uncle and kidnapped him yourself."

Ike started to get up.

"Stop," the officer said.

Face down on the wet cold deck, Ike said, "You're making a mistake."

Jack was now sitting up on the gurney. "My uncle took me."

The officer glanced back at Jack, then back to Ike. "We'll straighten this out at the station. Hands behind your back."

Ike complied. The officer held his aim on Ike and pulled out his cuffs as he circled behind Ike.

"No. He saved me!" Jack said.

As the officer lifted his head to reply, Ike rolled and swept the officer's feet from under him. The back of his head hit the deck hard and Ike ripped the gun from his hands. "Sorry about this—but you're wrong. I need to finish what I started."

An EMT next to Jack moved toward Ike. Ike swung around, stepped back, and put both the officer and the EMT in his field of fire. "Stop. Nice and easy." Ike directed the EMT with the gun. "Move back to Jack and stay there." Ike bent over and cuffed the officer, then aimed at the EMT at the helm. "Take me over there," he said, pointing back to the old marina. He put his foot in the officer's back and pinned him to the floor.

Ike was soaked, cold, and exhausted. He needed warmth.

"You. Give me your jacket and your shirt. Now," he said to the EMT who'd tried to approach him. The EMT removed his coat and shirt and tossed it to Ike as the boat pulled to the riverside edge of the wooden dock at the marina. Ike wanted to disable the radios, but while he'd give himself a little lead time, he'd also cut off any medical help for Jack. With the Shelby, he was sure he'd be gone before any patrol officers responded. He stepped off the boat.

"Ike. No, Ike. Stay with me."

Ike kept the gun on the crew and shoved the boat from the dock with his foot. "These are good people. They'll take good care of you." He nodded to the helmsman. "Drive away slowly and leave the officer on the deck. I'll be watching."

The boat pulled into the river and headed downstream to the lock. When it was out of sight, Ike tossed the officer's gun into the river. Sprinting to the Shelby, he ripped off his wet shirt and shrugged on the dry one and the coat. He jumped into the Shelby and raced down the narrow road to the traffic light at Washington Boulevard. He pulled his phone from his soggy pants and was surprised when the screen lit up. He put it in airplane mode and turned off the Wi-Fi. He tossed the phone onto the seat and jammed the Shelby into first. When the light turned green, he floored it.

CHAPTER 54

IKE CREPT ALONG the back roads as if on a razor's edge. He cut through East Liberty and entered Bloomfield the back way. He glanced at the iPhone on the seat. It held the keys to end Jack's troubles, and within a few minutes he was sure he'd unlock the secrets that would free Jack and dismantle the Falzones.

With each block, his eyes darted left and right, checking the dark side streets for any sign of a patrol car. He was certain the call had gone out, and after assaulting the police officer, he'd be a target of every cop in the department. Detection now meant failure. And failure meant yielding control back to the Falzones.

After a few turns, he arrived at the gate to DeSantis Auto Repair. Vinny and Danny lived above the shop. It was after midnight and he hoped their Saturday night antics had fizzled out. Vinny was a year older than Ike and Danny a year younger. They'd met in grade school but bonded in high school over their mutual love for cars.

Ike rolled down his window, reached for the rusted speaker, pressed the button, and waved to the security camera staring down on him. The gate jerked and then rolled open. He loved those DeSantis brothers—no questions. He pulled through the lot, with cars lined up on either side. Ahead, one of the three white shop doors lifted and Ike saw Vinny standing to the side, barefoot and wearing a Metallica T-shirt. His long black hair was wet and tucked behind his ears, belying the fact that he was forty-two. Ike drifted into the shop and Vinny closed the door behind him

"What's up, Ikey boy?"

Ike grabbed his phone and stepped out of the car. "I need to hide this for a while," he said, patting the roof of the Shelby. "And I need to borrow another car."

"No problem. Take the Charger." Vinny met Ike at the front of the car. "I know you didn't take the kid."

"You know about that?"

"Yeah. You're all over the news."

"What'd they say?"

"Said some rich guy said you slugged him and took the kid. Said you were troubled and he wouldn't be surprised if you ended yourself and the kid."

"He made that up. That asshole took Jack and I caught up to them on that boat. He tried to kill us, but we got away."

"Told you, Danny," Vinny yelled across the shop.

While Vinny was strong, Danny was built like a tow truck: square-shouldered and thick-necked with biceps that looked like they'd been carved from marble. His lips were thick and his teeth were darkened, stripped of their enamel. When he trudged across the shop floor like a gorilla, Ike was thankful they never played against each other in high school. Danny was the fiercest middle linebacker he'd ever seen at Peabody High. His career ended one winter when he broke his leg hanging Christmas lights while traveling hand over hand from the second-story gutter. But he'd quickly become the best muscle-car mechanic in the tristate area.

Danny came up to Ike, punched him in the arm, and grinned. "Yeah, I didn't think you had the balls to do something like that."

"Thanks, guys. Hey, can I use your office for a minute? Gotta look something up on the computer."

"No problem, dude. I'll log in so they can't trace you." Vinny led Ike to the office in the corner of the shop, flipped on the light and logged on. He opened the key holder on the wall and tossed Ike a set of keys. "Just don't wreck her. Danny worked on her for three months." He left and closed the door.

Ike pulled out his iPhone, removed his jeans, and set them in front of the space heater in the corner. He dropped into the ripped chair and grabbed the pen and notepad next the greasy desk phone. Opening his mail, he read the last message from Tom Cole he'd received while they were on the boat:

74+8+45–1+19

16+73+22+8+7 15

34+2–1

16+1+33–16+7+7+8+7

Surprised by the number of expressions in this e-mail, he jotted them down at the bottom of the blank page. He noted that for the first time, there was a number with no plus or minus sign. He simply wrote down that number next to the expression. Then he flipped through each e-mail from Tom Cole and wrote down each clue in the order he'd received them with a space between each one:

3–53+8x2+19

4+3–53+8+74

9+13+30–7+8+7+99

53+25–7+47+10–7

74+8+45–1+19

16+73+22+8+7

34+2–1

16+1+33–16+7+7+8+7

Then Ike turned the phone off and pulled up the periodic table.

Periodic Table of the Elements

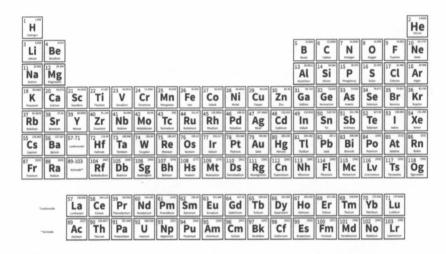

As soon as he saw it, the simplicity and genius of the key were obvious. For someone named after Isaac Newton, he wondered why he didn't see it sooner. The table was arranged by atomic number. He remembered from high school science that the numbers represented the number of protons in an atom. Hydrogen had only one, helium had two, and so on. He quickly assigned each number in the first expression he'd received from Tom to the corresponding element:

3–53+8x2+19

Li–I+OX2+K

Then he did the implied subtraction and multiplication of the letters:

LOOK

He leaned back and eyed the word. Look at what? Could this be the distraction he'd thought it was initially? Or the start of instructions? He repeated the process for the second clue received:

4+3–53+8+74

Be+Li–I+O+W

The letter math was easy on this one:

BELOW

He understood what Tom Cole was doing and he raced through the rest of the translation, putting each deciphered word below each expression on the page. The message puzzled him.

3–53+8x2+19

Li–I+OX2+K

LOOK

4+3–53+8+74

Be+Li–I+O+W

BELOW

9+13+30–7+8+7+99

F+Al+Zn–N+O+N+Es

FALZONES

53+25–7+47+10–7

I+Mn-N+Ag+Ne–N

IMAGE

74+8+45–1+19

W+O+Rh-H+K

WORK

16+73+22+8+7 15

S+Ta+Ti+O+N

STATION 15

34+2–1

Se+He–H

SEE

16+1+33–16+7+7+8+7

S+H+AS-S+N+N+O+N

SHANNON

Ike knew the seismic image held the key. Based on Bobby Scott's description of Tom's breakthroughs, he was sure the clarity and detail of the three-dimensional image of the target zone at over ten thousand feet deep would reveal detail never seen before. But Tom's clues said to look below the image—not at the potential oil reservoir but below. And whatever that image was, it was enough for Nick Falzone to kill Tom Cole and probably his half brother, Patrick.

The last clues were a dichotomy of logic and insanity. Workstations were the computers geophysicists used to do their seismic interpretation. They'd process the millions of pieces of seismic data generated by the seismic crews. Tom's process was state-of-the-art. And once the data was processed, a three-dimensional image was generated. The image Ike needed—the one that could possibly free Jack—was on Workstation 15.

The balance of the clues cut like a ripsaw against reality. If Ike interpreted Tom's meaning properly, Shannon Falzone either had the workstation or would willingly access it. Joseph Falzone's only daughter, who'd ripped Ike apart with zeal and skill beyond anything he'd seen from her father, was the person Tom Cole was asking him to contact.

Why would she help destroy her family? How would Ike get to her? Every cop in town was looking for him. He had a face and the kind of notoriety that most people remembered. And with Jack's kidnapping, the security around the Falzone family would be formidable.

Ike let go of the paper and let it flutter to the desk. It was clear, Tom Cole suspected the authorities were involved. Otherwise he could have sent this information directly to the police or the FBI. By encoding it, he'd ensured anyone else intercepting it would have difficulty deciphering the code. He'd anticipated his own death, and the thought of that realization, knowing how close he was to Jack, peeled a layer from Ike's heart. Ike remembered Lauren's reference to seeing Ike's name on an entry in her brother's planner well before his murder. Tom Cole had trusted Ike with his son's life before he died based solely on Ike's reputation.

Ike stepped to the heater and slipped his jeans on. He grabbed the paper off the desk, creased it hard, and shoved it into his back pocket. He snatched the keys to the Charger and remembered Jack's limp body in his arms just an hour ago—and the smug look in their would-be killer's eyes. The anger paced inside him, clawing at the bars his mind had wrapped around it. It was time to let it out and to unleash it on the Falzone empire.

CHAPTER 55

IKE CRUISED DOWN a deserted Wilkins Avenue weighing his approach. Shannon Falzone was his only hope, and getting her to turn on her family would be difficult. But he knew that within the Falzone family, loyalty could be a fragile thing. He'd sensed a chasm between Shannon and Nick and had seen it firsthand with Brenda. And Ike had information that could fracture the strongest bond.

It was one a.m. and the streetlights reached out and illuminated the Charger every fifty yards or so before he plunged back into the darkness between them. He'd cut through Shadyside and into swanky Squirrel Hill North. The restored '69 candy apple-red Charger was like a beacon in this neighborhood. It screamed for further investigation. So he ditched the car in front of an old apartment complex, two blocks from Shannon's townhome, and approached on foot.

Her address had been easy enough to find on the DeSantis computer, but Ike knew that after Nick's lies and thinking the kidnapper was on the loose, her father would have insisted on additional security. The street was dark and the light from the large homes on deep lots was blocked by giant elms and oaks that dwarfed the road. While a few cars were parked on the curb, the street was mostly deserted. Ike examined each car as he approached, looking for the security team. Thick landscaping consumed the cluster of townhomes. Two colonial brick buildings, housing three townhomes each, faced the street. A concrete drive split the buildings and led to six other units in the back. With no cars in front, Ike counted on someone watching the townhome from a car in the driveway. Shannon's unit was in the back. Ike chose to tangle with the landscaping, enter from behind the unit, and avoid the driveway.

Emerging from the shrubs between the units, he spotted a dark sedan directly in front of 515 Dogwood. The townhome would be alarmed, and Ike knew Shannon would have to let him in voluntarily. If he spooked her, she'd trigger the alarm and the two-man security team would be upon him in seconds. He'd have to gently spark her curiosity, and he'd have to do that from her backyard.

Working his way around the fences, he moved behind Shannon's unit and clawed his way over the six-foot cedar fence. The yard was dark, but Ike noticed light bleeding through the drapes of a second-story window. Based on their previous meeting, he assumed she was probably up working on the PR mess she'd have to deal with in the morning.

Ike only had one option, and while it was a cliché, it might just work. The entire plan hinged on three things: doubt about her own family, Tom Cole's apparent trust in her, and Ike's read of her incessant curiosity. If Ike was wrong on any point, he'd be easily trapped and captured.

He pulled the creased paper from his pocket and opened the page in his left hand. He bent down in the darkness and scooped a handful of pea gravel from the flower bed. Gently, he tossed a pebble against the lighted window. There was no movement. He repeated the toss and the pebble ticked against the glass. In seconds, the drapes stirred and Ike held the paper up in his left hand, with his right hand out to the side.

Ike knew the next seconds would be the difference between a nightmare and Jack's chance at freedom. The drapes wiggled again and then went limp. Ike held his pose despite wanting to assume a sprinter's position facing the fence. Then light appeared through the backdoor window, and the mounted porch lamp came on. The door cracked open, but Ike held his pose in the middle of the yard. He saw the gun barrel emerge first, then Shannon with a security system fob in her other hand.

"What the hell are you doing here?"

Ike had carefully chosen the next words. "I have a message from Tom."

Her rigid stance loosened, and Ike saw a glaze cover her eyes.

"He sent them to you?"

Ike held out the page. "He did." He dropped his arms to his sides and wondered how she knew about the mysterious e-mails. "Can we talk? I'm not armed and you can keep that gun aimed at my head." He nodded toward the car in front of the townhome. "I can't get caught yet."

Shannon glanced over her shoulder and back at Ike. "Okay. But come in slowly."

Ike walked to her and she held her ground until he was a few steps away.

"Slowly now. Come inside." She kept her aim on Ike and held the gun like she'd fired it before.

They moved down a narrow hallway and into the kitchen. Shannon walked around the island and Ike stopped on the opposite side, facing her. The thick plantation shutters covering the front windows were closed.

Ike laid the paper on the counter. "You knew about these?"

"No. I knew he was setting something up. He told me it was better if I didn't know the details."

"You and Tom were closer than I thought."

Despite holding him at gunpoint, Ike could see the tenderness in her eyes. "We were closer than anyone knew." She caught herself and tightened her grip on the gun. "Why did you kidnap Jack?"

"I didn't. Your brother did. Then he and his henchman tried to kill Jack and me. I saved Jack and left him with River Rescue."

Fury swept across her face like a hurricane making landfall. Her gun hand shook. "I knew he was lying. About everything."

Ike gently turned sideways in case the gun fired. "Can you drop that thing to your side? I'd hate to take your brother's bullet."

Shannon relaxed and lowered the gun.

Ike slid the paper closer to her. "Do you know why he set up these messages?"

He watched her eyes scan the paper. She tilted her head back. "The seismic." But then, as if discovering a ticking bomb, her expression widened. "Tom. This was about Tom."

It wasn't a question. She'd found the truth on her own. Ike would have to make the final link for her.

"Nick's muscle told us how he killed him before they set the boat on fire."

The hardness in her voice returned. "Nick, again."

Ike nodded. "I'm sorry, but there's more."

Shannon looked as if she knew what Ike was about to say. He didn't want to say it, but he had to. "I think he may have killed your brother."

The gun came back up. "You're lying." He waited as the wetness returned to her eyes. He could tell she knew the truth. The words were just too hard.

"Think about the timing. The data was processed by Tom, then your brother died just before Tom did."

"Patrick," she said softly. Tears rolled down her cheeks. She looked off somewhere in the distance.

Ike waited, knowing piling on wouldn't help this process.

She looked back at the note. This time Ike saw rage. "Patrick." Her gaze bored into the note.

He asked the question again. "Did you know that Tom set up the e-mails?"

"All I knew was that he said he was entangled in something he was trying to exit. Now I know what it was. He said it was better if I didn't know."

"Did you take that to the police when he died?"

"Yes. Detective Cassidy. He was at my father's house and I told him. I was certain Tom wouldn't do that to himself or Jack, but Detective Cassidy convinced us he killed himself."

"You and Tom, was it ser—"

"Serious. Yes. I know how it sounds with me being Brenda's half sister. But it just happened." She set the gun on the island. "We decided to keep it secret. Brenda was whacked out on coke—no telling what she'd do—and I was certain my father would demand I stop."

Ike wasn't there to judge her. He had little room to criticize based on his past choices. But they needed to get the image. "I need your help getting to the seismic image. Does Workstation 15 mean anything to you?"

Shannon nodded. "It's a computer on the eleventh floor."

"Not on the twelfth?"

"No. It's not part of the Minuteman prospect. It's a machine used by one of the Gulf of Mexico teams. One of Tom's people showed me some of their work on it. The machine belongs to Cole's Seismic, and the person operating it was contracted to the team."

"I need you to get me in there."

She looked back at the clues. "Why does Tom say, 'Look below'?"

"I don't know. But whatever it is, it won't be good for your family."

Shannon looked up at Ike with a hardened vengeance. "I'll take care of that."

"Can you get me inside? To the workstation?"

"I'll need something from you."

Ike was surprised by the negotiation. "Okay. What?"

"Let me be the first to tell my father and my brother."

"Done."

"Tom asked me to help you. That's the least I can do. But I don't know the passwords."

"That's okay, I'll get Bobby Scott to help us."

"Let's go," she said, heading for her purse on the kitchen counter. "You stay here and I'll let my father's security team know I'm going to the office. You meet me in the garage. You can hide in my backseat."

She walked to the front door and left, and Ike wondered what she'd do. She'd just found out her brother *and* her lover had been murdered. The words *loose cannon* came to mind. But he sensed she was a woman of her word. And that word would destroy one family and save another.

CHAPTER 56

IKE'S TRUST IN Shannon grew with every turn of her SUV. She'd concealed him in the back of her Range Rover as they left her townhome. She'd followed his instructions perfectly as they lost her security tail and trekked out to Southpointe to pick up a bleary-eyed Bobby Scott. By three a.m. they were on the nearly empty Parkway West. They headed through the Fort Pitt Tunnel and over the bridge into the city. Shannon's serious and determined demeanor told Ike he had a chance, but something was missing, like a gap in the bridge that led to her family's destruction. Ike hoped the discovery they were about to uncover would solidify her commitment.

Shannon swiped her card past the card reader for the security gate to the executive garage at Falzone Center. Ike and Bobby sat up in the backseat when they'd cleared the gate. She parked and they all headed to the executive elevators. Ike spotted the cameras, but at this point it didn't matter. A blue-blazered woman stood in the shadows at the lone elevator in the corner of the garage. Shannon had assured him that she knew the head of the overnight security team well and that access, despite Ike's robbery attempt, wouldn't be a problem.

"We okay, Jo?" Shannon asked as they approached the woman.

She eyed Ike and he recognized her from the lobby. "It's all good, Ms. Falzone. Just three on the graveyard shift, counting me. They're all good."

"Thanks, Jo. I'll owe you. Don't tell anyone else we're here."

Jo grinned. "No worries, Ms. Falzone. We ladies need to watch out for each other."

Once in the elevator, Bobby asked about the legality of the whole thing, explaining for the fifth time that his company couldn't afford to lose its leader again. Ike assured him that when they saw the image, it wouldn't be an issue. Shannon surprised Ike by adding that she'd attest to authorizing Bobby to access the data and he'd be off the hook regarding their confidentiality clause. It wasn't her offer itself that surprised him but what it implied about the depth of her relationship with Tom.

The executive elevator went straight to the fifty-second floor. Shannon led them down a long mahogany hallway that was the artery connecting the plush executive offices. She used her key card and pushed through a set of glass double doors to a bank of elevators. When the door opened, she turned to Ike.

"I'll get you to the eleventh floor and show you where the workstation is, but I need to get something up here when we're done. Then we should go."

Ike nodded and followed her into the elevator. They rode to the eleventh floor, which was a carbon copy of the twelfth. She led them down the hallway and stopped at the door marked *Gulf Team*. Swiping her card, she unlocked the door and then guided Ike and Bobby inside.

The room was filled with cubicles and rimmed with private offices. At the far end, Ike could see colorful maps and charts hung on the back wall marking the team area for the space. Shannon walked halfway down the right side and stopped at an outside office.

"Here it is. Workstation 15."

Two large flat screens sat side by side on a worktable with a key-board centered in front of them. To the left, Ike noticed the thick stubby tower connected to the monitors.

Ike gently corralled Bobby into the office. Bobby eyed the computer and then looked back at Ike. "Workstation 15."

"Can you access it?"

Bobby nodded, seemingly muted by his nervousness. He dropped into the chair and powered up the computer. He deftly worked through the log-in screens and began scrolling through the folders on the right-hand monitor. Ike knew the processed three-dimensional image could be a large file. Bobby had promised he could spot it by the file size. Ike watched the folder names race down the screen. The further Bobby scrolled, the more Ike felt his lungs tighten. It had to be here.

Bobby stopped the scrolling and pointed to the screen. "What about this?"

The folder name was "Jackknife."

"Might be. Open it."

Bobby clicked, and in seconds an image opened on the left screen. The background was black, but the image was a colorful array of hues covering what looked like a photograph of the surface of a lifeless planet, with a large mound surrounded by crevasses and pinnacles.

"No. Sorry. This block is in the Gulf of Mexico," Bobby said as he clicked the image away and the screen went dark.

He went back to the folders and continued scrolling. Ike spotted a fragment of another folder name that started with *Jack*. "There. Stop."

Bobby froze the screen.

"There. 'Jack and Jill.'"

Bobby opened the folder and again pulled up one of the images. This one looked like a high-definition picture of the wall of the Grand Canyon. Layers laid one atop the other, varying in color from red to blue to green and black. The layers were jagged and interrupted by thick vertical lines that seemed to form wedges across entire sections. Ike knew they were faults that ran miles into the earth. But this cross section was clearer than any other Ike had seen. The depth scale on the left showed that the cross section ran from eight thousand to sixteen thousand feet deep.

Bobby leaned closer to the screen. "This is it," he whispered. "Minuteman."

He scrolled down and stopped. See these facies here," he said, pointing to a bright blue line marking the top of one of the rock layers that rose and formed a giant hill. He moved the cursor just below the blue line to a thick continuous black layer that ran over the entire structure. "My God, that's probably all oil, and it covers all three blocks. Fifteen thousand acres." He moved the cursor to the depth reading on the left side of the image. "Sixteen thousand feet. That's the Jurassic Age."

Bobby looked at Shannon. "Congratulations. That's one of the biggest oil reservoirs I've seen offshore. The question is, why kill for it? Your family controlled the blocks. You'd have most if not all the oil under them."

Ike could see that one word cut her. *Kill.* Kill Tom and kill Patrick.

She stayed stoic, staring at the screen. "The clue Tom sent said look below the image."

Bobby turned back to the screen and scrolled down the image, looking deeper into the earth. As the image scrolled up Ike saw it. Bobby did, too, and he stopped scrolling.

Ike's mind didn't accept what his eyes were seeing. "What is that?"

Interrupting one of the layers was a series of what looked like perfectly formed pyramids. They went on for miles, according to the scale Bobby pulled up.

Then Ike's eyes froze on another image farther toward the right side of the screen. It was long and continuous, a quarter of a mile. Over four hundred yards. The image was sleek and looked like an elongated bullet.

Bobby saw it, too. He turned back and ogled Ike. "That can't be."

"Still Jurassic?" Ike said.

"Yes. I think so."

"What is that?" Shannon asked as she stepped closer to the screen.

"I'm not sure, but it shouldn't be there," Ike said.

Shannon dropped even closer to the screen. "It looks like pyramids and a craft of some sort. Buried—" her eyes widened when it clicked in her mind. "Buried by eighteen thousand feet of rock over millions of years!"

"Exactly. What are structures that are clearly engineered doing in a formation that was deposited one hundred and fifty to two hundred million years ago?"

For a moment, they all just stared at the screen. Ike knew nature wouldn't form those structures. He also knew that man had first appeared on earth between one hundred thousand and three hundred thousand years ago. That left one easy answer. One he'd never really given much credibility.

"This is crazy. Someone was here one hundred and fifty million years before we were."

"You're kidding, right?" Shannon said.

"Afraid not. Tom's processing is very precise. Now I know why they'd keep this covered up. They'd never get a permit to drill here until the U.S. government figured out what this is."

"Can you pull up the 3D image of that layer?"

"I'm sure Tom put that together. Let me see if I can find it."

Bobby had the image in less than a minute. The image looked like an aerial view of a large town covered with pyramids, with the long ship in the center.

Ike turned to Shannon and pointed to the screen. "This is the reason why Nick killed them." Shannon dropped her head and cried silently for a moment. Then she stopped and lifted her head. "Remember what you promised me."

"I've gotta get this to Jenna and maybe the FBI."

"Not until I talk to—"

Shannon's phone chimed. She read the message.

"They're here. Somehow my father or Nick found out we were here. Jo says they just pulled up out front."

Ike grabbed Bobby's shoulder. "Download the file."

"I'll meet you upstairs," Shannon said and headed for the door.

Ike grabbed her. "Where are you going?"

Ike could see the pain in her eyes.

"I've got to get something."

She pulled free and ran from the office.

Ike turned back to Bobby. "You got it?"

Bobby had his hand on the portable drive. "It's almost there."

Ike ran from the office to the doorway of the Gulf Team Section and checked the elevators. Three of the indicators showed the first floor and the last showed the fifty-second.

"We gotta go," Ike yelled.

Bobby barreled out of the office with the drive in his hand. Ike sprinted to the elevators and pressed the button. One of the elevators began to move from the first floor. Either it was empty and coming to pick them up or the Falzones and the security team had made it to the elevator and they were sitting ducks.

When Bobby arrived, Ike took the drive. His body crackled with anticipation as he tucked it into his pocket. He envisioned Jack's face when he was freed. A protective force swelled inside. They'd have to kill him before he surrendered it.

Ike watched the indicator count the floors. When it hit the ninth floor, he pulled Bobby back behind him against the wall. He unleashed the aggression he kept chained inside and readied for a fight, but then noticed that another elevator started to rise from the first floor. He pulled Bobby to the first elevator door as it arrived. It opened and Ike yanked Bobby in with him and hit "52." The elevator rose as if in molasses. Ike guessed the Falzones were headed to the eleventh floor first. He hoped he wasn't wrong. Either way, they'd quickly head to the fifty-second.

When the elevator opened, he headed to the glass double security doors. Shannon had left one wedged open with a notepad, and they headed down the long hallway. Ike stopped when he spotted Shannon in an office, glued to the computer screen. Tears streamed down her face.

"They're coming," he said.

Ike's warning jolted her from the screen. She grabbed the keys from her desk and tossed them to Ike.

"Go to the garage and take my car."

"What about you?" Ike said.

She glared at the computer screen, condemning it like a criminal. "I have to take care of this. Go."

CHAPTER 57

SHANNON HAD HEARD the footsteps all her life. They had a comforting rhythm and always carried the promise of something special. Most of her most precious moments had been with her father at the office. Now the rhythm of those steps was panicked, like she imagined a war drum would have sounded. Instead of joy, she hoped his footsteps carried an explanation for the terrible revelation on the screen. She exhaled and fortified herself just before he appeared in the doorway. The pain had aged his face and worry radiated from his eyes.

"What's going on, Shannon?" He edged into her office. "Why did you shake your security?" He looked like he already knew the answer.

Shannon tapped all her courage. "First, I have a question for you, Father."

A storm of indignation flashed across his face at the sudden insubordination. "Answer me."

Shannon redoubled her challenge and pointed to the screen. "I came to check the flight log."

"Where is he?"

"Who?"

"Rossi."

"He's not here."

A second set of footsteps, running, closed in on her office. Joseph's most trusted bodyguard, Kent, burst in. "The eleventh floor. She went to the Gulf of Mexico team room."

Joseph furrowed his brow, and she could see him instantly make the connection. "No. No! What did you do?" He turned to the bodyguard. "Tell Cassidy he has it. He's got the file." The bodyguard bolted out the door and down the hallway, yelling into his phone. Joseph turned back to Shannon. "You have no idea what you've done."

"Perhaps. But it's what *you've* done that may be my biggest problem."

"What are you talking about?"

Shannon crossed her arms, partly for effect but partly for comfort. She was about to find out if the man who'd given her everything was someone else. "On the night Patrick died, you took the plane to Houston."

"Of course I did. He was my son."

She turned the flat monitor toward him. "This says you left at 9:40 that night."

Joseph eyed the screen and refocused on Shannon. "Okay."

Shannon watched her father's face. Ever since she was a kid, she could read his heart in his expressions. As she readied to ask the next questions, she knew she was about to jump off a ledge into a bottomless ravine. "We didn't get the call from the Harris County sheriff until after eleven."

Joseph froze, and the split second before he spoke was enough to formulate a lie. "I had them wait until I made sure it was Patrick."

Shannon's core quaked and her red-hot disdain overflowed. "You didn't. Tell me the truth."

He held his resistance, but then his shoulders dropped as if surrendering to a truth neither of them wanted to hear. Sadness shaded his demeanor, and seeing that, she started to cry. This would be too hard—but it had to happen.

"The truth, Father." She felt her jaw quiver under the weight of the words about to cross her lips. "Did you kill Patrick?"

Her father looked like he'd been shot. "No. I didn't. I would never hurt Patrick."

"Then what happened?"

Her father scrubbed his face in his hands and sat on the corner of the desk. He didn't look at her but instead out the window at the cresting dawn. "I've always tried to do the best for all of you. I thought if I loved you all enough, we'd have the family I never had growing up. Nick and Brenda had it hardest, and that's on me. But you and Patrick brought such joy and pleasure to me. It was like a do-over. A wonderful do-over. I did everything I could to help Brenda, but she was too far gone. And I held on to Nick, hoping my love and support would overcome his anger. All I wanted was for all of us to be a family."

Shannon saw where this was headed. "What happened? Was it Nick?"

He dropped his head. "It got away from me before I could fix it."

"You knew. You knew Nick killed my brother?"

A tear leaked from his eye. "You have to know how much I loved Patrick. And it roiled my soul when I got the news."

Shannon found herself standing and punching her father on every word while he halfheartedly shielded himself from her blows. "So—you—helped—cover—it—up."

"Nick is my son, too. And his troubles were my doing."

His justification broke something inside her. He'd taught her everything. She'd always seen him as her hero. But all that admiration and love died in that instant.

"Where is he?"

Joseph shared a look with Shannon she'd never forget. Surrender, betrayal and guilt. He knew this was an end. His body relaxed. "He's headed to the plane—out of the country."

Shannon grabbed her purse and shoved him away as she passed. "I never want to see your face again." She ran down the hallway fully expecting to be stopped. But the guards let her pass all the way through the lobby. Jo stood dutifully and, with tears in her eyes, held the door. Shannon stopped and squeezed her shoulders, then left the building for the last time.

CHAPTER 58

DESPITE THE RISK, Ike knew there was nothing more important than this. Getting hard evidence into Jenna's hands would weaponize her case. On the other hand, he was sure that getting caught by the Pittsburgh Police might be the end. The thread of corruption ran through the force, but he knew neither its beginning nor its end. Bobby promised to get word to Jenna about the rendezvous, sidestepping Ike's risk of using his phone.

He'd picked the location based on a single childhood memory. In seventh grade, a friend had invited him to a party at the North Park skating rink, north of the city. The rink sat at the north side of the park, relatively isolated. With kids back in school and no ice at the outdoor rink, the facility would be abandoned. And at six a.m. on a Sunday, the whole area would be deserted. He'd snaked out of town, avoiding well-traveled roads and any police cruisers looking for him. He hoped no one had yet tied him to Shannon's Land Rover. That advantage was fleeting, so once he was out of the city, he jumped onto I-279 and raced north toward the park.

Ike cut through Wexford and entered the park from the north. He followed the narrow road divided by a single yellow line. The thick forest leaned from both sides. It provided both concealment and restriction. If detected, Ike had little maneuverability and no exit. The sun was still below the horizon, and the milky haze of first light seeped through the trees. The morning air chilled Ike's cheeks, but the cold air slicing through the open window sharpened his senses. Without the benefit of GPS, he followed the signage toward the rink. When he spotted the A-frame roof of the lodge, he slowed, then stopped short of the clearing that held three basketball courts and the parking lot.

Through the trees, Ike saw Jenna's BMW parked nose-in adjacent to the narrow footbridge leading to the rink. Ike scanned the remainder of the lot and asphalt loop in front of the rink. It was deserted, and the only sound was the chatter of the forest coming to life. Satisfied they were alone, he parked next to the BMW. He could see the front of the rink now but saw no sign of Jenna. About a dozen thick flagstone and concrete columns were spaced evenly along the front of the building. Each supported a heavy beam connected to the large overhanging roof. The roof's shadow and the columns provided concealment for anyone awaiting Ike.

One by one, he examined each column and didn't see Jenna. He checked the area one last time and got out of the Land Rover with the drive wrapped in his hand. Keeping his eyes cycling back and forth along the front of the building, he crossed the footbridge and stopped just short of the two center columns. Without a weapon, he felt exposed. He could see the front doors in the recessed entry but no sign of Jenna.

The sudden chill on his arms was the first sign of trouble. Instinctively, he backed away until Jenna abruptly appeared from behind a column. Her mouth was taped and her hands were pinned behind her. Her eyes cut to her right, warning of someone behind the column. The gun appeared next and then pressed against her temple. Ike saw the black gloved hand gripping her bicep. Then Vic Cassidy stepped from the shadow.

"I'd stop right there," he said. A satisfied grin swept across his face. "I knew if I followed her, I'd find you."

Ike angled himself to Cassidy, shrinking his target as he inched closer. Cassidy would get one shot off before Ike reached him, but right now that shot would be into Jenna's skull. "I knew you were getting your sport-coat money somewhere."

"No further or you'll be picking up her head in a baggie." Cassidy moved behind Jenna with the gun still against her skull. "And it's a lot more than sport-coat money, you dumb jock." He pressed Jenna's head forward with the gun barrel. "Now let's get to it. Toss the drive to me."

Even with her head pressed downward by Cassidy's gun, Jenna shook her head. But Ike had no other options. He wasn't close enough to reach Cassidy before he fired. And Ike assessed the likelihood of that happening at 100 percent if he tried. He also knew there was a 100 percent chance they'd both die once Cassidy got the drive. He'd have to sacrifice Jenna for Jack. He thought about her murder in the eyes of her family and it rattled through the hole in his own heart. She was still shaking her head, and Ike readied himself without Cassidy's detection.

"Well?" Cassidy said.

Ike saw Jenna's signal. She'd given him permission to do the unthinkable to save Jack.

"Drop it!"

Ike recognized the voice before he saw Mac emerge from the darkness at the side of the building. Cassidy didn't flinch. He kept the gun on Jenna's head. "Mac, my old friend, I'm glad you're here. Now your prodigy can hear the truth."

Mac stepped toward Cassidy, snapping his gun hand straight at him to make his point. "Shut up."

Cassidy kept the gun pressed against Jenna's skull. "He doesn't know you were the one who started all of this."

Cassidy's words jolted Ike, but Mac's silence ripped through him like a hunting knife.

Cassidy looked at Ike from behind Jenna's head. "Oh, the football hero looks like he's going to cry. Well try this on. He was the reason your dear mommy and daddy bit it."

Mac held the gun steady, but Ike felt the admission in his silence.

Ike's rage spun up like an ICBM and he nearly crushed the drive in his hand. "You, Mac?"

Cassidy swung his head back to the other side of Jenna's head to see Mac's reply. But a blast splintered the cold air and Cassidy's face atomized in a red mist. Jenna lunged to the left and Cassidy's body hit the concrete floor.

Ike ran to her. And while staring at Mac, he pulled the tape from her mouth and hands. Mac's gun was now pointed at them.

"What now, Mac? Is this it? All those years—all those times were just lies."

"No, Ike. Those were real. I never meant for your family to get involved. I'll never forgive myself for what happened to your mom and dad."

Ike pressed Jenna behind him. Any bullet from Mac's gun should hit him, not her.

Ike held up the drive. "You'll have to kill me to get this."

Mac kept his aim. "I know, son. I'm so sorry. Your mother didn't know what she was doing. Please know that I love you and your sister." In one fluid movement, he swung the gun into his mouth and fired.

"No." Ike ran to Mac's contorted body. The rage had abandoned him, replaced by a weight he'd felt twenty-two years ago. "Oh, Mac. Why?" He couldn't look at what was left of Mac's face.

Jenna stepped beside Ike, slipped off her jacket, and covered Mac's head. Ike felt her hand on his shoulder. "Ike?"

He looked back at Cassidy, dead on the concrete. Cassidy and Mac had been in on it together. He'd been fooled most of his life. Suddenly, reality seemed elusive. But one fact was clear: neither Mac nor Cassidy started this. Ike stood and looked at Jenna. "Are you okay?"

She nodded.

Ike handed the drive to her. "Call the FBI in Virginia. Not the local SAC. That will give you oversight and insurance against their involvement if there is any." He scanned the bodies on the concrete. "I can't be here. I've gotta end this."

Jenna gave Ike a trembling smile as if reading his mind. "Be careful."

He walked to Cassidy's body, picked up the Glock and pulled Cassidy's iPhone from his bloody sport coat. He lifted Cassidy's lifeless hand and pressed the thumb on the home button. The phone unlocked and he disabled the auto lock. The last text message was from Nick Falzone, received ten minutes ago. *Falzone Hangar PIT.* Ike showed the message to Jenna, and then his eyes drifted from the phone to Mac. After one last look at the man who had meant everything to him, he left Jenna and sprinted to the Land Rover.

CHAPTER 59

IKE RACED ALONG Hangar Road on the northwest side of the airport and prayed he wasn't too late. It had been an hour since Joseph had texted Cassidy and Ike wasn't sure they had enough evidence to justify Jack's shooting. As much as Ike wanted to put a bullet between his eyes, Nick Falzone would have to be captured so he could pay. Pay for Jack's father, pay for Maria, pay for Patrick, and even pay for Mac.

As he rounded the turn into Falzone Enterprises' hangar, the parking lot was empty. Ike rammed the chain-link security gate, skidded to a stop at the front entry, and jumped out. Immediately, he heard the whine of jet engines from the other side of the facility. He hit the glass doors hard and bounced back. Two shots from the Glock broke the lock and shattered the doors. An alarm sounded as he sprinted through the reception area and spotted the sleek G5 through the wide glass windows waiting just outside the open hangar doors. Ike raced through the door to the hangar and skidded to a stop when he saw them.

Shannon had her back to Ike, but he could see Nick over her shoulder. Her gun rigidly targeted Nick's head. Nick's hands were in the air and two bulging leather duffels sat at his feet. She flashed a glance over her shoulder but snapped her attention back to Nick.

"You know our deal, Ike. He's mine," Shannon said.

Ike stepped next to her and scanned the empty hangar over the barrel of the Glock. "I can see that," Ike said, settling his eyes and his aim on Nick. "Just remember, there is no payoff for Jack with this pig dead."

"Listen to your new friend, sister."

Shannon moved her second hand to the gun. "I'm no longer your sister. You killed the only real brother I had."

Nick seemed relaxed. "You may think that, but you'd be nowhere without me. While you were still in junior high, I was building our family's business. Your brother was going to destroy all that. I did what was necessary to preserve the Falzone legacy." His smug demeanor permeated every word. "That idiot thought it was our social responsibility to report the findings on the seismic survey to the damn government. Then, when Cole found out, he brought it to me and said the same thing. He and Patrick were buddies, so I had to end him, too. The only mistake I made was underestimating the kid. Never thought he'd blow Tanner's head off." Nick laughed halfheartedly as if reacting to a bad joke. "Guess Tanner did too good of a job setting up his daddy."

Ike could see the anger vibrating in Shannon's arms. A gargantuan battle appeared to be consuming her from inside. She'd obviously never killed in cold blood before, but the devil was winning ground with every word spewing from Nick's mouth. She could pull the trigger any second.

Ike knew he needed to say something to deflect Shannon's vengeance. "You talk like you still make the rules," he said. "That time is over. You'll go to jail and lose everything. And you'll rot in prison for the rest of your life for killing Patrick and Tom. Better yet, I'll execute you here and now and save us all the trouble."

"You need me alive. You won't shoot." Nick dropped his hands, and both Ike and Shannon prepared to fire.

"You may want to reconsider your position." Nick turned back to the idling jet and yelled, "Bring her out."

In seconds, Erin Falzone appeared in the doorway.

"Mom!" Shannon screamed.

Erin's face boiled, like a teakettle left on too long. A thick cluster of fingers gripped the back of her neck and shoved her against the doorjamb. The Roustabout appeared and pressed a long hunting knife against her throat.

"You see, when Cassidy told me you had the seismic image and he knew where you were headed, I thought I'd need an insurance policy. And with Joseph at the office looking for you, my answer was right in front of me." Nick stepped closer and Ike thrusted his Glock into Nick's face. "You might get a shot off and kill me, but my friend will probably have dear old Mom deboned by the time you get him."

"Let her go," Shannon said.

"Uh, no," Nick said. "You two are going to give me your guns." He reached out with both hands. "Grips first, please."

Ike eyed the Roustabout. From this distance, a head shot might miss and Erin would be dead. From the corner of his eye he saw Shannon drop her aim.

"Ike, please," she said, holding the barrel of the gun. "She's my mother. She's all I have now."

Nick reached for Shannon's gun.

Ike knew surrendering his weapon was a death warrant for both of them. "Nope," Ike said, holding his ground.

Nick looked back to the plane. "Show him."

The Roustabout slowly ran the blade over the side of Erin's neck, lightly slicing the skin. Blood ran down her neck.

"No." Shannon pulled Ike's arm down and Ike complied.

Nick took Shannon's gun, then Ike's. He tossed Shannon's gun toward the jet and it skittered along the shiny gray floor. "Bring Mommy dearest here," he said. He pointed the Glock at Ike and Shannon.

Ike watched the Roustabout force Erin down the stairs. She was crying now, and Ike didn't know if it was the pain from the cut or the pain of waiting for her daughter's death. He peered into the cockpit and saw the pilot staring straight ahead.

"They're with me," Nick said. "So don't get your hopes up."

The Roustabout dragged Erin to the hangar entrance. Then without warning a shot rang out and the Roustabout crumpled to the ground. Nick flinched but pressed the gun to Ike's head. Erin froze, then ran out of sight past the right side of the hangar door. Then, like a zombie, Joseph walked around the corner alone, with a gun hanging at his side.

"Why the hell did you do that?" Nick said.

"Is Mom okay?" Shannon asked.

Joseph kept walking directly toward them. "She's with Kent. It's time to end this."

Nick smiled, still holding the gun on Shannon and Ike. "That's what I was just telling them."

Joseph stopped a few feet from Nick. "No. That's not what I was talking about. I've put the family through enough for you just to give you the family I never had."

Ike heard sirens in the distance growing louder by the second. Nick was running out of time and Ike knew that desperate men, trapped by time, were as unstable as nitroglycerin.

Nick held his focus on Ike and Shannon but addressed Joseph. "I won't go back. It's gone too far now. It will be the end for me. You can't do that to me. You're my father."

Joseph pointed his gun at Nick.

"I'm sorry, son. Let them go."

The sirens were on the other side of the hangar now.

Nick's face transformed into a mask of destruction. In a split second, he tightened his aim on Shannon and closed his eyes. Ike shoved Shannon and heard two blasts. He hit the floor atop her. He turned to see Nick on his back, blood gushing from a chest wound. Joseph still held his gun in firing position. Ike could read surrender in Joseph's eyes. Standing up, Ike felt a trickle of blood down his arm. The bullet had nicked his arm. He helped Shannon to her feet.

"You okay?" Ike asked.

Shannon stared down at Nick. She seemed to realize Nick's death wasn't enough to bring Patrick back.

Ike walked to Joseph and gently slipped the gun from his hand just as the FBI SWAT team flooded in from all sides. They ordered Ike to drop the gun and lie facedown on the floor. Shannon and Joseph were ordered to the floor, too.

"Get these two up." The order came from a fed with a close-cropped haircut who was dressed in a tie and a sport coat. Ike assumed he was the special agent in charge for Pittsburgh.

Ike was helped to his feet and stood face-to-face with the SAC. "Jenna Price cleared up the kidnapping mess. She wanted me to tell you Jack is okay." Then he turned to Shannon. "Miss Falzone, are you okay?"

"My mother. How's my mother?"

"She's being treated around front, but she'll be okay."

Several SWAT team members boarded the jet and the engines immediately wound down.

Joseph remained facedown and cuffed, with two SWAT team members standing over him.

Ike stared down at Nick's blood-soaked body and wondered how much of Jack's case had died with him.

He felt Shannon at his side. "Thanks, Ike."

Ike nodded but kept looking at Nick.

"We can piece it together," she said as if reading his mind. She looked back at her father.

"Get him up," the agent ordered. The two SWAT team members pulled Joseph to his feet

"Wait," Shannon said.

She stood face-to-face with her father. "I'll never forgive you. You know that."

"I do. I'll never expect you to." He looked past her at Nick. "I did the right thing here."

Shannon nodded, then reached for her father and hugged his neck.

Over her shoulder, he looked at Ike and said, "I'll do the right thing for Jack, too."

CHAPTER 60

IKE SHIELDED MARIA from the gathering crowd and pressed toward the entrance to the courthouse. The radiant sunshine warmed his back and drove off the late September chill. It was Friday at four p.m. and police barricades deflected the rush-hour traffic for a three-block radius. The judge had scheduled the hearing for after normal hours to ensure complete control.

With Ike's help and Joseph Falzone's revelations, a tsunami of arrests had rocked the city since the FBI swarmed the hangar last Sunday. Conspiracy, fraud, bribery, and conspiracy-to-commit-murder charges electrified the online news outlets and fueled record newspaper sales that hadn't been seen since the Pens won the Stanley Cup for the third time. Ike's sense of justice was bolstered by the swift arrests that sidelined two judges, the DA, the assistant police chief, three detectives, and a dozen attorneys. The U.S. attorney had already assigned two assistant U.S. attorneys to help her prosecute the cases. But Ike suspected none of those cases were the focus of those gathered in and around the courthouse today. They were part of the #FreeJack movement that had gone viral on Wednesday when an exposé of the conspiracy was published in the *Pittsburgh Post-Gazette*.

Ike reached the door of the courthouse and the young sheriff's deputy at the barrier blocking the entrance stiffened when he recognized him. The deputy moved the barrier and Ike guided Maria to the doorway. The deputy stopped Ike and shook his hand. "A pleasure, Mr. Rossi. A real pleasure."

"Thank you, Deputy."

Maria gave Ike an I-told-you-so smile as they entered the courthouse. He'd denied her claims that he was a hero. After clearing the metal detector, they climbed the stairs to the second-floor lobby. The lobby was crowded but Ike easily spotted Jenna above the bobbing heads of reporters from around the country. When she spotted him, she smiled and waved him toward the ropes at the base of the stairway. Leading Maria by the hand, he met Jenna at the stairs. She hugged Ike and then Maria.

"Are you ready?" Jenna said.

At that moment, a feeling of weightlessness swept over Ike. He was immersed in a joy that required no thought or analysis.

"We're more than ready for this," Ike said, nodding to the deputy holding the rope open and smiling. They ascended the cavernous stairway and Jenna led them down the empty hallway, past a bailiff, and into the courtroom. It was packed like church on Easter and the crowd hummed with excitement.

Jenna led them to the first row and the only two vacant seats in the gallery, just behind the defendant's table. Maria sat first and Ike took the seat on the aisle. Just ahead, he saw Ed, Lauren, and Jack sitting at the table facing the bench. When Jenna reached the table, she bent down and whispered to Jack. He turned, smiled, and gave Ike a thumbs-up. Ike returned the gesture. He'd spent two days at the hospital with Jack and had seen him each day after. Their connection fed Ike's thoughts about starting his own family. Thoughts he'd buried with responsibility and the pain of his loss. His few attempts at relationships had convinced him his picker-outer was broken. But Jack and Lauren had changed that view.

Ike looked across the aisle and saw Shannon and Erin Falzone in the front row. Shannon leaned forward, smiled, and nodded to him. Erin, with her neck still bandaged, gave him a small two-fingered wave. Shannon had already taken the reins of the family business and was cooperating fully with the authorities. A team of U.S. scientists from Los Alamos, NASA, and several universities were now studying the seismic data and images. The images hadn't been released to the public. Ike guessed the government wanted to understand what it had before it made a statement.

Donna Martin, the court clerk who had helped Ike, took her seat and waved to Ike. Her boss, Judge Palmeri, had been assigned the case after the arrest of Judge Nowicki. Without Donna, Ike knew they wouldn't be there. He threw her a kiss and she laughed.

The bailiff ended her smile. "All rise."

Judge Palmeri swept in with his robe flowing like a superhero's. He mounted the bench and tapped the gavel.

"All right. Just a warning—no outbursts from the gallery will be tolerated. Anyone doing so will be immediately removed from my courtroom." He picked up a stack of papers. "I've read Ms. Price's motion to dismiss and the prosecutor's response. Ms. Price, please proceed."

Jenna rose but stayed at the table. "Your honor, statements and confessions received this week from the conspirators have been provided to the court and the acting district attorney. Late yesterday, after our motion was filed, the FBI released the results of a search of Mr. Franklin Tanner's residence." Jenna handed a copy to the clerk, who passed it up to the judge. "I'd refer Your Honor to page two of the summary. Paragraph two states that the legal briefcase carried by Mr. Tanner on the morning of his death contained alarm codes for my client's guardian's home, a layout of the house, a detailed accounting of her schedule, and instructions that indicated an associate of Mr. Tanner, a Mr. Derek Thorne, aka The Roustabout, was to enter the residence that day and kill my client." Jenna paused and allowed the judge to read the page.

The judge arched both eyebrows as he read, then set the report aside.

Jenna continued. "Since my client's actions were in self-defense, the defense moves for dismissal of all charges."

The judge zeroed in on Jack, and Ike's tension spun up again.

"Mr. O'Donnell?" the judge said without looking away from Jack.

Ike felt sorry for Assistant District Attorney O'Donnell, who'd been promoted to acting DA less than seventy-two hours ago and deposited into the middle of a Category 5 shitstorm.

"Your Honor, we've read the report and the statements, and considering the circumstance, we believe there is insufficient evidence to proceed and are dropping all pending charges against Mr. Jack Cole."

A rumble ripped through the crowd and Judge Palmeri slammed the gavel twice. "Quiet."

The gallery quieted and Judge Palmeri settled his attention back on Jack. "Will the defendant please rise?"

Jack eyed Lauren and Jenna, then wobbled to his feet. Jenna and Lauren joined him.

The judge's eyes softened. "Young man, you have what I hope is a long life ahead of you. Do you understand that going around shooting people is wrong?"

"Yes, Your Honor. I only did it to save my aunt and me."

"Okay then." Judge Palmeri focused on the gallery. "You're free to go, Jack. Court dismissed." He hit the gavel once and left the bench.

The gallery roared and Ike dropped his head into his hands. In an instant, the nineteen-year-old deep inside himself didn't feel so alone anymore. Maria wrapped her arms around him

"You did it," she said. "You did it."

Ike raised his head and hugged her. He felt a tap on his shoulder. He turned and saw Jack standing in the aisle. The bailiffs were herding the crowd out of the courtroom.

Jack's smile widened and Ike saw the joy of freedom in his eyes. Ike opened his arms and Jack hugged him, then looked up. "Will you walk me to our car?"

Lauren stepped around the bar and took Ike's hand in hers. "I'll never be able to repay you for what you've done." She sparkled with delight and leaned in and kissed him on the cheek.

"You already have," Ike said as he wrapped his arm around Jack's shoulders and started down the aisle. As they walked, escorted by two deputies, Jack and Ike took turns planning outings to the science museum, a Pens game, and dinner at Jack's. They descended the granite stairway to the second-floor lobby. The press had been cleared out and the lobby was empty. When Ike spotted the mural of Justice, he stopped and faced it. Jack stopped beside him and Ike felt his gaze. Ike had never studied it over the years, because justice held no meaning for him here. It was just a hollow promise. But today it felt different. Lady Justice sat atop her throne, comforting a woman with one hand and gripping a thick sword in the other. An angel floated to her right, casting out two perpetrators while an angel on her left cradled a victim. Just twelve days ago, on the thick wooden bench in front of them, he'd met Jack.

"Who's that lady?" Jack asked, examining the mural.

"She's Lady Justice," Ike said, staring at her.

"Justice. I guess that's what we have?" Jack said, grinning.

Ike faced Jack. "That's what we have today. You ready to go out there?"

Jack nodded.

Ike turned to Jenna. "You ready, Counselor?"

Jenna offered Ike her hand and he shook it. She held it and said, "Thanks, Ike. Thanks for everything."

"Congratulations, Counselor. I hope you and your dad can handle all the new business coming your way."

Jenna laughed and turned for the door. Across the lobby, Ike noticed Shannon and Erin eyeing Jack and him. Ike silently looked at Lauren and nodded in their direction. She gently put her arm around Jack and began to walk over to them with Ike.

"Congratulations," Ike said to Shannon. "CEO?"

"Yes, we've got a lot of work to do to repair the family name."

Erin nervously eyed Jack with tears rolling down her cheeks. "I'm sorry about all of that. I hope you know we weren't part of any of it," she said, opening her arms. Ike was surprised when Jack looked to him for his blessing. Ike smiled. "Go hug your grandmother."

Ike noticed Jenna by the stairs to the doorway.

Jenna tilted her head toward the door. "We have to go."

Shannon handed Ike her card. "I'd like you to consider joining us. Great perks and we can sure use the help. Name your price."

"I appreciate the offer," Ike said. He looked back at Maria. "But we have our own rebuilding to do." Ike, Jack, and Lauren joined Maria and walked down the stairs to the door.

"Here we go," Jenna said. She opened the door and Ike saw a sea of people. The cheer was as loud as he'd heard in any stadium and it echoed off the stone façades of the building. Men, women, and families filled the streets. Ike knew many were victims of the same system who'd probably got the same taste of closure he had through Jack's case and the ensuing arrests.

Jack's mouth dropped open, and then he grinned. A makeshift podium at the base of the steps held a bouquet of mics. As Jenna made her way down, Ike's phone vibrated. He pulled it out and saw he'd received an e-mail. He opened the app and shivered when he saw the sender. It was Tom Cole. He read on:

53

3–53+8+23+26–9

25–7+39

16+8+7

Tears welled in his eyes. He turned to Jack and handed him the phone. "It's for you."

Ike watched Jack's eyes scan the message. He knew Jack could translate it as fast as he did, and Jack's face filled with joy.

53

I

I

3–53+8+23+26–9

Li-I+O+V+Fe-F

LOVE

25–7+39

Mn-N+Y

MY

16+8+7

S+O+N

SON

THE END

If you enjoyed *The Victim of the System*, leaving a review will let other readers know how much you loved it and would be greatly appreciated.

To learn more about new books and exclusive content, sign up for my author mailing list and receive *The Sunset Conspiracy* free: http://eepurl.com/chqYJj

Keep reading for a riveting excerpt from *Genetic Imperfections*...

A NOVEL

GENETIC IMPERFECTIONS

STEVE HADDEN

November 8th, 1996 ...

PROLOGUE

CONNOR XAVIER WELLINGTON'S young life wasn't supposed to end this way. There was supposed to be a breakthrough— a dramatic last minute cure produced by his father's three year heroic effort at Rexsen Labs. But David Wellington knew he'd failed. There would be no cure, no last minute miracle, only suffering and guilt.

The decision to move Connor into Saint Michael's hospice in Irvine was his first admission of failure to his son. David sat anchored next to his wife in the dim glow of the single fluorescent light above the bed. Although they'd been at their eight-year-old son's bedside every minute for the past week, he could barely recognize him. Pale and melting into the white sheets, Connor's blue eyes peeked from underneath his eyelids as the morphine drip did its work and masked the pain of the multiple infections and failing organs, courtesy of the genetic imperfection that prevented his stem cells from developing into healthy blood. His thick brown hair was gone and replaced with a Dodger's bandanna. He hugged his baseball glove while his mother, Linda, stroked the bony outline of his legs.

David forced a smile and did his best to hide what they all knew was about to happen. Connor's eyes lifted for a moment.

"Daddy, are you still working on my medicine?"

The question cut through David's heart. He glanced at the green numbers on the monitor counting down his son's last heartbeats and reached deep for another smile. He rested his hand on his son's head.

"Yes, Sport. We are still working on it."

David looked at Linda and detected no evidence of blame. He'd quit his job at the investment bank in New York, moved the family to Newport Beach and dumped his seven figure bonus into a fledgling biotech firm in the hopes of finding a cure. But the Director of Research had delivered the bad news a week earlier. Without detailed mapping of the human genome it was like looking for a needle in a haystack. Despite three years of research, testing and prayer, David could do nothing to stop his young son's killer. He'd failed and God didn't care.

Connor sucked in a deep breath and sighed. "That's good Daddy."

Connor closed his eyes and David heard the rhythm of the monitor slow. He reached for his son's hand. Connor's skin was still soft, but the warmth was fading. David heard Linda sob and she rose next to David, leaned in and kissed her son's forehead. David squinted to force the tears back into his eyes. "No, no, *no!*" he begged through his clenched teeth. The monitor stopped and then warbled a continuous tone that David would never forget. Connor Xavier Wellington, the boy who was going to play third base for the Dodgers, was gone. The nurse quietly slipped in and shut down the monitor. Linda hugged her son and wailed. David wiped his eyes, stood and stared at Connor's limp body, and then grabbed the glove at his son's side and dropped it into the trash can on his way out the door.

Fifteen years later ...

CHAPTER 1

DAVID WELLINGTON FOUND it hard to believe an imperfection could be so profitable. He didn't tolerate them in his minions, hated them in his women, and acted as if he had none himself. After fifteen years of excelling at corporate politics and pretending he cared about his diseased and dying customers, the payoff of his life was at hand.

He celebrated, sipping his Hennessy X.O. from a Waterford crystal glass. His Gulfstream V, Rexsen Lab's newest corporate jet, streaked southeast from San Francisco to Newport Beach 29,000 feet above the chilly Pacific. Equipped with soft leather chairs, inlaid wood cabinetry, and state of the art LCD screens, he was surrounded by the luxury he expected.

The forty-five-year-old CEO had just completed the last of the road shows promoting the most talked about initial public offering Wall Street would launch this year. The FDA was on the verge of approving his company's first gene therapy treatment for leukemia. The institutional investors had been duly impressed with Wellington's plans and the solid backing of the company's seventy-five-year-old founder, Adam Rexsen, who slept peacefully in the seat across the aisle. Rexsen Labs would go public within two weeks, and David Wellington would become Newport Beach's newest billionaire.

As Wellington tilted the glass and anticipated the warm burn of the last sip of liquor, he felt the plane shudder and dive to the left. The crystal snifter was ripped from his hand as a blast roared through the cabin. Instinctively, he grabbed the leather armrests, locked his arms and braced himself. A yellow oxygen mask fell from the headliner and bounced wildly in front of his face. Paralyzed, his terror refused to allow him to let go and grab the mask. He pushed back hard on the armrests and fought the invisible force trying to rip him out of the seat.

He assessed the situation instantly, and the conclusion echoed in his head.

I'm going to die.

He struggled to get a breath as smoke filled the cabin. The jet's nose plunged steeper into the dive. For the first time since a genetic imperfection took the life of his son, he thought of his soul and its ultimate keeper.

Images flashed through his mind. Hell—Sister Theresa had described it as eternal flames and agony. "Heaven or hell—it's your choice," the nun had said.

For the past fifteen years he'd chosen money. It was how he kept score. Money was his drug of choice, and he was addicted. Suddenly, he understood the nun's warning. He'd already made his choice.

He felt the jet's fuselage start to vibrate. The black smoke thickened. His inner voice summed up the fruits of his time on earth.

I am selfish, greedy, and alone.

He knew the voice; it was the one he never listened to. He tried to ignore it, but it was strong and uncontrollable. Expensive leather briefcases and crystal glassware smashed into the bulkhead. He looked to the right at the old man who wagged his head in disbelief.

Adam Rexsen, the founder of Rexsen Labs, was about to die, but *he* had dedicated his life to finding a cure for cancer. *His* life had served a purpose, he'd said so just minutes ago; his wealth was simply a by-product. At the time, Wellington pitied the old man and thought the world had passed him by. Panicking, he now wished he'd listened to his mentor years earlier.

Purpose! What's my life's purpose? Shit, it's too soon, too soon!

Wellington had seen no purpose in his life, at least not since he'd stood by helplessly and watched Connor wither away. His son's disease was the reason he'd started with Rexsen. He had left his lucrative future as an investment banker and signed on with Adam Rexsen and a team of scientists who were focused on a genetic cure for cancer. He'd decided he'd dedicate his life to finding the sinister imperfections in the human genome that caused so much pain and heartache. But despite being a brilliant businessman with a Harvard MBA who'd built Rexsen into the leader in genetic oncology research, he could do nothing to stop his son's killer. After three years of research, testing, and prayer, Connor died. God abandoned him in his time of need, he'd concluded, so he'd decided to return the favor. From that point forward, his only purpose in life was to use Rexsen to fill the hole in his heart with money and distract his mind from the pain with self-indulgent behavior.

Now, facing death, an avalanche of guilt and regret for the life he'd lived engulfed him. He struggled to look aft at Jeff Reese. Minutes ago, Reese had said he was grateful not to have to fly commercially from San Francisco with the peons. Now Wellington could barely see him through the smoke, as Reese fumbled with a family photograph taken from his wallet. The most money-hungry man he knew, who'd just presented the medical breakthrough of the century to the most powerful investment bankers and investors in San Francisco, stared at the picture.

Fifteen years ago, Wellington had lost his chance at a happy family. After his son's death, his marriage broke apart. Wellington had given up—sold out. His current wife was the founder's daughter and nothing more than a good career move—a means to more money.

He glanced at Reese again. Reese cried and clutched the picture. Wellington cried for himself.

I miss my son! God, why did you take my son!

He hadn't invoked God's help in fifteen years. Now his name was attached to every thought he had. His body was crushed into the seat as the nose of the jet lifted.

"Multiple system failure. Can't make Vandenberg. Prepare to ditch. Prepare to ditch!" the pilot screamed over the cabin's speakers.

Please God, it's too soon, too soon!

He choked as the thick black smoke burned his lungs. He was smothered with the smell of burning oil and rubber.

"Brace for impact! Brace for impact!" the co-pilot squawked.

"Oh, God!" he screamed out loud.

Wellington was driven into the bulkhead, face first. His ears throbbed from the roar, and he gagged on several broken teeth. The whole cabin tumbled: the ceiling, the window, the floor and the ceiling, again and again. Still belted in his captain's chair, Wellington's face smashed against a bloody stump of jagged flesh and bone, dangling between Adam Rexsen's shoulders.

He felt a sharp pain rip through his chest. Still tumbling, the pain and his vision began to fade. He smelled jet fuel and felt searing heat. Then, the crush of seawater overwhelmed him. He tasted blood and saltwater and sank in the darkness. He considered surrendering his pointless existence, but something inside him refused to give up. Even *his* life seemed too precious.

Light—there's light! Swim! Don't breathe! Swim to the light!

He flailed and fought towards the light. The closer it got the harder he struggled. His lungs were still burning and about to explode. He bobbed to the surface and gasped for breath. Burning jet fuel covered the water behind him. Everything seemed fuzzy, as if in a dream.

A piece of cherry wood floated past. Fabric, liquor bottles, pieces of soundproofing foam, and oil surrounded him. Suddenly he felt cold, freezing cold. The frigid saltwater sloshed into his mouth and burned his bleeding gums. He coughed up the water and a few teeth.

A white mist fogged his vision. He couldn't stay conscious much longer. His eyes were swelling shut. He spotted something yellow just off his right shoulder as it surfaced in the rush of bubbles coming from below. He remembered the safety briefing.

The raft! Reese must have opened the raft before impact.

His arms burned when he reached for the raft. He felt the slippery-cold, rubberized canvas. All his pain faded. There was no noise. The bitter taste of saltwater mixed with blood and jet fuel disappeared. Exhausted, he began to give up. There was no point in continuing to fight it; his pointless life wasn't worth it. He surrendered to death's grip, and, in a strange way, it warmed him. His vision narrowed to a small hole surrounded by white light, and then nothing but his inner voice's final condemnation.

Heaven or hell? Probably hell.

If you enjoyed the excerpt, you can buy your copy of *Genetic Imperfections* here:

https://www.stevehadden.com